"Well, it's not what I bloody corl a picture." Mrs Cornelius waded across the foyer on old, flat feet and lowered her tray of Lyons Maids and Kia-Oras to the counter. "I mean, in my day it was love an' adventure an' that, wannit."

Lifting a crazed eye from behind the hotdog warmer Sergeant Alvarez opened his disturbed mouth.

"Who...?" he began. But his attention was already wandering.

"Now it's all vomit an' screwin'," she continued. "I wouldn't mind if it was Clark Gable doin' it. *An'* there's no bloody adventure, Sarge. Wot you grinnin' at?"

"Who?"

"Oh, shut up, you pore littel bugger. It's that Mrs Vicious I feel sorry for."

"Killed...?" said Sergeant Alvarez.

"Too right." Mrs C. heaved her tray around. "Oh, well. Back into the effin' fray."

from GOLD DIGGERS OF 1977

Also by Michael Moorcock in VGSF

WIZARDRY AND WILD ROMANCE

CASABLANCA

MICHAEL
MOORCOCK

VGSF

For Rabia, Sedik, Mohammed, Moustafa
and all our friends in
North Africa

First published in Great Britain 1989
by Victor Gollancz Ltd

First VGSF Paperback edition published 1993
by Victor Gollancz
An imprint of Cassell
Villiers House, 41/47 Strand, London WC2N 5JE

A catalogue record for this book is available
from the British Library

ISBN 0 575 05445 X

Printed and bound in Great Britain
by Cox & Wyman Ltd, Reading

Acknowledgements

Gold Diggers of 1977 was first published by Virgin Books, 1980, as *The Great Rock 'n' Roll Swindle*, and was revised for this publication. *The Frozen Cardinal* first appeared in OTHER EDENS, ed. Evans and Holdstock, 1987. *The Murderer's Song* appeared in TALES FROM THE FORBIDDEN PLANET, ed. Roz Kaveney, 1987. *The Last Call* appeared in FANTASY TALES, ed. Stephen Jones, 1987. *Mars* appeared in OTHER EDENS II, 1988. *Hanging the Fool* was written for Rachel Pollock's and Caitlin Mathews' TAROT TALES. *Casablanca* appears here for the first time.

Anti-Personnel Capability and *A Fiercer Hen* first appeared 1976, 1977 in THE NEW STATESMAN. The piece on Mervyn Peake first appeared in BOOKS AND BOOKMEN, 1979. The piece on Harlan Ellison was for THE FANTASIES OF HARLAN ELLISON, 1979. The piece on Angus Wilson was for RADIO TIMES, 1983. The piece on Andrea Dworkin first appeared in THE NEW STATESMAN, 1988. *Taking the Life Out of London* was done for THE LONDON DAILY NEWS, 1987. *Maeve Gilmore* and *Covering Up* first appeared in THE GUARDIAN, 1988. *Building the New Jerusalem* is from TIME OUT, 1988. *Scratching a Living* and *Literally London* are from PUNCH, 1985 AND 1988. *The Smell of Old Vienna* first appeared in THE LOS ANGELES TIMES, 1988. *London Lost and Found* appeared, as described, in an edited form in THE DAILY TELEGRAPH, 1988. *What Feminism Has Done For Me* and *The Case Against Pornography* were commissioned by the TIMES LITERARY SUPPLEMENT and THE SUNDAY TELEGRAPH MAGAZINE respectively and not used. Thanks to all editors who commissioned the pieces, including Martin Amis, Nicholas Shakespeare, W. L. Webb, Dominic Wells, Stanley Reynolds, Carole Mansur, Waldemar Januszczak and Harriett Gilbert.

CONTENTS

SHORT STORIES

NON-FICTION

People

Places

FICTION

SHORT STORIES

CONTENTS

INTRODUCTION

As with all my recent collections, I include fiction and non-fiction without apology. Much of the non-fiction is political and some of the stories have a political cast. I believe they're compatible and hope you do, too. We're living through times when the writer is under increased and subtle pressures from governments and their supporters to tell only the truths which will maintain the status quo. Most genuine radicalism is under attack from various forms of Thatcherism and Reaganism and few people seem to care about the threat to our hard-won freedoms.

Our present governments are not only changing the rules to suit them—they are also trying to change the language to make words like democracy, freedom, citizenship, civil rights and so on mean almost the opposite of what they meant, say, in the late 1960s. Perhaps this is the inevitable result of their old-fashioned economic remedies.

The current climate of increased authoritarianism, of almost suicidal nostalgic reactionaryism, seems dangerous to those of us committed to progressive politics since the 1950s and who began to see an enormous improvement in society's acceptance of minority rights, women's rights and freedom of speech. We have seen most of our gains in those areas subjected to cynical commercial exploitation. We have seen dreams go sour to be replaced by lazy and simplistic social and economic remedies which, in a crueller and more dramatic version, gave the Third Reich a temporary prosperity at the expense of every democratic reform Weimar had tried to achieve.

I mention elsewhere how I believe we have returned not to the Victorian Age, which was one of fairly steady social progress, but to the careless greed and short-sighted, selfish money-grubbing which characterised the Second Empire. That society stifled criticism and opposition, went to great lengths to cover up its immoral politics, its heartless misuse of power, encouraging in its nouveaux riches, its monstrously wealthy brokers and industrialists, a celebration of the kind of greed which symbolises a deep and dangerous decadence far more perturbing than the excesses of the late 60s and 70s. The rationales for the same behaviour which are presented to us now are as depressing as they are familiar.

In 1983 I wrote a rather hastily argued essay called *The Retreat From Liberty* in which I suggested we had, among other things, lost our nerve in the face of a genuine chance of social change, a move towards greater liberty (and therefore greater personal responsibility). I made the point that I saw in the Women's Liberation movement the only real chance left to us for genuine progress and I haven't altered my view. I was depressed by the numbers of people who turned away from that movement, who willingly embraced the language and attitudes of reactionaryism and all too thoroughly offered their support to the male power elite. What sometimes frightens me most about people is how readily they are frightened and, once frightened, how they rush to placate their oppressors.

Present government policies are producing a disenfranchised and consequently demoralised working class which is easily manipulated through vulgar rhetoric, vague threats and even vaguer promises. Such demoralised people do not stay demoralised for ever, especially when offered a different sort of vulgar rhetoric which promises them *immediately* everything that they want.

Better commentators than I have pointed out how dangerous it is to dismantle the Welfare State and destroy the ideals of egalitarianism on which post-war Britain was based. With those ideals destroyed, we face an increasingly violent and unjust future. And it is up to those of us who fear such a future to try to do something about it, to speak up now. A time could come when any form of mild criticism of authority could, as in South Africa, seem like an act of immense courage.

Michael Moorcock
London 1989

CASABLANCA

AN EPISODE IN THE THIRD WORLD WAR

"We are betrayed by what is false within."
George Meredith

Beyond the deserted huts and artificial pools, far out to sea, like a cold wall around our world, a mist had formed. I saw an oil tanker moving through it, coming away from the Gulf, while on the harbour and the unkempt flat roofs, where TV dishes were raised like broken shields, a thin drizzle settled. I turned from the window but found no warmth in the room.

"Well, darling, you told me so! Panos is a complete bastard." She advanced on me, put her hand on my arm, her head against my shoulder. "Forgive me?" Her lips anticipated the pleasure of my assent.

Again I resisted the ritual. The effort was considerable. "I'm tired of what you do," I said. "I'm going to leave you."

"Sweetie!" Her disbelief was observably turning to fury at the prospect of being denied her usual blessing. I wondered if she had always loathed me and if every betrayal I had so far accepted had been from fear of that one terrible truth.

"Faithless . . ." I began, but moralising was beyond me. I had known her from the beginning. Any pain she caused was of my own seeking. I felt disgust. I stepped back from the balcony. "We have to separate, Nadja."

"That doesn't suit me." She controlled herself. "I need you."

"I've nothing left to give. I'm exhausted."

"I've been selfish. I didn't think." But she gave up this approach almost at once, retrieving her dignity and her sense of perspective at the same time. She laughed. I had confirmed her view of the world. Her golden skin glowed like metal and her eyes were ancient stones.

"I'm going," I said. "I'm in an hotel on Rue de la Radiance du Sol. We'll be in contact, eh? I shan't want the flat immediately." I was tempted to touch her hair for the last time; hair as delicate and as coarse as her love-making, as black as her most secret despair.

I turned my back on her. I turned my back on Africa. She went past me and stood on the balcony, deliberately re-entering my field of vision. She let the moisture settle in her hands, combing it into her hair, spreading Casablanca's oily atmosphere over her face, arms and shoulders and cleansing whatever vestiges of sin she imagined to be still visible on her body.

I wish that she had not made an awful sort of choking noise when I left.

My chief met me in the Travel Bureau, which was closed for the afternoon, its plate glass staring on to an almost deserted Boulevard Emile Zola, where a few cars moved in the brightening afternoon light. He was a thin man with a moustache modelled on Georgian lines, I would guess, so he looked like a wolfish caricature of Stalin, something he was unconscious of and would have been horrified to know. His name was Yagolovski. He had been born in Riga and was of that new breed of traditionalist who emerged from the Gorbachev period. We sat together in the empty chairs watching a video of the Barbados beaches reflected in the shop's window. "You've made your plans?" he asked.

"She and I are finished."

"And you're happy with that?" Yagolovski became avuncular with approval. "You're a strong one. Good boy!"

I had not suffered such praise for many years.

All this happened some time ago, before I took up my last post in England and during that prolonged "phoney" period prior to the outbreak of the World War. After my spell in Athens and before I settled in London, I was working in Casablanca. Most people will tell you that Casablanca is not the real Morocco but she remains my favourite. She was big, even in those days, with a population of around seven million, much of it in shanty towns, had few remarkable features and even her Medina was sleazy in the way of the most industrial ports. The tourist trade, primarily dependent on the Bogart myth, had established holiday villages along the somewhat bleak and dangerous beaches, a series of bathing lagoons and some restaurants with names like *Villa Tahiti* and, of course, *Café Americaine*, which looked even grubbier in the foul weather which blew so frequently off the Atlantic.

The years of rain, following the drought of the 70s and 80s, were, of course, to Morocco's benefit and helped establish her as one of Africa's richest nations, but during my time in Casablanca most people were worried about what the wet weather would do to their vacation business.

If the rain had no serious effect on the port traffic and the factories, it was a relief for the people living in the countless shanties, since it cut down Casa's smog, the equal to Los Angeles', and made the city a little healthier. For a while local entrepreneurs had managed to sell copied Burberry trenchcoats to tourists determined to milk at least a little romance from a city having more in common with the reality of Liverpool than the fantasy of Hollywood.

As usual I was working as an art dealer, specialising chiefly in North African antiquities, and had been established in the name of Erich Volker, a Czech émigré, in the old harbour quarter's Rue Sour el Djedid, a street becoming fashionable amongst successful Moroccan bohemians, chiefly painters and photographers.

"Women are grief," said Yagolovski. "You should know that." Out of deference to me he did not light the cigarette between his fingers. I was making one of my attempts to stop smoking. "You're lucky this job came up." Even in his sympathetic mood he reminded me of a jocular Stalin about to betray some old comrade. "It will take you away from Casablanca. And, when you return, never fear—she'll have discovered some new supporter." He cleared his throat and picked up a file. "They're ten a penny."

I welcomed his remarks. I did not need comfort at that stage. I was glad to be going.

"You like Marrakech, don't you?"

"For a holiday. Is that my destination?"

"Initially. You'll be staying at the Mamounia. It's well-known, of course."

The Mamounia had remained Morocco's most famous hotel for half a century and, like similar legendary hotels across the world, had never quite lost its romance or failed to disappoint, very slightly, those who had imagined for years how they might get there. I preferred the smaller hotels in the Medina, or the Es Saadi, where the French show people went and which could offer an equally magnificent view of the High Atlas. But at least I had never

been to the Mamounia with Nadja. "It was Churchill's favourite."
I looked out past the reflected waves and consciously took control
of myself. "He painted in their gardens. And I think de Gaulle,
Roosevelt went there. Possibly Stalin. John Foster Dulles. And of
course all those emirs and kings from the other side of Suez. It
sounds as if I'm to hob-nob with a better class of people."

When I looked at him Yagolovski was grinning. "Just a richer
class. No Saudi princes or Gulf sultans, I'm afraid." He outlined
the first part of my assignment, which was to make contact with an
Algerian agent who would book into the Mamounia as an Egyptian
businessman.

Although officially Morocco was no longer at war with Algeria,
who had apparently given up ambitions in the old Spanish Sahara
and withdrawn support for the Polisario guerillas, there was still a
great deal of political activity under the surface, much of it, of
course, in relation to Libya and Algeria's frustration at having no
Atlantic seaboard. For that reason we continued to maintain a
department in Casablanca and another in Algiers.

"I suppose you want me to leave tomorrow," I said.

Raising his unlit cigarette to his heavy moustache Yagolovski
chuckled as he shook his head. "Tonight," he said. "You meet
your Egyptian businessman in the morning. But, believe me, this
should take your mind off your troubles."

The Marrakech plane was full of pale tourists going on to Agadir
whose beaches were golden and whose hotels were high and white.
A town destroyed by God, they said of the earthquake, restored by
Man and populated by Satan. I think Satan was a euphemism for
Europe. The nearest thing I had seen to even a simple *djin* in that
Moroccan Miami Beach was a German holiday-maker creeping
out before dawn to lay claim to a pool-chair with his towel. The
place consisted entirely of hotels, restaurants and tourist shops and
was, I thought, an unfortunate vision of Morocco's future.

My own country was also eager for hard currency in those days,
so I sympathised with Moroccan policies, even as I regretted the
signs of standardisation which threatened to place a Laura Ashley
and a McDonald's in every identical shopping mall from Moscow
to Melbourne. Marrakech had kept so much of her character
through her position in one of the country's richest agricultural

areas while the Berbers in particular did not so much resist the evils of capitalism as ignore those aspects of it they did not need.

It was not in my nature to express judgements, but I would have been happy if the tourist industry had confined itself to North Africa's Atlantic coast.

The journey was short. By the time we landed at Minar Airport I was thinking of nothing but Nadja and already, of course, weakening. Walking from the plane to the embarkation building I put on my wide-brimmed Panama and drew a deep breath of the relaxing heat, turning my face to a heaven which had something of that dark, moistureless desert blue of skies beyond the High Atlas. The soldiers on duty smoked and chatted, showing us only casual interest. I remembered what I had liked about Marrakech and why I feared her attraction. Of all Maghrebi cities, she possessed the greatest love of pleasure, a carelessness, a good humour, that reminded me of Cairo. The French had never been very secure in Marrakech. Her easy-going confidence derived, I think, from her once superior position as the centre of a great Berber Empire from the Pyrenees to the Sahara, successfully resisting all would-be outside conquerors. I suppose Casablanca's cautious cynicism, developed in the service of a dozen masters, was preferable to me.

After suffering the irritating passport and customs rituals which refused to distinguish residents from visitors, I found a taxi to take me to the Mamounia. I chatted in French with a driver who assumed me to be a tourist and recommended a variety of relatives for whatever goods or services I might require. I did not reveal any knowledge of Arabic. It is my habit to seem unfamiliar with languages. People have a way of revealing much more if they think you have only a word or two of their native tongue.

As we drove along the broad red avenues of the Menara quarter of the new town, I remembered how Nadja and I had wandered these streets when we were first together. Now I felt more pain than I had imagined possible. I wondered if this were an important job or if my chief, knowing that it was in my interest to stay away from Casablanca as long as possible, had done me a favour. He, like all his kind, possessed a fatherly and sometimes unwelcome concern about the private lives of his officers. It is in the tradition of our Service and goes back long before the Revolution.

For my part, I should have been unhappy without that concern.

"Follow the rules and enjoy the love of the Father," as the priests used to say in our little town. My mother was fond of the phrase and would repeat it sometimes like a litany. My own father's rules were inviolable but I could not say he loved any of us.

I grew up in the shadow of Stalin and, even though he was dead by the time I could read, the old habits lived on. It makes us slow to take decisions sometimes, even now. But that is often no bad thing.

A case in point was our decision to remain in the Maghreb when almost everyone else removed their agencies altogether, usually leaving one officer at their consulate. An American friend of mine, who had guessed my job as I had guessed his, was amused by it. "You Russians keep as many staff in warm countries as you can possibly justify. I don't blame you, with your hideous climate, but it's a standing joke amongst most intelligence crews. Your chiefs want to be sure of a few days of sunshine every year." I was reminded of all the engineers, military experts and technicians volunteering for work in, for instance, Libya, and how Afghanistan with her awful winters had proved such a disappointment to certain colleagues.

We drove through broad streets cooled by tall palms, flanked by red-brown walls, by wrought-iron which gave glimpses of villas decorated with bright tile and pastel lime-wash, with vibrant trailing flowers and vines, lush shrubs and trees, the New City, which we used to call the French City, lying outside the walls of the Medina. The Mamounia was almost as famous a landmark as the tall, elegant outline of the Katoubia Mosque, the Mosque of the Booksellers, where from the surrounding shops, it was again possible to buy exquisitely printed editions of Ibn Rushd's Aristotle commentaries, al-Khwarizmi's mathematical treatises, as well as any number of editions of the Qu'ran. Unlike the Mosque, however, the Mamounia, lying just within the high crenellated walls of the Medina at the Djedid Gate, had changed to meet changing times. My suitcase was taken from the taxi by a man dressed for a touring production of *The Desert Song* who carried it into a foyer half reproduction deco, half the interior of Los Angeles' *Dar Maghreb* restaurant.

I was a little shocked and at the same time amused. The place was a vulgar Arabian Nights fantasy, an authentic extension of Hollywood. I reflected that as Morocco grew richer she resembled

18

California in all her ways. Perhaps this was the logic of wealth? Perhaps our notions of value and culture and human dignity were old-fashioned? Certainly nobody suffered in modern Marrakech as when the Caids held power.

I went to sleep in a bed whose canopy of red silk, whose massive purple pillows and yellow sheets would have put to shame the ostentation of a Turkish pasha and in the morning was served, on a tray of rosewood, silver and mother-of-pearl, coffee and croissants the rival of anything I had tasted in Paris. I showered in a black and silver stall almost the size of the flat I had been born in, then shaved and dressed, started down to the pool to keep my appointment, seemingly a casual meeting, in the shade of some palms flanking the hotel garden.

I remembered when Nadja and I had stayed at a little hotel just outside the Medina and seen the dawn rising in a pale mist of pink and blue: the palms and eucalyptus dark green against the red walls of the city. From some shuttered shop came the resonant lute and drum music of Rouicha Mohemed while elsewhere Azzahia sang of metaphysical love to inspire images of birds, animals and flowers as vivid as any picture. This was the perfect life of Marrakech or, at least, a perfect moment, a pause before the day began. The smell of sweet mint tea joined the aroma of baking bread and wood-smoke. She had told me how much she loved me and how she would always love me and I had had her again, as the sounds of the city rose around us like a symphony.

There were already a few Americans and Germans around the pool, distinguished from one another only by the tone of their tanning agents. My man stood smoking under an orange tree, apparently fascinated by the brilliant pinks of a bougainvillaea. He was tall and handsome, reminding me of an Egyptian film-star I saw frequently on billboards in Casablanca. About thirty-five, with dark, sardonic eyes, carefully groomed black curly hair and moustache, he wore a grey silk suit which had not been bought this side of the Italian Riviera. His name, even his cover name, was unknown to me, but we had a rather childish conversation code for mutual identification.

"A beautiful morning," I said.

"Like the first morning in Paradise." He smiled. "Have you been in Marrakech long?" He purred his words like a Cairene.

"A matter of hours. I live in Casablanca. I have a business there." I replied in French.

We walked away from the pool. On the other side of the hotel wall came sounds of the city's ordinary commerce, the muezzin, a radio playing Rai hits.

I yawned. "I'm still a little sleepy. I arrived late last night. The mountains are magnificent from my room."

"Unfortunately I have only a concourse. You're in business in Morocco? That's interesting."

"I deal in antiques."

"Quite a coincidence," he murmured in what was virtually an aside to the tree. "I sell cotton. I'm at present in Esna but my home's in Alexandria. You know Egypt, I suppose?"

"Fairly well. I do very little buying there now."

"The export restrictions on that sort of thing are pretty much total. And if they're not there, it's clear what you buy is a fake!"

We talked a little longer, then shook hands and agreed to meet before lunch. At about noon, in a horse-drawn taxi, we toured the city's pink sandstone walls which served, among other things, to protect the Medina from fierce winter sandstorms.

My contact smoked constantly. Eventually I accepted his offered Marlboro and, with a sense of considerable relief, lit it. I felt I gave my liberty up to a familiar and not unkind master. I had always understood the basic meaning of Islam, which was "Surren-der". The Egyptian's name was Tewfik al-Boulekh, he said. We used English, of which our driver had only a few words.

"You'll be wanting to interview the boy?" He tossed a dirham coin towards the group of shouting children now running beside our carriage. Some scrambled for the money while others kept pace with us. I admired their stamina. "*M'sieu!*" they called. "*Un dirham! Un dirham!*" I was reminded of an English friend telling me how he had pursued American jeeps during the Second World War pleading for gum. Across the road men used materials and methods unaltered for a thousand years to rebuild the walls. The red mud blended with older remains of houses and stables. "The Maghreb is so much cleaner than Egypt."

"I know very little." I thought it wise not to admit my complete ignorance. "Is he here in Marrakech?"

"No, no." He turned his head as our driver reined in suddenly to begin a passionate argument with a man whose donkey was almost hidden by a huge bundle of newly-picked mint. Clutching at his brown-and-white-striped djellabah in a gesture that was as obscene as it was obscure, the Berber further enraged our cabman and brought another donkey-owner into the argument while passengers boarding a nearby bus, on to which one man was forcing two sheep he had just bought, turned with interest to witness the argument concerning the first donkey's absolute refusal to move from the tarmac to the strip of hardened mud beside it and so give the taxi a clear passage. Meanwhile we were joined by a score of astonishingly lovely Marrekshi children asking us for stylos and money. I ignored them until we were on the move again then threw them a cheap ballpoint and some small change.

Al-Boulekh continued: "The boy was born in France but his papers are absolutely authentic. There can be no question of his lineage."

"Are his ancestors well-known?"

The Egyptian laughed heartily. "Oh, indeed!"

"Provenance is so important in my walk of life," I said.

He dropped his voice. "There is no question that our young friend is a direct descendant of the Prophet. If anything his blood is better than any ruling Fatimid."

I hid my surprise and cursed my chief for not warning me of the fantastic nature of the assignment. I regarded the Algerian agent with increased suspicion. Was I to be involved in some bizarre kidnapping? Even during my early days with the Service such schemes had fallen out of fashion.

We went together to Djemaa al-Fna. The great central square of Marrakech was crowded as always with every kind of produce, with entertainers, with tourists. It always reminded me, I told my companion, of London's Portobello Road. There were spice-sellers and food-stalls, fruit and vegetables, pots and pans, and two great hand-cart displays of every type of Japanese digital timepiece. The modern goods were offered side by side with rugs, pottery and tools in use since the city's foundation when William the Conqueror was making London his capital.

We sat at a table outside the *Café de France*. I had the *simple* and my Algerian-Egyptian had the *filtre*.

"You know where we are going tomorrow?" he asked.

"I believe I am to travel to the other side of the mountains." I gestured with my cup at the distant peaks.

"We have to be pretty cautious at this moment." Chiefly because I had no cigarettes myself I refused his offered Marlboro.

After lunch, we walked through the souk and then went to see the Majorelle Gardens, the *Bou Saf Saf*, whose entrance was in a little side-street in the Gueliz district not far from the Doukkala Gate. As usual the botanical gardens were almost deserted and I was immediately captured by their peacefulness. I am always impressed by the Arab appreciation of zones of tranquillity, little bits of paradise on earth, though this particular garden was the creation of a French painter.

"There's nothing like this in Cairo now." Al-Boulekh was impressed. "People have to go out to the pyramids if they want some space. That city should be a warning to us."

I told him Cairo was one of my favourite cities. Given her thirty million inhabitants, she was a splendid example of how people of disparate religions and politics could survive together, however tenuously.

This did not suit his own views. Changing the subject, he said he had known a Volker in Munich who ran a little private toy museum there, near the open market. Was I a relative? I told him I was not German but had been born near Prague and emigrated with my parents in the 1950s. He accepted this lie as readily as he accepted any other story from me. He had that way of Mediterranean and African peoples, who seem to judge you not by the accuracy but by the quality of your accounts. For his benefit I next invented a trek across no-man's-land, guards shooting at us, my little sister being killed.

"Yet now you work again for the Russians?" He introduced a sudden reality into our exchange.

I laughed aloud and he joined me; just, I decided, for the relief of it. Since we demanded no superficial logic of our ancient myths and legends, why should we demand it of our modern ones?

We paused beside a mosaic fountain, under great feathery branches of trees which had covered the Earth before the first fish crawled to land and filled its lungs.

"There's an economic crisis coming here." He blew smoke

towards a sky so blue and still it might have been painted by a New York pop artist. "Until now King Hassan has been able to control the Left. But with the population explosion, with the collapse of their European markets, with a restless and newly-educated and largely unemployable middle-class, with the Libyan trouble, the situation will soon become volatile, wouldn't you say?"

I agreed his projection had some basis in truth, though privately I believed Morocco could solve her problems and maintain a stability already making her one of the most progressive countries in Africa.

"The Left on its own has no one to lead a successful coup. We've nobody left in the UNFP. And anyway all the attempted coups have come from the Right. The Left needs a good alternative to Hassan. His sons won't do, of course. Hassan can't last very much longer. It's at that point we have the chance to win the country over."

"You expect us to co-operate with you in financing a revolution?" I was incredulous.

"It wouldn't amount to anything hugely disruptive. Not with the cards we have to play."

"I thought your people had stopped supporting the Polisarios?" The guerrillas of the old Spanish Sahara had been neutralised in their bid for an independent nation controlling the phosphate mines which gave Morocco so much of its hard currency.

"You know the pressure we were under." He began to walk down one of the brick paths towards a group of sinuous plants whose brilliant, spiky blossoms suggested they had been brought from the continental interior. "We expected the United States to reduce her aid. Instead she increased it. For a while she was almost as generous to Morocco as she was to Israel. Yet somehow Hassan kept faith with everyone. Largely because of his importance to Islam. There are not many like him left." He meant, I assumed, that Hassan was a descendant of the Prophet's daughter, Fatima, which many accepted as the purest of all royal bloodlines. "His survival has proved to many Islamic leaders, even those directly opposed to his policies, that he is Allah's chosen. Well, you know that. His *baraka* has never been more evident."

This was European logic, of which I was always suspicious if presented by an Arab, yet again I was bound to agree with him.

23

The word, distinctly Arabic, had a wealth of meaning—a mixture of status, *charisma*, *chuztpah*, glamour and good fortune which, in a world whose rulers, even socialist presidents, were regarded as God's representatives as well as the State's, was of crucial significance now that the fundamentalists gained so much power. My chief always complained how our Moscow people refused to understand that to Moslems, even our own Moslems, politics and religion were synonymous.

"The problem," my companion continued, "has never been how to overthrow Hassan, but who will replace him."

Again I agreed. Sentimentally, of course, I could see no possible point in replacing Hassan, who had proved himself since 1976 (when, leading his people into the desert, he had peacefully occupied the Spanish Sahara) a brilliant politician. His esteem in the country and throughout the world had never been higher. Moroccan troops had fought bravely beside Syrians in the Golan Heights while at the same time Hassan had encouraged Jews to return to his country, displaying that tolerance for other faiths which his greatest ancestors had exercised throughout their long rule in Africa and Europe. He had demonstrated ethical and pragmatic judgement at least equal to Sadat's and any hint of our interfering with his rule would lose us authority throughout the world.

I wondered why my chief, who knew my admiration for Hassan, had given me this task. Hassan was everything great that Stalin could have been. But Stalin was a failed priest, ever unable to placate his own ghosts or reconcile his past with a future for which he had relinquished his place in heaven. Self-sacrifice is always borne with greater dignity if that sacrifice is proved of value.

The Egyptian again revealed his obsession. "This boy has Almohad, Fatimid and Abbasid blood. By showing increased support to orthodoxy he could win unprecedented influence through the entire Islamic world. It might be truly united for the first time in history!"

"Under whom?" I asked. He did not reply.

We walked back from the gardens and visited some of the shopping streets of the French Quarter. He paused in the Place du 16 Novembre outside a motorbike showroom. Staring through the display window al-Boulekh was surprised by a poster on which three Japanese women in one-piece bathing suits advertised a new Kawasaki.

"Doesn't it occur to you how behind the times we are in this profession?" I said. "The Japanese concern themselves with commercial espionage, with the empire of the market place. It makes a great deal of sense."

He was predictably disapproving. "It certainly does, if you've something to sell. These days Moscow has very little people want. You relied on exporting an ideal."

"But that's a bit obsolete now. These days we're trying for the consumer market. We're out of practice."

He was dismissive. "If the war doesn't escalate, you'll do it, I'm sure. You still have a low paid and extremely well-disciplined work-force."

I found myself unamused by his irony. I remained suspicious of Arab socialists. I was more comfortable with traditional power-seekers.

We returned to the Mamounia and I went to my room, having agreed to see him for dinner. On impulse I put through a call to Casablanca but was told that there was no reply. Trying to avoid thinking of Nadja, I watched a James Cagney movie on television, *Yankee Doodle Dandy* dubbed into French with Arabic sub-titles. Eventually I turned the TV off and listened to the radio news. As usual England was justifying some piece of American gunboat diplomacy to her EEC allies while Israel accused Syria of arming the Jews for Palestine guerrillas recently allied to the PLO. South Africa's invasion of Mozambique and Libya's 'border dispute' with Tunisia seemed to be taking place unopposed.

These familiar reports were almost comforting. When the Folklorique performances followed I was irritated and found a Tunisian discussion on the changing face of France. Maghrebis share that complicated fascination with their former rulers which Indians have with the British. Not everyone benefits from colonialism and there are many losses in the name of Western progress, but I cannot dismiss all imperialist expansion as harmful. I was raised in a tradition, old-fashioned in the non-Communist world almost before I was born, and it is still hard for me not to take a paternalist view of what was once the Third World, especially since paternalism prevails there. We Russians understand and accept the nature of power rather more readily than the ambivalent English, for instance, or those who inherited and developed their particular brand of imperialism, the Americans.

Until I was on the edge of sleep I gave no thought to what al-Boulekh had told me. The Egyptian's story seemed the fantastic concoction of some distant intelligence agency without enough real business. According to the Algerians I was to meet a young man whose Sharifian lineage, just on one strand alone, went back to the 17th century Alouite sultans of Marrakech. With such potent blood, the Egyptian claimed, Hassan and his family could be deposed and a regime more closely aligned to the socialist world be installed in Rabat. To me the scheme, even if the boys' ancestry were perfect, was so pointless and reminiscent of a foolish 19th century Ottoman plot, that I was hardly able to stop scoffing at it on the spot. Yet the Egyptian revealed himself as being closely involved with and committed to the scheme. Doubtless he had supplementary ambitions.

"Wait until you meet him," he had said. 'You'll be won over."

I had my orders. I had no choice. The next morning we were to drive over the High Atlas to a small town on the edge of the Sahara which had been colonised by Club Med and was primarily patronised by middle-class French people in their late thirties. In 1928 Ouarzazate had been a Foreign Legion garrison town on the site of an old kasbah and was more than once attacked by various bands of determined irregulars, who refused to accept European protection and were still not completely pacified at the outbreak of the Second World War.

At that time Route P31 over the Tizi 'n' Tichka Pass to the Draa Valley was, after the first few miles, somewhat bleak, rising about 8,000 feet amongst peaks still snow-capped and frequently as barren as those parts of the Lake District where as an exchange student in the 1960s I used to hike. Until spring, when wild flowers make them vibrant, they are unremarkable mountains, dotted with ruined kasbahs from which local chieftains, controlling the caravan routes and trails, had raided as successfully as the Scottish robber barons in the Highlands.

Obviously familiar with the range, my companion drove our Avis Renault at headlong speed around the mountain roads, his horn frequently in use, occasionally missing a collision with a truck or a tourist bus. The radio was turned up to full volume. "*Too tired to make it, too tired to fight about it*," sang al-Boulekh with the Eagles. As we descended towards the Draa we followed the river, the Oued Imini, south-east through shale slopes and grey-black rock occasionally brightened by a little foliage, a narrow strip of cultivated land, a small goat herd or a dusty, broken tower.

For twenty years Old Ouarzazate, the provincial capital, had been the location of so many Hollywood films that it immediately struck a romantic chord. The low, pleasant houses, the crenellated walls, the half-ruined kasbah, the palm-trees and oases where nomads came to trade, were familiar to anyone who ever saw *Lawrence of Arabia*. The reality confirmed the fantasy so thoroughly it seemed they were the same.

Al-Boulekh told me a little of his work with the Polisario guerrillas. Until recently he said they had camped not a hundred miles from here. The Algerians were too cautious to involve directly any of their own people, so the contact officers had been, like al-Boulekh, from friendly Arab countries or else were disaffected Berbers, sometimes Moroccan Touaregs considering a career move. Pressured by us, the Americans and the Arab League, Algeria had agreed to stop even her indirect Polisario support. That war drained everyone and had only strategic results for the Polisarios. Ironically, Morocco was at one time forced to put more men and money into that particular field than the French spent maintaining power over the whole Maghreb.

Al-Boulekh was tired by the drive and wanted a drink. I suggested stopping at a little place called *Zitoun*, the Olive Grove, but he shook his head.

"It's hard now to find a public bar in Ouarzazate. *Zitoun* doesn't sell alcohol. For a while, you know, Club Med had the monopoly. Did you ever try to get a beer in Moulay Idris?"

"That's hardly a good example. It's a holy town."

He shrugged. Like so many younger Arabs he equated drinking with modernity. He would no more patronise a café which did not sell liquor than he would sit and listen to the love-songs of Oum Kal Thoum, the classical Egyptian singer I admired. He only listened to American pop, he had said, like Dire Straits. So he preferred, I replied, to hear middle-aged millionaires from San Luis Obispo wailing their contempt for microwaves and colour televisions? There had been a familiar note of puritanism in his voice, echoing writers I had known who dismissed narrative, or painters who loathed anything remotely figurative: an attitude which in Europe had seemed radically progressive twenty years earlier but which I nowadays found embarrassing. We had entered a more conservative phase of our cultural history and I was consoled by it. But at least he had revealed something of his moral view and I felt pleasantly satisfied by this, as if I had mysteriously gained an advantage in an unfamiliar game.

Near the old Glaovi Kasbah we found a pleasant restaurant with rooftop seats looking down on to Ouarzazate's ever-expanding main street, where stalls now sold trinkets, handicrafts and Pakistani brasswork to tourists. In the uncompromising near-desert heat German automobiles manoeuvred for space with donkeys, bicycles, horsemen and ancient trucks whose gaudy decoration was reminiscent of the nomad tents we had passed coming in. Once a detachment of smart Moroccan soldiers marched by. I almost mistook them for paras. Their presence surprised me.

"Is the Sahara trouble starting up again?" I asked as I sipped my Valgrave.

"Who knows?" He had stretched out his long legs and was as relaxed as the hopeful cats who sat politely around us.

"You, possibly?" I was sardonic. I guessed he had high ambitions.

"Oh, we're nothing but intermediaries. You understand that. Messenger boys at best. Even you, M. Volker, in spite of your rank."

I was mildly amused by this display of knowledge. I had no information about him, but someone had shown him a dossier on me.

"I'm a simple antique dealer," I said. "A Czech emigré."

"I had forgotten." It seemed a genuine apology.

When he had finished his beer we drove to the Club Med buildings. The great kasbah-style walls looked as if they might have resisted the whole of Abd el-Krim's 1920s tribal army. Had it not been for some kind of special pass displayed by al-Boulekh, I think we could have found it impossible to reach the reception area.

The place was decorated in French-Moorish, a rather unhappy

combination of two splendid aesthetics, and we were greeted by a pretty young Berber woman stylish in Parisian casuals. Her name was R'Kia and she was the Customer Relations Liaison Officer. She had been told to expect us. Normally, she said, visits from relatives were discouraged by the Club. She was charming. She was sure we could understand why these rules existed.

I told her I too was a great believer in rules, and she was winningly grateful. She led us around the pool where near-naked women stretched themselves on loungers and their men played water-football or lay reading paperback spy thrillers, through an archway, up a short stair until we stood outside a bright blue door on which she tapped.

During the pause I said: "You have a world of your own here." We were all speaking French.

"Yes. You never need to leave, if you don't want to. Everything is provided." She called through the door. "M. Maquin. Your uncle and his friend are here."

The door was opened by a handsome boy of about twenty dressed in shorts and grey silk beach shirt. He was below middle height but had the physique of a body-builder. He shook hands, greeting us in an educated Parisian accent. I guessed that French was his first language. It was immediately obvious why al-Boulekh was convinced and why our Odessa office had given credence to the scheme. The boy radiated *baraka*.

Alain Makhainy knew nothing of my people's involvement and, I would guess, had not been told of any historic destiny planned for him by whatever Algerian Secret Service department had concocted this Ruritanian scheme to replace him at the head of the Moroccan state. Al-Boulekh had described his vision of a shining new monarch coming out of the desert at the head of an Algerian-Soviet equipped army to unite the Maghreb, including Libya, into one powerful nation. Wild as the plan was, many people in those days of flux would have given it credence. Myths of hope were in short supply. It was not the most bizarre plan invented by the world's intelligence agencies, nor the most dangerous. Indeed, in retrospect, it has for me a certain innocence. At that time, however, in a very different climate, I was utterly sceptical.

Makhainy took us to a bar with a wide balcony looking out over the battlements to palms and a shallow stream. When I tried to pay for our drinks he laughed and gave the waiter some coloured beads from his pocket. "This is the only currency we're allowed here."

The boy believed he was to be interviewed for a sensitive job representing one of the main international banks where his lineage would stand him in unusually good stead with Arab clients.

I questioned him about his parents, who were both second-generation Parisians. His grandfather had come from Lebanon and his grandmother from Sinai. During the War they had lived in Casablanca. His maternal grandparents were both Palestinian Arabs who had emigrated to Lyons after 1947. He had birth-certificates, family photographs, documents of every kind from half-a-dozen French and Arab authorities, including references to his ancestors in a variety of Islamic historical texts. His paternal grandfather was the son of a mutual ancestor of the Moroccan Sultans. They had been a distinguished family of Islamic judges and scholars. In France, as merchants, they had experienced great wealth for a while. I was in no doubt about his bloodlines, neither was I surprised by his family's recent past. Not everyone desires to be a prince or even an eminent holy man. "My parents are French citizens," he said. "My father was a socialist."

"And you?" I asked casually.

He shrugged. "I am a child of my age. I need a well-paid job which will make the best use of my talents."

"You are fluent in Arabic?" I asked in that language.

"A bit rusty," he told me. "But practice should take care of that. Eh, m'sieu?" He offered me a wonderful smile. I think he had the measure of his own gifts.

The Egyptian and I stayed overnight at a local *fonduk*, rather like one of those pensions you used to find in provincial France, and which had the same air of fly-blown cosiness. We each had a single iron-framed bed and the Turkish toilet facilities were on the floor below.

Al-Boulekh was elated by what he was certain had been a successful encounter. "Isn't he perfect?" He had removed his European clothes and sat on his bed's edge wearing a blue and white Alexandrian gelabea.

"He's certainly convincing and he has personality." I carefully folded my clothes and sat them on the tiled floor. "Let's hope he does well at the doctor's examination."

He frowned from where he lay with a book supported by his pillows. "A doctor? What for?"

"Oh, it's one of our rules," I said. "You know what bureaucracies are like. Moscow will want it."

"He doesn't look the type to have a heart attack." Then he smiled. "I know. You're worried about AIDS. I'm sure he's fundamentally heterosexual."

I said nothing to this. Neither did I tell him how much I had liked the young man and, unusually for me, did not wish him to be destroyed by what I considered an already doomed adventure. Algeria had taken the wrong lessons from us. Times and methods were changing rapidly. At that stage we were hoping to avert what the Americans called "a major conflict".

"And he can always brush up his Arabic," said al-Boulekh.

Next morning we returned to Marrakech. The Egyptian was exceptionally friendly on the journey back and even turned off the radio at my request, whereupon he outlined the great benefits of the Maghreb's unification. "What Hassan did for Morocco, Hamed—his original name—will do for the whole of North Africa. Imagine! A unified socialist Arab alliance the length and breadth of the Mediterranean from the Atlantic to the Red Sea. And what an example for the rest of Africa! Within a couple of generations they could form a bloc as powerful as Europe!" Was this naïveté a display for my benefit?

I envied him, I said, his old-fashioned optimism. In my own country Lenin's great ideal was giving way to Lenin's equally great pragmatism and it was fashionable to describe how Stalin had lost the way, that Lenin had foreseen what could go wrong and thus had introduced the New Economic Policy which, essentially, most well-established socialist states were now reproducing. There is sometimes nothing worse than being taken for the representative of an ideal—or even a sexual preference—one has discarded in the light of experience.

In Marrakech I tried to phone my flat from the airport while I waited for the delayed plane but my operator was unable, he said, to make the connection, though I insisted I had heard the number ring. I had decided to try one last time to come to an agreement with Nadja and felt urgently she should know.

The plane eventually came in from Agadir. It was packed with sun-reddened tourists wearing locally-bought straw hats, Rose Sarkissian shirts covered in rhinestones and gilded cowboy emblems, and cheaply-made kaftans. I found a seat on the smoking side of the plane. Moroccans had solved the problem of non-smoking accommodation by simply dividing the plane down the middle. Halfway to Casablanca I bought a packet of English cigarettes from the stewardess but did not light one until I was outside the airport waiting for my car.

I went straight to the office and gave my report to my chief.

"You seem unimpressed," he said. It was still raining heavily. The water poured like mercury down the plate glass. "This is a little awkward for me."

"He's a very personable young man. Simply tell him he has to have a medical before we can give him a firm answer."

"You're not normally so assertive." Without comment he accepted a Silk Cut from my packet. "Very well. I'll tell Odessa. And they'll tell Moscow. And we'll hear in a month. You think the scheme's crazy, don't you?"

"And you?"

I expected no reply.

He shrugged. "Otherwise, you'd say he was what he claims?"

"I think claims are being made for him. All he wants is an easy, well-paid job. But yes—he's kosher." And I smiled as I picked up my bag. "I think the Algerians are trying to get back into the game. He's all they have at present."

He was equally amused. "Very romantic, Erich. Just like the Great Game, eh?" Typical of his years, he was a keen reader of Kipling and Jack London. "More like a plot from the turn of the century. Don't you feel nostalgic? Like a character in John Buchan. Or one of those old Alexander Korda movies?"

"Our destinies are just as determined by mythology as were our ancestors'. I used to be frightened by the idea."

"That girl of yours, by the way, has a new gentleman friend. A Tunisian sardine wholesaler. Named Hafid. You'll be at your hotel?"

"My flat. I have some stuff there I want."

He said nothing as he watched me leave.

I enjoyed the walk through the rain to the taxi stand. The car took me along the seafront with its closed-down bars and abandoned night-clubs, its waterlogged beach umbrellas and torn red-, white- and blue-striped awnings, its drunks in their filthy European suits, its desolate whores. I was sure the boy would be found to be uncircumcised. An uncircumcised Moslem is a contradiction in terms. If he did not know Arabic well, he did not know the Qu'ran and therefore had no prospect of a crown by that route. Without our support, he was not the slightest threat to Hassan or his sons, all of whom were thoroughly educated in Islam. The Egyptian clearly had some sort of financial stake in this scheme.

The taxi dropped me off outside the whitewashed walls of my building. When I pressed the code on the electronic lock there was some trouble with it and I could not get in. I shivered as I put my finger to my own bell and was answered by Nadja's voice.

"It's Volker," I said. "I'm back from Marrakech."

After a short pause she pushed the button to admit me. I walked up the stairs, obscurely thinking I should give her a little time before I reached the door, but she had opened it and was waiting for me as I walked in. Her clothes were unfamiliar. She wore a tight red skirt and a gold blouse. Her make-up had created a stranger. She was already established in her newest role.

"I'm leaving in the morning," she told me. There were a few boxes and suitcases packed. "I shan't take much."

"Perhaps you'll let the concierge have my keys," I said.

"Of course," she said. "You look tired. Your trip didn't do you much good."

"Oh, I enjoyed myself, I think. A little." I turned to go. "The department knows about your Tunisian. You'll be careful, I hope. No mistakes. Nothing about me."

She took my warning without expression and then kissed me gravely. "For a while," she said, "I thought I had worked a miracle. I convinced myself I had brought the dead to life."

My answering smile appeared to disturb her.

Casablanca &
Marrakesh April 1988/
Oxford & London,
January 1989.

33

THE FROZEN CARDINAL

Dear Gerry,

I got your last, finally. Hope this reaches you in less than a year. The supply planes are all robots now and are supposed to give a faster service. Did I tell you we were being sent to look over the southern pole? Well, we're here. Below zero temperatures, of course, and at present we're gaining altitude all the time. At least we don't have to wear breathing equipment yet. The Moldavian poles have about twice the volume of ice as those of Earth, but they're melting. As we thought, we found the planet at the end of its ice-age. I know how you hate statistics and you know what a bore I can be, so I won't go into the details. To tell you the truth, it's a relief not to be logging and measuring.

It's when I write to you that I find it almost impossible to believe how far away Earth is. I frequently have a peculiar sense of closeness to the home planet, even though we are light years from it. Sometimes I think Earth will appear in the sky at 'dawn' and a rocket will come to take me to you. Are you lying to me, Gerry? Are you really still waiting? I love you so much. Yet my reason cautions me. I can't believe in your fidelity. I don't mean to make you impatient but I miss you desperately sometimes and I'm sure you know how strange people get in these conditions. I joined the expedition, after all, to give you time by yourself, to reconsider our relationship. But when I got your letter I was overjoyed. And, of course, I wish I'd never signed up for Moldavia. Still, only another six months to go now, and another six months home. I'm glad your mother recovered from her accident. This time next year we'll be spending all my ill-gotten gains in the Seychelles. It's what keeps me going.

We're perfectly safe in our icesuits, of course, but we get terribly tired. We're ascending a series of gigantic ice terraces which seem to go on forever. It takes a day to cross from one terrace to the wall of the next, then another day or so to climb the wall and move the equipment up. The small sun is visible throughout an entire cycle of the planet at this time of year, but the 'day', when both suns are visible, is only about three hours. Then everything's very bright, of course, unless it's snowing or there's a thick cloud-cover, and we have to protect our eyes. We use the brightest hours for sleeping. It's almost impossible to do anything else. The vehicles are reliable, but slow. If we make any real speed we have to wait a consequently longer interval until they can be re-charged. Obviously, we re-charge during the bright hours, so it all works out reasonably well. It's a strangely orderly planet, Gerry: everything in its place. Those creatures I told you about were not as intelligent as we had hoped. Their resemblance to spiders is remarkable, though, even to spinning enormous webs around their nests; chiefly, it seemed to us, for decoration. They ate the rations we offered and suffered no apparent ill-effects, which means that the planet could probably be opat-gen in a matter of years. That would be a laugh on Galtman. Were you serious, by the way, in your letter? You couldn't leave your USSA even to go to Canada when we were together! You wouldn't care for this ice. The plains and jungles we explored last year feel almost deserted, as if they were once inhabited by a race which left no mark whatsoever. We found no evidence of intelligent inhabitants, no large animals, though we detected some weirdly-shaped skeletons in caves below the surface. We were told not to excavate, to leave that to the follow-up team. This is routine official work; there's no romance in it for me. I didn't expect there would be, but I hadn't really allowed for the boredom, for the irritation one begins to feel with one's colleagues. I'm so glad you wrote to say you still love me. I joined to find myself, to let you get on with your life. I hope we both will be more stable when we meet again.

The gennard is warmed up and I'm being signalled, so I'll close this for the time being. We're about to ascend another wall, and that means only one of us can skit to see to the hoist, while the others go up the hard way on the lines. Helander's the leader on this particular op. I must say he's considerably easier going than old IP whom you'll probably have seen on the news by now, showing off his eggs. But the river itself is astonishing, completely encircling the planet; fresh water and Moldavia's only equivalent to our oceans, at least until this ice age is really over!

8/7/17 "Dawn"

A few lines before I fall asleep. It's been a hard one today. Trouble with the hoists. Routine stuff, but it doesn't help morale when it's this cold. I was dangling about nine hundred metres up, with about another thousand to go, for a good hour, with nothing to do but listen to Fisch's curses in my helmet, interspersed with the occasional reassurance. You're helpless in a situation like that! And then, when we did all get to the top and started off again across the terrace (the ninth!) we came almost immediately to an enormous crevasse which must be half-a-kilometre across! So here we are on the edge. We can go round or we can do a horizontal skit. We'll decide that in the "evening". I have the irrational feeling that this whole section could split off suddenly and engulf us in the biggest landslide a human being ever witnessed. It's silly to think like that. In relationship to this astonishing staircase we are lighter than midges. Until I got your last letter I wouldn't have cared. I'd have been excited by the idea. But now, of course, I've got something to live for. It's peculiar, isn't it, how that makes cowards of the best of us?

9/7/17

Partridge is down in the crevasse at this moment. He thinks we can bridge, but wants to make sure. Also our instruments have picked up something odd, so we're duty-bound to investigate. The rest of us are hanging around, quite glad of the chance to do nothing. Fedin is playing his music and Simons and Russell are fooling about on the edge, kicking a ration-pack about, with the crevasse as the goal. You can hardly make out the other side. Partridge just said he's come across something odd imbedded in the north wall. He says the colours of the ice are beautiful, all dark greens and blues, but this, he says, is red. "There shouldn't be anything red down here!" He says it's probably rock but it resembles an artefact. Maybe there have been explorers here before us, or even inhabitants. If so, they must have been here relatively recently, because these ice-steps are not all that old, especially at the depth Partridge has reached. Mind you, it wouldn't be the first practical-joke he's played since we arrived.

Later

Partridge is up. When he pushed back his visor he looked pale and said he thought he was crazy. Fedin gave him a check-up immediately. There are no extraordinary signs of fatigue. Partridge says the outline he saw in the ice seemed to be a human figure. The instruments all suggest it is animal matter, though of course there are no life-functions. "Even if it's an artefact," said Partridge, "it hasn't got any business being there." He shuddered. "It seemed to be looking at me. A direct, searching stare. I got frightened." Partridge isn't very imaginative, so we were all impressed. "Are we going to get it out of there?" asked Russell. "Or do we just record it for the follow-up team, as we did with those skeletons?" Helander was uncertain. He's as curious as the rest of us. "I'll take a look for myself," he said. He went down, said something under his breath which none of us could catch in our helmets, then gave the order to be hoisted up again. "It's a Roman Catholic cardinal," he said. "The hat, the robes, everything. Making a benediction!" He frowned. "We're going to have to send back on this and await instructions."

Fedin laughed. "We'll be recalled immediately. Everyone's warned of the hallucinations. We'll be hospitalised back at base for months while the bureaucrats try to work out why we went mad."

"You'd better have a look," said Helander. "I want you to go down one by one and tell me what you see."

Partridge was squatting on his haunches, drinking something hot. He was trembling all over. He seemed to be sweating. "This is ridiculous," he said, more than once.

Three others are ahead of me, then it's my turn. I feel perfectly sane, Gerry. Everything else seems normal—as normal as it can be. And if this team has a failing it is that it isn't very prone to speculation or visual hallucinations. I've never been with a duller bunch of fact-gatherers. Maybe that's why we're all more scared than we should be. No expedition from Earth could ever have been to Moldavia before. Certainly nobody would have buried a Roman Catholic cardinal in the ice. There is no explanation, however wild, which fits. We're all great rationalists on this team. Not a hint of mysticism or even poetry among us. The drugs see to that if our temperaments don't!

Russell's coming up. He's swearing, too. Chang goes down. Then it's my turn. Then Simons'. Then Fisch. I wish you were here, Gerry. With your intelligence you could probably think of something. We certainly can't. I'd better start kitting up. More when I come up. To tell you the absolute truth I'm none too happy about going down!

Later

Well, I've been down. It's dark. The blues and greens glow as if they give off an energy of their own, although it's only reflections. The wall is smooth and opaque. About four metres down and about half a metre back into the ice of the face you can see him. He's tall, about fifty-five, very handsome, clean-shaven and he's looking directly out at you. His eyes seem sad but not at all malevolent. Indeed, I'd say he seemed kind. There's something noble about him. His clothes are scarlet and fall in folds which suggest he became frozen while standing naturally in the spot he stands in now. He couldn't, therefore, have been dropped, or the clothing would be disturbed. There's no logic to it, Gerry. His right hand is raised and he's making some sort of Christian sign. You know I'm not too hot on anthropology. Helander's the expert.

His expression seems to be one of forgiveness. It's quite overwhelming. You almost find your heart going out to him while at the same time you can't help thinking you're somehow responsible for his being there! Six light years from Earth on a planet which was only catalogued three years ago and which we are supposedly the first human beings to explore. Nowhere we have been has anyone discovered a shred of evidence that man or anything resembling man ever explored other planets. You know as well as I do that the only signs of intelligent life anyone has found have been negligible and certainly we have never had a hint that any other creature is capable of space-travel. Yet here is a man dressed in a costume which, at its latest possible date, is from the twentieth century.

I tried to stare him down. I don't know why. Eventually I told them to lift me up. While Simons went down, I waited on the edge, sipping ade and trying to stop shaking. I don't know why all of us were so badly affected. We've been in danger often enough (I wrote to you about the lavender swamps) and there isn't anyone on the team who hasn't got a sense of humour. Nobody's been able to raise a laugh yet. Helander tried, but it was so forced that we felt sorry for him. When Simons came up he was in exactly the same state as me. I handed him the rest of my ade and then returned to my biv to write this. We're to have a conference in about ten minutes. We haven't decided whether to send back information yet or not. Our curiosity will probably get the better of us. We have no specific orders on the question, but we're pretty sure we'll get a hands off if we report now. The big skeletons were one thing. This is quite another. And yet we know in our hearts that we should leave well alone.

"Dawn"

The conference is over. It went on for hours. Now we've all decided to sleep on it. Helander and Partridge have been down for another look and have set up a carver in case we decided to go ahead. It will be easy enough to do. Feeling very tired. Have the notion that if we disturb the cardinal we'll do something cataclysmic. Maybe the whole planet will dissolve around us. Maybe this enormous mountain will crumble to nothing. Helander says that what he would like to do is send back on the cardinal but say that he is already carving, since our instruments suggest the crevasse is unstable and could close. There's no way it could close in the next week! But it would be a good enough excuse. You might never get this letter, Gerry. For all we're told personal mail is uninspected I don't trust them entirely. Do you think I should? Or if someone else is reading this, do they think I should have trusted to the law? His face is in my mind's eye as I write. So tranquil. So sad. I'm taking a couple of deegs, so will write more tomorrow.

10/7/17

Helander has carved. The whole damned thing is standing in the centre of the camp now, like a memorial. A big square block of ice with the cardinal peering out of it. We've all walked round and round the thing. There's no question that the figure is human. Helander wanted to begin thawing right away, but bowed to Simons, who doesn't want to risk the thing deteriorating. Soon he's going to vacuum-cocoon it. Simons is cursing himself for not bringing more of his archaeological gear along with him. He expected nothing like this, and our experience up to now has shown that Moldavia doesn't *have* any archaeology worth mentioning. We're all convinced it was a living creature. I even feel he may still be alive, the way he looks at me. We're all very jittery, but our sense of humour has come back and we make bad jokes about the cardinal really being Jesus Christ or Mahomet or somebody. Helander accuses us of religious illiteracy. He's the only one with any real knowledge of all that stuff. He is behaving oddly. He snapped at Russell a little while ago, telling him he wasn't showing proper reverence.

Russell apologised. He said he hadn't realised Helander was superstitious. Helander has sent back, saying what he's done and telling them he's about to thaw. A *fait accompli*. Fisch is unhappy. He and Partridge feel we should replace the cardinal and get on with "our original business". The rest of us argue that this *is* our original business. We are an exploration team. "It's follow-up work," said Fisch. "I'm anxious to see what's at the top of this bloody great staircase." Partridge replied: "A bloody great Vatican, if you reason it through on the evidence we have." That's the trouble with the kind of logic we go in for, Gerry. Well, we'll all be heroes when we get back to Earth, I suppose. Or we'll be disgraced, depending on what happens next. There's not a lot that can happen to me. This isn't my career, the way it is for the others. I'll be only too happy to be fired, since I intend to resign as soon as I'm home. Then it's the Seychelles for us, my dear. I hope you haven't changed your mind. I wish you were here. I feel the need to share what's going on—and I can think of nobody better to share it than you. Oh, God, I love you so much, Gerry. More, I know, than you'll ever love me; but I can bear anything except separation. I was reconciled to that separation until you wrote your last letter. I hope the company is giving you the yellow route now. You deserve it. With a clean run through to Maracaibo there will be no stopping the old gaucho, eh? But those experiments are risky, I'm told. So don't go too far. I think I know you well enough to be pretty certain you won't take unnecessary risks. I wish I could reach out now and touch your lovely, soft skin, your fine fair hair. I must stop this. It's doing things to me which even the blunn can't control! I'm going out for another walk around our frozen friend.

Later

Well, he's thawed. And it is human. Flesh and blood, Gerry, and no sign of deterioration. A man even taller than Helander. His clothes are all authentic, according to the expert. He's even wearing a pair of old-fashioned cotton underpants. No protective clothing. No sign of having had food with him. No sign of transport. And our instruments have been scouring a wider and wider area. We have the little beeps on automatic, using far more energy than they should. The probes go everywhere. Helander says that this is important. If we can find a vehicle or a trace of habitation, then at least we'll have the beginnings of an answer. He wants something to send back now, of course. We've had an acknowledgement and a hold-off signal. There's not much to hold-off from, currently. The cardinal stands in the middle of the camp, his right arm raised in benediction, his eyes as calm and sad and resigned as ever. He continues to make us jumpy. But there are no more jokes, really, except that we sometimes call him "padre". Helander says all expeditions had one in the old days: a kind of psych-medic, like Fedin. Fedin says he thinks the uniform a bit unsuitable for the conditions. It's astonishing how we grow used to something as unbelievable as this. We look up at the monstrous ice-steps ahead of us, the vast gulf behind us, at an alien sky with two suns in it; we know that we are millions upon millions of miles from Earth, across the vacuum of interstellar space, and realise we are sharing our camp with a corpse dressed in the costume of the sixteenth century and we're beginning to take it all for granted . . . I suppose it says something for human resilience. But we're all still uncomfortable. Maybe there's only so much our brains can take. I wish I was sitting on a stool beside you at the Amset having a beer. But things are so strange to me now that *that* idea is hard to accept. This has become normality. The probes bring in nothing. We're using every instrument we've got. Nothing. We're going to have to ask for the reserve stuff at base and get them to send something to the top. I'd like to be pulled back, I think, and yet I remain fascinated. Maybe you'll be able to tell me if I sound mad. I don't feel mad. Nobody is behaving badly. We're all under control, I think. Only Helander seems profoundly affected. He spends most of his time staring into the cardinal's face, touching it.

Later

Helander says the skin feels warm. He asked me to tell him if I agreed. I stripped off a glove and touched the fingers. They certainly feel warm, but that could just be the effect of sun. Nevertheless, the arm hasn't moved, neither have the eyes. There's no breathing. He stares at us tenderly, blessing us, forgiving him. I'm beginning to resent him. What have I done that he should forgive me? I now agree with those who want to put him back. I suppose we can't. We've been told to sit tight and wait for base to send someone up. It will take a while before they come.

11/7/17

Russell woke me up. I kitted up fast and went out. Helander was kneeling in front of the cardinal and seemed to be mumbling to himself. He refused to move when we tried to get him to stand up. "He's weeping," he said. "He's weeping."

There did seem to be moisture on the skin. Then, even as we watched, blood began to trickle out of both eyes and run down the cheeks. The cardinal was weeping tears of blood, Gerry!

"Evidently the action of the atmosphere," said Fedin, when we raised him. "We might have to refreeze him, I think."

The cardinal's expression hadn't changed. Helander became impatient and told us to go away. He said he was communicating with the cardinal. Fedin sedated him and got him back to his biv. We heard his voice, even in sleep, mumbling and groaning. Once, he screamed. Fedin pumped some more stuff into him, then. He's quiet now.

Later

We've had word that base is on its way. About time, too, for me. I'm feeling increasingly scared.

"Dusk"

I crawled out of my biv thinking that Helander was crying again or that Fedin was playing his music. The little, pale sun was high in the sky, the big one was setting. There was a reddish glow on the ice. Everything seemed red, in fact. I couldn't see too clearly, but the cardinal was still standing there, a dark silhouette. And the sounds were coming from him. He was singing, Gerry. There was no one else up. I stood in front of the cardinal. His lips were moving. Some sort of chant. His eyes weren't looking at me any longer. They were raised. Someone came to stand beside me. It was Helander. He was a bit woozy, but his face was ecstatic. He began to join in the song. Their singing seemed to fill the sky, the planet, the whole damned universe. The music made me cry, Gerry. I have never heard a more beautiful voice. Helander turned to me once. "Join in," he said. "Join in." But I couldn't because I didn't know the words. "It's Latin," said Helander. It was like a bloody choir. I found myself lifting my head like a dog. There were resonances in my throat. I began to howl. But it wasn't howling. It was chanting, the same as the cardinal. No words. Just music. It was the most exquisite music I have ever heard in my life. I became aware that the others were with me, standing in a semi-circle, and they were singing too. And we were so full of joy, Gerry. We were all weeping. It was incredible. Then the sun had set and the music gradually faded and we stood looking at one another, totally exhausted, grinning like coyotes, feeling complete fools. And the cardinal was looking at us again, with that same sweet tolerance. Helander was kneeling in front of him and mumbling, but we couldn't hear the words. Eventually, after he'd been on the ice for an hour, Fedin decided to sedate him. "He'll be dead at this rate, if I don't."

Later

We've just finished putting the cardinal back in the crevasse, Gerry. I can still hear that music in my head. I wish there was some way I could play you the recordings we've made, but doubtless you'll hear them in time, around when you get this letter. Base hasn't arrived yet. Helander said he was going to let it be their responsibility. I'm hoping we'll be relieved for those medical tests we were afraid of at first. I want to get away from here. I'm terrified, Gerry. I keep wanting to climb into the crevasse and ask the cardinal to sing for me again. I have never known such absolute release, such total happiness, as when I sang in harmony with him. What do you think it is? Maybe it's all hallucination. Someone will know. Twice I've stood on the edge, peering down. You can't see him from here, of course. And you can't see the bottom. I haven't the courage to descend the lines.

I want to jump. I would jump, I think, if I could get the chance just once more to sing with him. I keep thinking of eternity. For the first time in my life I have a glimmering of what it means.

Oh, Gerry, I hope it isn't an illusion. I hope you'll be able to hear that voice on the tapes and know what I felt when the frozen cardinal sang. I love you Gerry. I want to give you so much. I wish I could give you what I have been given. I wish I could sing for you the way the cardinal sang. There isn't one of us who hasn't been weeping. Fedin keeps trying to be rational. He says we are more exhausted than we know, that the drugs we take have side-effects which couldn't be predicted. We look up into the sky from time to time, waiting for base to reach us. I wish you were here, Gerry. But I can't possibly regret now that I made the decision I made. I love you, Gerry. I love you all.

Ladbroke Grove
May 1967

HANGING THE FOOL

1 THE HERMIT

His wife, he said, had negro blood. "It makes her volatile, like Pushkin."

Watching him later, as he played the table, I saw him show panic twice. He recovered himself rapidly on both occasions. He would tap his wedding ring sharply with his right index finger. His hands were long, not particularly thin, and as tawny as the rest of him—a lion, lazy and cruel, quick as a dagger. "Lord, lord," he would say as his wife made her appearance every evening just before dinner, "she is magnificent!" And he would dart towards her, eager to show her off. Her name was Marianne Max and she loved him in her careless way, though I thought it more a mother's affection, for she was at least ten years his senior.

He would escort her into the dining room and afterwards would never gamble. Together they would stroll for a while along the promenade. Frequently I saw them silhouetted with the palms and cedars, talking and sometimes embracing before returning to the hotel and the suite permanently booked to them. The Hotel Cumberland was older than most and cared more for pleasing its regular customers than attracting the new money which had come to St Crim; it was a little run down but maintained its elegance, its superiority over more modern buildings, especially those revivalist deco monstrosities which had risen across the bay on the French side, upon the remains of the old Ashkanasdi mansion, where the so-called Orient Express brought rich Americans in large numbers.

I had been spending the summer with my ex-wife, who had a villa just above the town, in the pine woods. Every evening I would go down to dine at the hotel and perhaps indulge in a little baccarat.

De Passoni was the chief reason for the regularity of my visits. The man was so supremely unselfconscious, so unguarded, few would have believed him a convicted murderer, escaped from the notorious Chatuz Fortress outside Buenos Aires some years earlier. There was no sign that he feared recognition or recapture. He appeared to live entirely for the day. And there was, of course, no deportation treaty between Argentina and St Crim.

I had not by the middle of the season found any means of approaching him, however. Every time I tried I had been rebuffed. His wife was equally impossible to engage in anything but light conversation.

She was the Countess Max, one of the oldest titles in Wäldenstein. Her first husband, Freddie Max, had been killed during the Siege, leading a cavalry charge against the Prussians across the ruins of the St Maria and St Maria Cathedral. She had remarried after a year, regaining her estates by her alliance with Prince Osbert, the new prime minister. He had died of influenza in 1912, whereupon she had appeared openly with de Passoni, who was already her lover, until the scandal had forced them to St Crim where they now lived in unofficial exile.

De Passoni had his own money, from his father's locomotive works, and it was this he gambled. He took nothing from her. Neither did she expect him to take anything. Residents of the Hotel Cumberland said they were a bloodless pair. I thought otherwise.

2 THE NINE OF PENTACLES

When I came home from North Africa, the following spring, my ex-wife told me that the couple had disappeared from the Hotel Cumberland, although their suite was still booked and paid for. There was a rumour that they were in the hills outside Florence and that the Italian police were resisting an attempt to extradite him. His father had investments in Milan and considerable influence with the authorities. My ex-wife became vague when I asked her for more details, a sure sign that she possessed a secret which she hoped would add to her power.

While she was in her private sitting room taking a telephone call my ex-wife's companion approached me that evening. The woman, Pia, knew through a friend of hers that Countess Max had been seen in Florence and then in Genoa. There was talk of her having bought and equipped a steam yacht. De Passoni had not been with her.

I asked Pia, who disliked me, why they should have left St Crim. She did not know. She shrugged. "Perhaps they were bored."

Returning, my ex-wife had laughed at this and then grown mysterious; my sign for leaving them.

I borrowed her horse and rode down to the cliffs above Daker's Cove. The Englishman's great Gothic house was a shell now, washed by the sea he had attempted to divert. Its granite walls were almost entirely intact and the towers showed well above the water line even at high tide, when waves washed foam in and out of the tall windows, but the great weather vane in the shape of a praying mantis had broken off at last and lay half-buried in the sand of the cove. Daker himself had returned to England and built himself a castle somewhere in the Yorkshire Dales. He lived there the year round, I heard, a disappointed recluse. The remains of his great garden were as beautiful as ever. I rode the chestnut down overgrown paths. Rhododendrons, peonies, lilac and great foxgloves filled the beds, and the whole of the ground was pale blue with masses of forget-me-nots, the remaining memories of England.

What had he learned, I wondered, from all his experience? Perhaps nothing. This was often the fate of those who attempted to impose their own reality upon a resisting and even antagonistic world. It was both a failure of imagination and of spirit. One died frustrated. I had known so many politicians who had ended their days in bitterness. The interpreter, the analyst, the celebrant, however, rarely knew the same pain, especially in old age. Neither, I thought, was that the destiny of those whose politics sought to adjust genuine social ills, who responded to the realities of others' suffering.

The paths joined at an abandoned fountain, a copy of the Kassophasos Aphrodite. Even though she was half-obscured by a wild clematis which clambered over her torso and shoulders like a cloak, she retained her air of serene wisdom. I reined in my horse and dismounted.

Struck by her similarity to the Countess Max, I wondered if I, in my turn, were not imposing my own fancy on the reality.

3 THE ACE OF WANDS

I had returned to Paris for a few days. My investments there were under attack from some manipulations on the Bourse which it soon emerged were fraudulent. By careful covering I was able not only to counter the threat and recover my capital, but make a handsome and honest profit from those whose actions might well have caused me considerable financial embarrassment.

Hearing I was at my house my friend Frere came to see me. He had a message from my father to say that he had been taken ill and was in Lucerne to recover. My own business was over. I went immediately to Switzerland to find my father in reasonable health and breathing almost normally. He was working on his book again, a catalogue of the important buildings destroyed in France and Belgium during the Great War. It was to be his acknowledgement, he said, to an irrecoverable moment in our history, when peace had seemed a natural condition of civilised mankind.

My father asked me to visit my brother at our estates. I had not been to Bek since the last family gathering immediately following the Armistice. Uncle Ricky was long since gone to Italy, obsessed as usual, with a woman, but my brother Ulrich, whom we called Billy, was running the place very well. He was most like my father, more prepared than I to accept such rural responsibilities.

When I left Lucerne the summer had come. Mountains were brilliant with wild flowers and the lake shone with the tranquillity of steel. The train wound down to the French border first and then travelled across to Germany. I changed in Nuremberg, which always reminded me of a gigantic toy, like the one made by the Elastolin firm, with its red castle and walls, its neat cobbles and markets, the epitome of a Bavarian's dream of his perfect past. I had a light lunch at the excellent station restaurant and was disturbed only once, by a gang of men, evidently ex-soldiers, who marched in military style through the lanes shouting of revenge against the French. I found this singularly disturbing and was glad to get on the train which took me to Bek's timeless woods and towers, her deep, lush fields, so like the countryside of Oxfordshire which I had explored while at Balliol before the War.

Billy met me himself, in a dogcart, having received my telegram that morning. "You've been in Africa, I gather?" He looked me over. "You'll be black as an Abyssinian, at this rate!" He was curious about my mining interests in Morocco and Algeria, my relations with the French.

Since I had taken French citizenship, I explained, I had had no trouble. But I was disturbed by the Rif and Bedouin rebels who seemed to me to be growing in strength and numbers. I suspected German interests of supplying them with weapons. Billy said he knew little of international politics. All he hoped was that the Russians would continue fighting amongst themselves until Bolsheviks, Whites, Anarchists, Greens, and whoever else there were, had all wiped one another out.

I had less unsophisticated views, I said. But I laughed. Ivy-covered Bek came in sight at last. I sighed.

"Are you ever homesick?" Billy asked as he guided the dogcart up the drive.

"For which home?" I was amused.

4 THE HIGH PRIESTESS

From Marseilles I took the train down the coast. The sun had given the olive trees and vines an astonishing sharpness and the white limestone glared so fiercely that it became for a while unbearable. The sea lacked the Atlantic's profundity but was a flat, uncompromising blue, merging with a sky growing hotter and deeper in colour with every passing hour until by three o'clock I drew the blinds and sat back in my compartment to read.

I determined not to go to Cassis where Lorna Maddox, the American, had told me she would wait until she returned to Boston in September.

I had met her at dinner when I visited Lord St Odhran at the opening of the grouse season, the previous summer. She had told an extraordinary story about her own sister receiving in the post a piece of human skin, about the size of a sheet of quarto writing paper, on which had been tattooed an elaborate and, she said, quite beautiful picture. "It was the Wheel of Fortune, including all the various fabulous beasts. In brilliant colours. Do you know the Tarot?"

I did not, but afterwards, in London, I purchased a pack from a shop near the British Museum. I was curious.

Lorna's sister had no idea of the sender, nor of the significance of such a grotesque gift.

I discovered that the card indicated Luck and Success.

For at least a week, whenever I had time on my hands, I would lay out sets of cards according to the instructions in the book I had bought at the same time. I attempted to tell my own fortune and that of my family. I recall that even my Uncle Ricky had "Safety" as his final card. But I made no notes of my readings and forgot them, though I still kept the pack in my luggage when I travelled.

"She was told by the police that the tattoo was quite recent," Lorna had said. "And that if the owner were still alive she would have a trace of the design still, on her flesh. The ink, apparently, goes down to the bone. The theory was that she had regretted having the thing made and had it removed by surgery only a month or so after it had been done."

"You're sure it was a woman's skin?" I had been surprised.

"The police were pretty certain."

"What did your sister do with the thing?" St Odhran had asked.

"The police held it for a while. Then they returned it to her. There was no evidence of foul play, you see. My brother wanted it. It fascinated him. I believe she gave it to him."

I knew her brother. His name was Jack Hoffner and he often visited St Crim. I had no great liking for him. He was a bad loser at the tables and was reputed to be a cruel womaniser. Possibly the piece of skin had belonged to some deserted paramour. Had she sent it to Hoffner's sister as an act of revenge?

5 THE NINE OF WANDS

It was raining by the time I reached St Crim. Huge drops of water fell from the oaks and beeches on to tall irises and there was a sound like the clicking of mandibles. Mist gathered on the warm grass as my car drove from the station up the winding road to the white house with its gleaming red roof and English chimneys. The scent of gardenias in the rain was almost overwhelming. I found that I was suddenly depressed and looking back through the rain saw the sea bright with sunlight, for the cloud was already passing.

Pia waited for me on the steps, her hair caught in some multi-coloured gypsy scarf. "She's not here. But she'll be back." Pia signed for a servant to take my bags from the car. "She told me you were coming."

"She said nothing of leaving."

"It happened suddenly. A relative, I gather."

"Her aunt?"

"Possibly." Pia's tone had become almost savage and it was clear she had no intention of telling me anything else.

It had always been my habit not to enquire into my ex-wife's life but I guessed she had gone somewhere with a lover and that this was disturbing Pia unduly. As a rule she kept better control of herself.

My room was ready for me. As soon as I had bathed and dressed I took the car back to the Cumberland. Almost the first person I saw as I stepped through the revolving door into the foyer was the Countess Max who acknowledged my greeting with a warmer than usual smile. Her husband came hurrying from the elevator and shook hands with me. His palm was moist and cool. He seemed frightened, though he quickly masked his expression and his face grew relaxed as he asked after mutual friends.

"I heard you had gone to Genoa to buy a boat!" I said.

"Oh, these rumours!" Countess Max began to move away on de Passoni's arm. And she laughed. It was a wonderful sound.

I followed them into the dining room. They sat together near the open French doors, looking out to the harbour where a slender steam yacht was moored, together with several other large vessels chiefly the property of visitors. I was on the far side of the room and a party of Italians came in, obscuring my view, but it seemed to me that the couple talked anxiously while preserving a good appearance. They left early, after a main course they had scarcely started. About half-an-hour later, as I stood smoking on the balcony, I saw a motor launch leaving a trail of white on the glassy water of the harbour. It had begun to rain again.

6 THE LOVERS

By the following Sunday I suspected some radical alteration in the familiar routine of life at St Crim. My ex-wife had not yet returned and it was impossible for me to ignore the gossip that she had gone to Tangier with Jack Hoffner. Further rumours, of them disappearing into the interior wearing Arab dress, I discounted. If every European said to be disguised as a Touareg was actually in the Maghreb then I doubted if there were a single tribe not wholly Caucasian and at least ninety per cent female!

However, I began to feel some concern when, after a month, nothing had been heard from them while the *Shaharazaad*, the steam yacht owned by Countess Max, was reported to have docked in El Jadida, a small, predominantly Jewish port south of Casablanca. They had radio equipment aboard.

I took to laying out my Tarot pack with the Hermit as Significator. I constantly drew the Ten of Swords, the Ace of Wands and Justice, always for the future but the order frequently changed so that although sadness, pain and affliction lay forever in my future they were not always the finale to my life. The other card drawn regularly for the future was the Lovers.

We turn to such methods when the world becomes overly mysterious to us and our normal methods of interpretation fail.

I told myself that my obsession with the Tarot was wholesome enough. At least it lacked the spurious authenticity of psychoanalysis. That particular modern fad seemed no more than a pseudo-scientific form of Theosophy, itself pseudo-religious: an answer to the impact of the twentieth century which enabled us to maintain the attitudes and convictions of nineteenth-century Vienna. Everyone I knew was presently playing at it. I refused to join in. Certain insights had been made by the psychoanalystic fraternity, but these had been elevated to the level of divine revelation and an entire mystical literature derived from them. I was as astonished by society's acceptance of these soothsayers as I was by the Dark Age rituals in St Crim's rather martial sub-Byzantine cathedral. At least these had the excuse of habit. Doctor Freud was a habit I did not wish to acquire.

I remained at St Crim until early September when I received a letter from my ex-wife. She was recovering from typhus in a hospital run by the White Sisters in Tangier. She was alone and had no friends there. She asked me to cable funds to the British Embassy or have my agent help her. There was no mention of Jack Hoffner or de Passoni and the Countess Max.

I chose one card at random from my pack. It was the Wheel of Fortune. I went down to the hotel and telephoned my friend Vronsky. That afternoon his Van Berkel seaplane landed in the harbour and after a light supper we took off for North Africa, via Valencia and Gibraltar.

The machine was a monoplane of the latest type and was built to race. There was barely room for a small valise and myself. Vronsky's slightly bloated, boyish face grinned at me from the rear cockpit, his goggles giving him the appearance of a depraved marmoset. Since the Bolshevik counter-revolution Vronsky had determined to live life to the absolute, convinced that he had little time before someone assassinated him. He was a distant cousin of the Tsar.

The plane banked once over St Crim, her wooded hills and pale villas, the delicate stone and iron of her harbour and promenade, the mock-Baroque of her hotels. It would only be a matter of seven years before, fearing the political situation in Italy, she gave up her independence to France.

The plane's motion, though fluid, filled me with a slight feeling of nausea, but this was quickly forgotten as my attention was drawn to the beauty of the landscape below. I longed to own a machine again. It had been three years since I had crashed and been captured by the Hungarians, happily only a matter of weeks before the end of the War. My wife, a German national, had been able to divorce me on the grounds that I was a traitor, though I had possessed French citizenship since 1910.

Gradually the familiar euphoria returned and I determined, next time I was in the Hague, to order a new machine.

After refuelling stops we were in sight of Tangier within a few hours. As always, the shores of Africa filled me with excitement. I knew how difficult, once one set foot on that continent, it was to leave.

7 THE PAGE OF WANDS

The Convent of the White Sisters was close to the British Consulate, across from the main gate to the Grand Socco, an unremarkable piece of architecture by Arab standards, though I was told the mosque on the far side was impressive. Apart from the usual mixture of mules and donkeys, bicycles, rickshaws, the occasional motor car and members of almost every Berber and Arab tribe, there was an unusually large presence of soldiers, chiefly of the Spanish Foreign Legion. Vronsky spoke to a tall man he recognised from before the War. The exchange was in Russian, which I understood badly. There had been some sort of uprising in a village on the outskirts of the city, to do with a group of Rif who had come in to trade. The uprising was not, as it had first seemed, political.

"A blood feud," Vronsky informed me as we crossed the square from the shade of the great palms, "but they're not complaining. It brought them in from the desert and now they have a day's unexpected leave. They are going in there"—he pointed through the gate—"for the Ouled Näil. For the women." And he shuddered.

We knocked on a rather nondescript iron door and were greeted by a small black nun who addressed me in trilling, birdlike French which I found attractive. Since they did not accept divorce, I simply told her I was visiting my wife and she became excited.

"You got the letter? How did you arrive so soon?"

"Our aeroplane is in the harbour." I lifted my flying helmet.

She made some reference to the miraculous and clapped her little hands. She asked us to wait but Vronsky said he had some business in the new town and arranged to meet me at the Café Stern in three hours. If I was delayed I would send a message.

The little negress returned with a tall olive-skinned old woman who introduced herself as the Mother Superior. I asked after my wife.

"She is well. Physically, she's almost fully recovered. You are Monsieur von Bek? She described you to me. You'll forgive me. She was anxious that it should only be you."

The nun led me down whitewashed corridors smelling of vinegar and disinfectant until we entered a sunny courtyard which contained a blue mosaic fountain, two Arab workmen repairing one of the columns and, in a deck chair reading a book, my ex-wife. She wore a plain lawn dress and a simple straw cloche. She was terribly pale and her eyes still seemed to contain traces of fever.

"Bertie." She put down her book, her expression one of enormous relief. "I hadn't expected you to come. At least, I'd hoped—" She shrugged, and bending I kissed her cheek.

"Vronsky brought me in his plane. I got your letter this morning. You should have cabled."

Her look of gratitude was almost embarrassing.

"What happened to Hoffner?" I asked. I sat on the parapet of the fountain.

"Jack's . . ." She paused. "Jack left me in Foum al-Hassan, when I became ill. He took the map and went on."

"Map?" She assumed I knew more than I did.

"It was supposed to lead to a Roman treasure—or rather a Carthaginian treasure captured by the Romans. Everything seemed to be going well after we picked up the trail in Volubilis. Then Michael de Passoni and Countess Max came on the scene. God knows how they found us. The whole business went sour."

"Where did Hoffner come by a map?"

"His sister gave it to him. That awful tattoo."

"A treasure map? The Wheel of Fortune?"

"Apparently." The memory appeared to have exhausted her. She stretched out her arms. "I'm so glad you're here. I prayed for you to come. I've been an absolute ass, darling."

"You were always romantic. Have you ever thought of writing novels? You'd make a fortune."

On impulse I moved into her embrace.

8   THE QUEEN OF PENTACLES

I remained at St Crim for several months while my wife grew stronger, though her mental condition fluctuated considerably. Her nightmares were terrifying even to me and she refused to tell me what they involved.

We were both curious for news of Jack Hoffner and when his sister arrived at the Cumberland for a few days I went down to see her. My visits to the town had been rare. In the evenings my wife and I played cards. Sometimes we read each other's Tarot. We became quite expert.

Lorna Maddox believed that her brother was dead. "He hadn't the courage for any prolonged adventure—and North Africa sounds dangerous. I've never been there. Someone killed him, probably, for that map. Do you really think it was sent by a deserted mistress?"

"Perhaps by the one who actually inscribed the tattoo."

"Or the person who commissioned it? I mean, other than the recipient, as it were?"

"Do you know more about this now?" I asked. We sat indoors looking through closed windows at the balcony and the bay beyond.

"I'm not sure," she said. "I think Michael de Passoni had it done."

"To his victim?"

"Yes. To a victim."

"He's murdered more than once?"

"I would guess so. I heard all this from Margery Graeme who had quite a long affair with him. She's terrified of him. He threatened to kill her."

"Why would he have told her such secrets?" A waiter came to take our orders and there was a long pause before she could speak again.

She had magnificent blue eyes in a large, gentle face. She wore her hair down in a girlish, rather old-fashioned style identified with pre-War Bohemia. When she bent towards me I could feel her warmth and remembered how attractive I had found her when we had met in Scotland.

"Margery discovered some papers. Some designs. And a set of Tarot cards with the Wheel of Fortune removed. The addresses of several tattooists in Marseilles were there. And the piece of skin, you know, came from there. At least the postmark on the envelope was Cassis."

"Everyone goes to Cassis." I was aware of the inanity of my remark which had to do, I was sure, with my wish to reject her information, not because it seemed untrue but because it seemed likely. I was beginning to fear a moral dilemma where previously I had known only curiosity.

9   THE WHEEL OF FORTUNE

Business at last forced me to return to Paris. Dining at Lipp's in St Germain on the first evening of my arrival I was disturbed to see the Countess Max. De Passoni was not with her. Instead she was in the company of a dark man who was either Levantine or Maghrebi. He was strikingly handsome and wore his evening clothes with the easy familiarity which identified him, as we used to say, as some sort of gentleman.

Countess Max recognised me at once and could do nothing but acknowledge me. When I crossed to greet her she reluctantly introduced me to her companion. "Do you know Moulay Abul Hammoud?"

"Enchanted, monsieur," he said in the soft, vibrant voice I associated always with the desert. "We have already met briefly, I believe."

Now that we stood face to face I remembered him from a Legation reception in Algiers before the War. He had been educated at Eton but was the religious leader of the majority of clans in the Southern- and pre-Sahara. Without his control the clans would have been disunited and warring not only amongst themselves but making desultory raids on the authorities. Moulay Abul Hammoud not only kept order in large parts of the Maghreb but also maintained enormous political power, for upon his orders the desert Berbers as well as large numbers of urban Arabs, could forget all differences and unite to attack the French or Spanish.

It was commonly agreed that Moulay Abul was only awaiting the appropriate moment, while the benefits of colonial occupation outweighed the ills, before declaring the renewed independence of the Saharan kingdoms. His influence was also recognised by the British who acknowledged his growing power in North India and in their own Middle Eastern interests.

"I'm honoured to meet you again, sir." I was impressed by him and shared a respect many had expressed before me. "Are you in Paris officially?"

"Oh, merely a vacation." He smiled at the Countess Max. She looked darker, even more exotic than when I had last seen her.

"Moulay Abul was of great service to me," she murmured, "in Morocco."

"My wife has only recently returned. I believe you met her there. With Jack Hoffner?"

The countess resumed her familiar detached mask, but in spite of seeming ill-mannered I continued. "Have you heard anything of Hoffner? He was meant to have disappeared in Morocco or Algeria."

Moulay Abul interrupted quickly and with considerable grace. "Mr Hoffner was unfortunately captured by hostile Tuaregs in Mauretania. He was eventually killed. Also captured, I believe, was the poor countess's husband. The authorities know, but it has not been thought wise to inform the Press until we have satisfactory identification."

"You have some?"

"Very little. A certain map that we know was in Hoffner's possession."

It seemed to me that the Countess Max tried to warn him to silence. Unconsciously the Moulay had told me more than he realised. I bowed and returned to my table.

It seemed clear that Hoffner and de Passoni had failed in their adventure and had died in pursuit of the treasure. Possibly Moulay Abul and Countess Max had betrayed them and the treasure was in their hands. More likely the answer was subtler and less melodramatic.

I was certain, however, that Moulay Abul and the Countess Max were lovers.

10   THE TEN OF SWORDS

The tragedy eventually reached the Press. By coincidence I was in Casablanca when the news appeared and while the local journals, subject to a certain discretion, not to say censorhip, were rather matter-of-fact in their reporting, the French and English papers were delighted with the story and made everything they could of it, especially since de Passoni was already a convicted murderer and Hoffner had a warrant for fraud against him issued in Berlin at the time of his disappearance.

The Countess Max emerged more or less with her honour intact. The Press preferred to characterise her as an innocent heroine, while my wife was not mentioned at all. Moulay Abul remained a shadowy but more or less benign figure, for the story had been given a Kiplingesque touch by the time the writers had licked it into a shape acceptable to a wide public.

The opinion was that de Passoni and Hoffner had duped the Countess Max, getting her to buy the steam yacht they needed to transport the treasure back to Europe as soon as it was in their possession. The map, drawn on the skin of a long-dead Roman legionary, had become the conventional object of boys' adventure fiction and we learned how the two adventurers had dressed as Bedouin and ridden into the Sahara in search of a lost city built by Carthaginians who had fled conquering Rome. More in fact was made of the mythical city than the map, which suited Hoffner's family, who had feared the sensational use journalists would have made of the bizarre actuality.

I was invited to dinner by General Fromental and his wife and should have refused had not I heard that Moulay Abul was also going to be present.

By chance it was a relatively intimate affair at one of those pompous provincial mansions the French liked to build for themselves in imitation of an aristocracy already considered impossibly vulgar by the rest of Europe. My fellow guests were largely of advanced years and interested neither in myself nor the Moulay, who seemed glad of my company, perhaps because we shared secrets in common.

When we stood together smoking on the terrace, looking out at palms and poplars, still a dark green against the deep blue of the sky, and listening to the night birds calling, to the insects and the occasional barking of a wild dog, I asked after the Countess Max.

"I gather she's in excellent health," he said. He smiled at me, as if permitting me a glimpse of his inner thoughts. "We were not lovers, you know. I am unable to contemplate adultery."

The significance of his remark completely escaped me. "I have always been fascinated by her," I told him. "We were frequently in St Crim at the same time. She and de Passoni lived there for a while."

"So I understand. The yacht is moored there now, is it not?"

"I hadn't heard."

"Yes. Recently. She had expressed some notion of returning to

Wäldenstein but the situation there is not happy. And she is a cold-natured woman needing the sun. You've a relative there, I believe."

"An ex-wife. You know her?"

"Oh, yes. Slightly. My other great vice is that I have difficulty in lying." He laughed and I was disarmed. "I make up for this disability by the possession of a subtle mind which appreciates all the degrees and shades of truth. Hoffner deserted her in Foum al-Hassan. I was lucky enough to play some small part in getting her back to Tangier. One should not involve women in these affairs, don't you think?"

"I rather understood they involved themselves."

"Indeed. A passion for excitement has overwhelmed Western females since the dying down of war. It seems to have infected them more than the men."

"Oh, our women have always had more courage, by and large. And more imagination. Indeed, one scarcely exists without the other."

"They do define each other, I'd agree."

He seemed to like me as much as I liked him. Our companionship was comfortable as we stood together in the warm air of the garden.

"I'm afraid my wife mentioned nothing of your help," I told him.

"She knew nothing of it. That man Hoffner? What do you think of him?"

"A blackguard."

"Yes." He was relieved and spoke almost as if to someone else. "A coward. A jackal. He had a family?"

"Two sisters living. I know one of them slightly."

"Ah, then you've heard of the map?"

"The one you mentioned in Paris? Yes, I know of it. I don't think his sister recognised it for a map."

"Metaphysically, perhaps, only?" His humour had taken a different colour. "Oh, yes, there is a map involved in many versions of that design. I thought that was common knowledge."

"You're familiar with the Tarot?"

"With arcana in general." He shrugged almost in apology. "I suppose it's in the nature of my calling to be interested in such things. Hoffner's death was no more unpleasant than any he would have visited on—on me, for instance." He turned away to look up at the moon. "I believe they flayed him."

"So he's definitely dead. You saw the corpse?"

"Not the corpse exactly." Moulay Abul blew smoke out at the sky. It moved like an escaped ifrit in the air and fled into invisible realms. "Just the pelt."

11 JUSTICE

My return to St Crim was in the saddest possible circumstances, in response to a telegram telling me that my wife was dead. When I arrived at the house Pia handed me a sealed envelope addressed to me in my wife's writing.

"You know she killed herself?" The voice was neutral, the eyes desolate.

I had feared this but had not dared to consider it. "Do you know why?"

"It was to do with Hoffner. Something that happened to her in Africa. You know how she was."

We went down to the kitchens where Pia made coffee. The servants were all gone, apart from the cook, who was visiting her sister in Monaco. The woman and her husband who had kept the house for her had found her body.

"She cut her wrists in the swimming pool. She used Hoffner's razor."

"You don't know why? I mean—there wasn't anything she discovered? About Hoffner, for instance?"

"No. Why, did you hear something?"

I shook my head but she had guessed I was lying. Handing me the coffee cup she said slowly: "Do you think she knew what was going on? With Hoffner and de Passoni?"

"She told you."

"The Countess Max stayed with us for several days. She went down to the hotel. She plans to remain there until the funeral. Hoffner's sister is there, too. A bit of a reunion."

"You think my wife was guilty? That she had a hand in whatever happened in Morocco?"

"She knew Hoffner was involved in every sort of beastly crime and that half the Berlin underworld was after him—not to mention the New York police and the French Secret Service. He betrayed men as well as women. She told me he was threatening her but I think she loved him. Some bad chemistry, perhaps. He excited her, at least. The Countess Max, on the other hand, was thoroughly terrified of him. He had a hold over her husband, you know."

"So he forced them into his adventure?"

"Apparently. They needed a boat."

I found that I could not bear to open the envelope my wife had left for me and walked instead down to the Hotel Cumberland where I found Lorna Maddox and Countess Max taking tea together in the cool of the salon. They both wore half-mourning in honour of my wife and greeted me with sincerity when I presented myself, asking me to join them.

"It must have been frightful for you," said Lorna Maddox, "the news. We were appalled."

"Her nerves were terribly bad." The Countess Max remained distant, though less evasive, less cool. "I thought she was brave. To go inland with the men like that. I refused, you know."

"But you believed the map?"

"I had no reason to doubt. Jack was completely convinced. The woman—the woman on whom it had been inscribed was—well, you know, of very good family over there. She was no more than a girl. The secret was passed from mother to daughter, apparently. God knows where Jack heard the story originally, but he made it his business to find her."

"And seduce her," said Lorna in a small, chilling voice.

"He was proud of that. I gather it was something of a challenge." The Countess Max raised china to her lips.

"Surely he didn't—he couldn't . . . ?" I was glad to accept the chair Lorna Maddox offered me.

"Take the skin?" she said. "Oh, no. That was sent to my sister by the girl's uncle, I gather. There was for a while some suspicion of a blood feud between her family and mine."

"Moulay Abul put a stop to that." The Countess was approving. "Without his interference things might have become considerably worse." She frowned. "Though poor Michael's not entirely convinced of that."

I was shocked. "You husband's still alive? I understood that he had died in North Africa."

"Moulay Abul saved him also. Through his influence he was given up to the French police and is now at sea, escorted back to Buenos Aires by two Sûreté sergeants. He was relieved at first. . . ."

She stared directly back into my eyes. "He saw it."

Although it was not yet five I ordered a cognac from their waiter. I marvelled at the self-control of such women. It was still impossible to guess their real feelings—one towards her brother, the other towards her husband.

There was little more to say.

"The matter's been resolved in the best possible way." Lorna Maddox sighed and picked up a delicate cup. She glanced at me almost in amusement. "You are very upset. I'm sorry. We were fond of your wife. But she would encourage men to such extremes, don't you think?"

I returned to the house and opened the packet, expecting some explanation of my wife's part in the affair. But she had written nothing.

The envelope contained a folded section of almost transparent skin on which had been tattooed a Wheel of Fortune. It had been wrapped around the Tarot card representing Justice. There was also a visiting card bearing the printed name of Moulay Abul Hamoud and on the reverse, in clear script, a few words— 'With my compliments. I believe this is morally, madame, your property.'

The note was, of course, unsigned.

Majorca/Oxfordshire
June 1987

THE MURDERER'S SONG

". . . and then, from that dungeon in the West,
  There rises up a melody, beguiling and forlorn.
  It is the sweet, sad, self-deceiving murderer's song,
  And it will not end 'til morn . . ."
—Wheldrake, The Prisoners.

I

BABY SHOT IN WOMB SURVIVES
A baby girl has been born in a Belfast hospital with a gunman's bullet
lodged in her side, it was revealed last night. The baby was born
prematurely in the Mater Hospital late on Friday a few hours after her
mother was sprayed by shots from a passing car in Crumlin Road.
—*Sunday Times, 4th July 1976*

Rolling through the twisting twitterns of his idea of Camelot,
clad in scarlet velvet stitched with an excess of gold thread,
black fur jumping on his head, flapping gallant's boots upon his
feet, the tune of some uncomplicated galliard slipping from tongue
and teeth, Romain de la Rose raised bottle to lips, revelling in the
effect which the alcohol was having upon his brain. "Quite unselfconscious!" He was amazed. The stuff was not at all disappointing.
Unlike so many things discovered from the ancient world, this
booze, this grog, this fruit of the vine was everything its original
inventors claimed. He sought control of his legs, his vision; he
failed. He saw a blank stone wall ahead. He fumbled for a power
ring, forgot his intention, and sat down.

Miss Una Persson, her co-ordinates as conservative as ever, had
landed in Camelot's central plaza. Until now the location had been
a deserted pine mine, an abandoned artefact of the Duke of
Queens. She had left her time-machine (merely a gent's Royal
Albert black bicycle) where it was and had been stretching her legs
when she bumped into the inebriated recreator of Arthur's ancient
seat—in a cul-de-sac he had not meant to invent.

Romain de la Rose was not one of Una's acquaintances at the
End of Time. His round blue eyes regarded her from handsome, if

plump, pink features. His legs moved a little, as if he were trying to regain his feet. He smiled at her. He studied her.

It was unusual for her to feel, these days, embarrassed. She wondered what was remarkable about her dark green military greatcoat with its red facings, the cavalry boots, the beret, which were her standard time-travelling costume.

She had already swallowed her translation pill. "Excuse me," she said, "but until today this spot was always deserted."

"The old ruin was yours?"

"Not at all. Although there was a sentimental attachment . . ."

He regained his feet; made a leg. Bottles fell from his pockets as he bent. They smashed on the flagstones (he wasn't sure if the flags were contemporary; he had chosen them primarily for their colours) and scents of whisky, gin and Cinzano gathered under her nose. She took a backward step.

"My drunkenness is not to your taste?" He could be as sensitive to nuance as his friend Werther de Goethe.

"Ah . . ." She waved an ambiguous hand.

"I can produce any beverage." Another bottle materialised. Sake.

She refused. "This is the End of Time?"

"A chrononaut!" He began to fiddle with one of the power rings of his left index finger.

She reached to stop him. "I've no desire to join your collection."

"Forgive me." He drew pink brows together. "It was unbionic of me." He explained. "The appropriate slang for the period." He indicated Camelot, its minarets, turrets and skyscrapers.

Una smiled and accepted the bottle. One sip. It was pure alcohol and could kill her. She spat politely and returned the sake. "Have you any idea where I might discover the Duke of Queens? Or Lord Jagged, perhaps?"

"They're both adrift, I heard. In Time." He made no further attempt at coherence. He sank down. He grinned, his head on one side. He hiccupped.

"There go my hopes," said Una.

His lids fell.

She walked back towards her bicycle.

"Sometimes," (she spoke to herself), "there seems no point at all in trying for a linear mode."

II

MYSTERY BOY
A teenager was suffering from loss of memory yesterday after staggering off the beach at Polperro, Cornwall.
—*Daily Mirror, 6th July 1976*

Jerry Cornelius was peering at his chest, picking at the hairs. He held something up. "Is that gangrene?" he asked her. "Or egg?"

"Egg." She was tired of rowing. She let the current take the boat, now that they were past Oxford's filthy ruins. He sat in the stern, the tiller lines over his thin, silk-clad shoulders. The shirt was dirty, as were his black velvet britches. There was a dash or two of blood on one sleeve.

"A lot of people resent me for that," he told her, lighting a soiled Sullivans. "My wounds heal so quickly."

She yawned and leaned forward to take the cigarette from his lips. She still wore her greatcoat, although the temperature was in the nineties. The river was low. Consequently the rocks were higher. She puffed. "Where to, now?" They peered together at the bank and the fire-blackened landscape beyond. "I've never known it so quiet at this time of year."

"It's the same everywhere," he told her. He tried to get his cigarette back, but failed. He contemplated the slime at his feet.

As a concession, she put on a pair of government shades which gave her the appearance of a surprised lemur. He seemed to think this gesture significant, for he looked over his shoulder. "Is anyone following us?"

"Probably not."

He was disappointed. "The freedom of pursuit," he said. "It's the only one we've got."

As was normal of late, he had automatically assumed his Pierrot posture, just as she fell into the Harlequin mode. Back at base Columbine was controlling the Time Centre's operations as best she could. Catherine had always preferred to take the important passive roles when they came up. She said she only thoroughly relaxed if type-cast. Besides, she was still mourning her short-lived colleague, the American-Greek, Minos Aquilinus, who had been killed in the line of duty while on a visit to an obscure half-focussed zone; some mythical 20th century Atlanta where a black emperor ruled over a Utopian Western Hemisphere. Aquilinus, who specialised as a metatemporal investigator, had been asked to look into the only case of suspected corruption in Atlanta in fifty years. Almost certainly he had been able to find confirming evidence and had been put out of the picture before he could pass his information on to the authorities. He had been the only Greek on regular call. Now Catherine would have to find a replacement.

"You'd better take over the oars," said Una. She rose and rocked the boat.

Jerry was reluctant to move. "I'm not well," he complained. "I was shot." He frowned. "Wasn't I?"

"You should be used to it. Row."

He obeyed, muttering, taking her place and pulling on the oars with deliberate clumsiness. "It's time I had a more important part. I used to be famous, you know, in some places. I was a living legend. Now I'm just a bloody stale joke."

"Every dog has his day. And you've had yours." She enjoyed being ruthless when he was in his moods of self-pity.

He continued to mutter. "Apoca-bloody-alypse after apoca-bloody-alypse. Arma-fucking-geddon on Arma-fucking-geddon. I was promised a reward."

"Heaven?"

"Full control."

"Of heaven?"

"I thought that's what they all meant."

"Con men like you, Jerry, are always the easiest men to con."

"Shit!" His oars found mud. "Oh, shit!" He hesitated on the edge of hysteria, eyeing her, wondering if he'd be able to get away with it. He withdrew the oar and pushed the boat further into the stream that had been the Thames. "Are you sure this is the way to London?"

"It was."

"Sod you!" He attempted to blame her for their predicament. His eyes filled with tears. "Oh, sod you!"

"You were told you could have a spell of R and R, but you had to come and see the damage."

"I always hated Oxford. Pater and that."

"It was the hardest bloody gem-like flame I ever saw."

67

"It happened too fast," he said. "I had my back turned."

"It's the story of your life."

Having failed to involve her, he improved his rowing. The landscape became brown and then an indeterminate green. Undamaged houses appeared on the banks. Children and stockbrokers gambolled on smooth lawns; tea-things clattered; women with well-bred voices called to their loved ones, terrifying Jerry so much that his speed doubled. They left the china, the deck-chairs, the climbing-frames, the garden hoses and sprinklers behind. Again the landscape grew black: stumps of trees, dark roots, and the smell.

"Oh, fuck," said Jerry trembling. "All that work. Everything wiped out except the middle-classes."

"They're like ants," said Una, commiserating. "They survive anything." She chewed on some slices of meat.

"I've got to get away," he said. "Where did you leave the bikes?"

"You shouldn't rely on bikes."

"You do."

"That's habit, not reliance. There's a difference." She became uncomfortable. "I left them in Oxford. We'll have to go to London to get some new ones."

Jerry cheered up at this admission of incompetence. "We all make mistakes," he said.

She rejected his attempt. "Nobody makes as many as you."

Relationships were, as always, breaking down as a result of the ambiguous nature of the disaster. She could not for the life of her determine the exact nature of the catastrophe. She felt guilty. "I'm sorry."

He shrugged, letting his intelligence through for an instant. "Tropes," he said. "That's all. They might have a function, though. And all the time I thought I'd found Romance."

III

CLIMBDOWN AFTER LANGUAGE RIOTS
South Africa yesterday gave in to demands to drop Afrikaans as the compulsory language to schools for black children—the cause of last

month's bloody race riots in which 176 people died. In future the staff of black schools will be able to teach in English if they want to.
—*Daily Mirror, 7th July 1976*

"I suppose that my faith is based firmly on the principle that people are stupider than they look and talk," said Una. She puffed on the cheroot which Catherine lit for her. They were on a verandah, facing the jungle. Various harsh-voiced birds blundered about in the foliage.

"That's not fair." Catherine wore a sarong. She kissed Una's gauze-clad shoulder. "Some people are very clever. Quite ordinary people."

"That's indisputable." Una lay back in the rattan chair and tried to see if there were any clouds in a sky only barely visible through the leaves. "But it isn't what I said. That is, you didn't understand me."

"You're not in a very democratic mood." Catherine pushed sweaty blonde hair back from her face. "Did you have a bad trip?" She glanced into the darkened interior of the bungalow. The instruments were operating normally. She was not really listening to Una's arguments. "Feeling a bit élitist, eh? You're always like this when you come home."

"Not at all. Experience shows that most people are thick. They are insensitive. They lack imagination. They are boring. I regard such qualities as pernicious."

"They can't help it . . ."

"They can help it if they don't possess the decency, the humility, to realise what fools they are."

"You used to try to encourage people to have self-confidence. You believed in Education and that."

"I still do. I'm all for improving the tone, if not the quality, of life."

Catherine signed to her poor brother Frank who mindlessly began to work the punkah with his big toe. She was anxious to cool Una down. Frank, dressed in a ragged pair of tennis shorts, his body covered in large sores of identical size and shape, smiled into the distance as he sat on one side of the bungalow's front door. Una continued:

"Most intellectuals are pretty stupid, which is why the education systems of the world remain so bad. A perfect system would reveal the best of us. Then we could do away with democracy which nobody really wants anyway. I know it's unfashionable, but we could certainly do with an intelligent intellectual élite running the world. Like in H. G. Wells or some of those others."

"Nobody thinks that any more." Catherine seated herself beside her friend. She stared with some dismay at the unchanging rain forest. "Do they?"

"Not in the democracies," said Una, "only in the Marxist countries. And what lets them down, of course, is their puritanism, their certainties. Only idiots are certain of anything."

"I can't disagree with you there." Catherine took one of the glasses from the tray between them and sipped her julep through a big straw.

"Bugger democracy." Una took the other drink. "I'm fed up with it. It forces intelligent people to pretend to be stupid. What good does that do for anybody?"

"You're just disappointed things haven't worked out too well."

"If you like."

For an instant a great macaw perched on the verandah railing and regarded them through chilly black eyes before flying off into the jungle. It seemed to be laughing.

"In lieu of sane politics we're forced towards drama." Una shifted her weight. "But how many are prepared to admit we spend most of our lives in a fictive mode? We're all characters in a bad novel. The best we can hope for is to have some share in the writing."

"But once we realise that, surely time travel becomes a possibility?" Catherine continued to stare at the forest. "There are advantages."

"Instinct forces us again and again towards catharses that are unnecessary and often destructive. But if one picks one's own ground, says goodbye to that sort of instinct; follows, perhaps, a higher, more human instinct, then one begins to smell freedom. Identity, time, the human condition, no longer enslave one. Then one can choose any slavery one desires, for as long as one desires it." She removed the cheroot and threw it as far as she could towards a clump of magnolia trees of a particularly vulgar variety.

"You mean it all comes down to nothing more than a choice of slavery?"

"Don't expect too much of yourself," said Una. "Most of us seek only that. True freedom is terrifying. It involves a high risk of destruction."

"And one's immortal soul?" Catherine smiled sardonically. "You sound like any black magic fascist." She sighed. "I can't resist them."

Una held firmly to her sad philosophy. "You can see why the Arabs are astonished by the Jews. A race like that will do anything for a catharsis, no matter what the cost. Heaven save us from Zionism."

As if summoned by an incantation Sebastian Auchinek showed his miserable face on the stoop. "Am I the only one doing any work around here?"

Una smiled at an unsmiling Catherine. "Don't worry, Seb. Glogauer will relieve you in an hour or two." She sank back into the luxury of the cane, the cushions and the Campari-soda. She giggled at the expression of hopeless pain in Auchinek's martyred eyes.

IV

THE HI-JOKER

A man who hijacked a Libyan airliner on an internal flight was flown to Majorca yesterday. There he meekly gave himself up to police and surrendered his weapons . . . two toy guns.
—*Daily Mirror*, 7th July 1976

"People seem to get angry about the silliest things." Una put down the half-read paperback copy of Guy Boothby's *The Beautiful White Devil* and looked again at Auchinek's incoherent note to her. "Can he survive in the jungle? What's the time in the outside world?"

"About 1070," said Catherine. "This part of the continent's virtually unpopulated, but there are all kinds of beasts."

"I'll drink to that." Una used the note to mark her place.

V

PEOPLE
Dai Llewelyn, brother to Roddy (you know, Princess Margaret's friend),
has been escorting three American girls around town. They're all black
and from New York. "They're my ethnic friends," says Dai who is shortly
going to America, and, I am told, will stay in their empty flat.
—*"The Inside World", Daily Mirror, 7th July 1976*

Auchinek was weeping when they found him on the banks of a
stagnant lagoon four miles from the Centre. "You're all fascists.
Fucking fascists!" Leeches covered his neck, shoulders and upper
arms. He had been trying to drown himself—lying on the shore
and immersing his head—in his usual compromising fashion. Una
took some salt from her kit and began to remove the creatures.
Shadows moved in the jungle. Captain Bastable, in his khaki
tropical kit, his solar topee on his fine crown, fiddled with the heavy
dial of his Banning cannon, using all his strength to keep the
weapon off the ground. He had forgotten to bring the stand. Una
supposed it was unfortunate that Bastable had been the only
member of personnel available for the expedition; his remarks
about Jews had not gone down at all well with Glogauer or
Auchinek in the canteen a few nights before. His attempts to
explain that "he meant no harm" and that his remarks didn't apply
to "an awful lot of Jews who are jolly good sorts" had made matters
worse.

Una pulled off the last leech. Auchinek continued to swear at
her. "You're the kind of people who put Hitler in power!"

Bastable, of course, had no idea what Auchinek was talking
about, since he didn't come from Auchinek's zone, but Una
couldn't help telling the truth. "As a matter of fact," she said, "I
did."

Auchinek fell silent.

"Everybody agreed later that he went too far," she added.

Auchinek was shocked, disbelieving. "You played a part in the
Russian revolution!"

"That's right. But not the counter-revolution. The Bolsheviks
kicked me out. What's that got to do with it? The Slavs have never
been fond of Jews either, you know."

"Oh, my God!" Auchinek shrieked. He loved Una. He still loved her.

"I'm only stating facts," she continued reasonably, helping him towards the trees. "It's this way." She supported him as he limped. "You Jews always bring things down to a personal level."

"Oh, Una! Una! Una!"

She looked sardonically at a bemused Captain Bastable and shrugged.

After they had returned to the bungalow and sedated Auchinek, putting him to bed, she confided to Catherine.

"It seems I'm getting up everyone's noses here. I'd better move on."

Catherine could only agree.

"There are times, Una, when you're less than tactful."

VI

PUBLIC OPINION
The Israelis are magnificent. They must be the only people in the world with the courage to deal with terrorists, hijackers, bombers, hooligans or the like. What a pity that this country cannot act in such a forthright manner. We used to, many years ago.
H. J. Smith, Banbury, Oxfordshire.
—*Daily Mirror, 7th July 1976*

Shakey Mo Collier came running out of the blazing building with oil and blood all over his face, an M16 in his fearful hands, a grin on his face. From the upper floors of the building issued wailing of a kind Una hadn't heard since Kiev, 1919, during one of the pogroms which had relieved the tensions and uncertainties of the civil war for so many of the citizens. "They nearly got me, Miss P. Christ! It's appalling in there . . ." He stood beside her, looking up, panting. "I suppose there's nothing we can do for them now?"

"We've got to go." She glanced at her calendar. The figures fluttered and died on the display panel. "It's 1943. Only another three years before Einstein's Revenge. You have to hand it to them. They know how to get back at people."

Mo was disapproving. "Well, I call it discrimination."

Una made no attempt to follow his logic. He was suffering from minor shell-shock and would continue to do so for the rest of his days, no matter what part of the twentieth century he operated in.

"Reprisals are all very well," Mo went on, "but why take it out on the innocent?"

"We're all innocent," said Una. "We're all guilty. What does it mean?"

She was in worse shape than he was.

VII

PEOPLE
Marlene Dietrich is to make her first appearance since before the Hitler era in Berlin where her stage career began more than half a century ago. But it is not purely a sentimental journey for Miss Dietrich, now 75. She is being paid £4,000 a show—plus expenses and travel.
—*Daily Mirror, 7th July 1976*

Jerry shuffled towards the gas-ring and took the aluminium pot from it, pouring coffee into two earthenware bowls. He was naked, but on a nail on the door of the room hung his white Pierrot suit, the black skull-cap.

"I haven't worked in two years," he said. "The drink."

He was unshaven. The room smelled of urine and rotting food. Una had heard about it. She now held a handkerchief to her nose. The handkerchief was soaked in Mitsouko, her favourite perfume.

"You don't have to black up for this one," she told him.

He showed a fraction of interest, explaining: "It was those bloody Panthers gave the whole coon business a bad name. I blame them for the death of Vaudeville."

"It wasn't just them," Una said reasonably. "It's like the boxing business. Improved educational opportunities lured the talent away." She was being as conventional as possible. She still regretted opening up to Auchinek. "Look at England. All those Irish and Pakistani jokes. No wonder they bombed the Palladium."

"It was my first big break." He sighed. "I was going on the next day. Minimum of two weeks. Then the sods take out the venue. You must be able to understand why I'm so bitter."

"I've had the same experience myself." Una inspected his costume. It was covered in stains. "You'll have to get this cleaned. I know what it's like. But it was probably all for the best."

Jerry poured the last of his brandy into his coffee. "You're going to pay my fare home, then? Things haven't been easy. Surabaya's a tough town to find work in."

She chucked him under the chin. "Mein Gott, und ich liebe dich so."

He was not to be placated. "Warum bin ich nicht froh?"

"Because you're not in your natural element. Because you're not doing the work which suits you best." She ignored his coffee. "Come on. There's a schooner waiting in the harbour."

"I seem to remember a time," he murmured, climbing into the Pierrot suit, "when racialism was punishable by death. Where was that?"

She was on her knees, drawing his battered wickerwork suitcase from under the bed. "Oh." She was vague. "That must have been before the war."

VIII

FOUR WOMEN ANARCHISTS ESCAPE
Four women anarchists, including Inge Viett, 32, whose release was demanded by pro-Palestinian hijackers in Uganda last week, escaped from a top security women's jail in West Berlin yesterday. Police are concentrating their search on border crossings.
—*Daily Telegraph, 8th July 1976*

Jerry as Pierrot and Una as Pierrette danced across the tiny stage erected on the beach at St Ives while behind the curtain Shakey Mo, Catherine and Frank Cornelius played their banjos for all they were worth.

"Hello again! Hello again! We're here to entertain you!" Jerry and Una sang as brightly as possible to the four or five stern-faced children who so far made up their audience. They lifted their legs, they crossed their legs, they tap-danced, they grinned.

Soon they were singing the last number of the show, the reprise of the Entropy Tango, at something more than twice its normal speed.

For a while at least it's all right
We're safe from Chaos and Old Night
The Cold of Space won't chill our veins
And Fimbulwinter's fazed again
We have danced the Entropy Tango.

Now the curtain fell back and there was the entire ensemble to join in. Jerry and Una went to their respective corners and found their ukuleles, came back to the centre of the stage while Catherine, Frank and Mo formed up behind them.

And it's kiss, kiss, kiss
Fear and hate we have dismissed
And it's wish, wish, wish
For a better world than this . . .
So say goodbye to pain and woe
And we'll stop the Entropy Tango . . .

For the first time, the children began to clap enthusiastically, whistling, stamping their feet in the worn-out sand, yelling for more.

The company took its bow. It took several more. It gave them an encore.

"Well," Jerry removed his skull-cap as the curtain fell. "If we can get the same response from an adult audience this evening, we're on our way to the big time. It could mean a renaissance of the Concert Party." He was panting. "A come-back for Variety."

"It's the variety I miss," said Frank vaguely. A little saliva inched down his chin.

IX

AMIN ALERT ON AIR RAID THAT NEVER WAS

President Amin yesterday mobilised Uganda to face what he said was imminent attack from the air. At the same time reports in East African capitals indicated that Col. Gadaffi, the Libyan leader, had stepped in to restore the strength of the shattered Ugandan Air Force. The dramatic warning broadcast over Radio Uganda early yesterday and repeated throughout the day was made by a military spokesman—generally believed to be President Amin himself. He said that 30 Israeli and American

warplanes were approaching Uganda from Kenya and that they had been picked up on radar.
—*Daily Telegraph*, 8th July 1976

Success had given Jerry a bloom which Una found sickening. She discovered him checking his heat in his hotel room and waited until he had finished. He slipped the needler into the shoulder holster and grinned at her. "Tasty," he said.

"Tasteless, I'd call it. What a vulgar little wanker you are. Now that the show's over, where are you going?"

"Tel Aviv, I thought. Some unfinished business."

"Not you too! Auchinek's there."

"So I understood." He pulled on his well-tailored black velvet jacket. "How do I look?"

"Handsome," she said disapprovingly. "When are you coming back to work?"

"I'll be working over there." He winked. He was cheeky. He was loathsome. "I've got four weeks at the Tel Aviv Apollo and then, if I'm lucky, another fortnight at the Sydney Steak and Opera House. Auchinek says that it's almost certain I'll be picked to represent Israel in next year's Eurovision Song Contest." He opened his wardrobe and chose a striped tie. "Then it's on to South Africa."

"So you're selling out?" She sank onto his neat bed.

"Not exactly. Buying in, really." He knotted the tie about his throat. "I'm grateful to you, Una. You restored my confidence."

"Heaven forbid!"

"I had to take the jobs offered. You weren't exactly specific."

"You can't afford to be."

"That's the difference between us, Una. I believe in positive action. Cutting through the ambiguities."

"All that attitude produces is further complications."

"Complications aren't necessarily ambiguities, though. Life is action." He condescended to kiss her. The kiss was cold on her forehead. "I'll never forget what you've done."

But it was evident he had already forgotten. That was what made him a survivor of sorts.

X

PRETORIA TO BE WHITE BY NIGHT
Building will start next April of hostels to house 26,000 to 30,000 Black
Africans miles outside Pretoria the South African capital so that the city
can be 'white by night'. The scheme will cost millions of pounds and is due
to be completed by 1983. Each hostel will accommodate about 1,000 men.
All Blacks who are not considered officially to be key workers in the
White area—such as those in hotels, hospitals, old people's homes,
blocks of flats—will be affected.
—*Daily Telegraph, 8th July 1976*

Una's co-ordinates were evidently out. The whole landscape was
seething, semi-liquid. Terrifying shapes formed and disappeared.
Armies of half-human figures rode through billowing black smoke
and hungry flame. Confronting them, on a rearing stallion, a
white-faced warrior in dark baroque armour lifted a shrieking
sword to the skies, voicing a challenge in a rich, lilting language
only vaguely familiar to her. She remounted her Royal Albert and
began to pedal as fast as she could, studying the instrument
strapped to her left wrist. It told her nothing. Chaos controlled
everything. She was drifting. She concentrated and reset the
speedometer on her bike. Gradually the world turned to ice and
became peaceful. Somewhere in the distance a huge clipper ship
raced by. She considered trying to reach it, but her tyres would not
grip the ice. Again, she reset her instruments and a burning wind
seized her. She was in a desert and above her the sun was small,
dull red. In this world, the society at the End of Time had almost
certainly failed to flourish. She went sideways through the Shifter,
desperately. She knew what was happening to her now. She pulled
herself together, hitched up her greatcoat and pedalled as fast as
she could. The bike crossed the desert and reached a thick, salt sea.
Her concentration faltered. She tried again. Her attempts to get
back to her original base had been foolish; she had been too long
away from it. Linear logic was virtually a mystery to her now. The
larger world beckoned. She accepted it. It was what she had always
wanted. She gave up her soul.

    Auchinek, in tweeds, came running towards her across a lawn.
"Una! We thought we'd lost you."

"Fat chance," she said. "Hello, Sebby. Nice to see you." Behind him was a large country mansion, probably Georgian, with the usual offensive Adam flourishes. There were ornamental hedges, yews, cypresses, poplars, creating a pleasant Romantic landscape. "Is this your new house?"

"Do you like it?" He flung an arm around her shoulders, wheeling the bike for her with his free hand.

"It suits you."

"Thanks." He took a deep breath of his air.

"I thought most of these places were owned by Arabs, these days."

"Oh!" He was expansive, relaxed. "There's still a few of the original old Jews left, you know."

Frank Cornelius came shuffling through the gravel of the wide drive. He had a scythe in one hand and a bucket in the other. He touched his cap as they passed. "Evening, squire."

Sebastian Auchinek took Una through the French windows and into the library, showing her his Buchan first editions, his collection of Chesterton manuscripts, his illustrated Tolkiens and Lewises. "And for politics—" He knew her tastes. He drew back a velvet cloth to reveal a case. "Beaconsfield manuscripts!"

She was disappointed. "No Marx."

"For what?" He became agitated and replaced the velvet. "What do you mean?"

"Nothing. Honestly."

"Catherine's here. And Jerry, of course. It's going to be quite a week-end. Maxwell's coming down from London. De Fete, and Tome, and Markham will represent the Arts. The Nyes live quite near and they've promised to call over on Sunday. There's not much shooting, but there's plenty of fishing." They entered a cool hall. "And I know you like riding. You must ask the groom to pick you out a horse. I'd recommend the chestnut filly." They walked into a sunny room full of soft furniture covered in some sort of tapestry work. A dark-skinned servant was already pouring tea into thin cups. Bishop Beesley, in purple and black, rose from his chair, a large slice of yellow seed-cake in his chubby hand. "Miss Persson. Such a long time."

"It doesn't seem it, Bishop."

From the security of her sofa, his daughter Mitzi regarded Una with naughty eyes. "So you've turned up," she said. She licked a crumb or two from her thin, experienced lips.

"It's a good old reunion," said Auchinek with considerable innocence.

XI

THE AMBASSADOR OF ISRAEL, MR GIDEON RAFAEL
unable to reply individually to the stream of messages, wishes to thank the great many well-wishers who expressed, by telephone, telegram, or by letter, their congratulations and rejoicing at the rescue of the hijacked hostages held captive by terrorists in Entebbe.
—*Advertisement, Daily Telegraph, 8th July 1976*

Catherine, Jerry and Una lay cuddled together in the huge four-poster. Candlelight filled the room with shadows. It was about three in the morning and outside, on the lawn, peacocks were hooting. It was this noise which had awakened them all from their semi-slumber.

"I'm thirsty." Jerry, after his Oxford experience, had become rather more attractive again. "Do you think there's any sort of room service, Una?"

"I doubt it. But one of us could go down and get some drinks from the cabinet. Or the kitchen, perhaps."

"I'm not going downstairs on my own!" Jerry was adamant. "Christ. I've seen too many thrillers on telly. You know what happens to the first one."

"We could all go," suggested Catherine.

"I'm not thirsty." Una was too tired to move. Her recent experiences had taken a great deal out of her. She stared stupidly at Jerry's clothes, piled on the floor near her. She saw that he still had his weapons. "Take a gun."

"And get blamed when I find the corpse in the library? Not likely!" Jerry was openly contemptuous. "I'm too fly for that."

"Oh, sod. I'll go." Catherine began to climb out of the tangle of sheets. "Blimey, you don't half sweat a lot these days, Jerry."

"That wasn't me," he said. "It was Una."

"I never sweat." She sat up, offended. "Not that much, anyway. It must have been you, Jerry."

"I don't sweat. Not at the moment. Really."

"Well, it must have been me," said Catherine, to keep the peace as usual.

"It was him," said Una.

"It bloody wasn't." Jerry was on his knees facing her. "Smell it! That's your Mitsouko. It reeks of it." He held up part of a sheet.

"Just because it smells of my perfume doesn't mean it was my sweat," said Una evenly. "You little shit. What are you trying to put over?"

"It was me!" cried Catherine, falling between them. "Me! Me! Ahhh!"

The door had opened. Sebastian Auchinek, in dressing gown and slippers, stood there. He looked horrified. "Oh, Una!"

"I'm sorry, Sebby. We got carried away."

"Oh, Christ." Una reached towards him as Jerry and his sister slowly got off the bed and rose to their feet.

Auchinek raised his arm. There was something in his hand. Una pulled the sticky sheet over her head. "Go away, the lot of you! Vampires!"

There came a movement, a sound, then a strong smell of burning meat. She sat up. In the doorway was Auchinek's quartered corpse. There was no blood, just blackened edges to the wounds. Jerry had used his heater. A box lay near Auchinek's hand. From the box spilled some sort of jewellery. A gift.

Jerry began to apologise. Una rounded on him. "You knew it wasn't a weapon!'

Jerry began to sulk. "What if I did? It could have been."

"He hardly ever used one."

"Just the fucking eyes. Just the fucking guilt." Jerry holstered the heater. "I couldn't stand it. He wasn't going to pull that one on me again. I remember when he could handle a machine gun with the best of them. In Macedonia. In Chile. In Kenya. But he couldn't keep it up. He fell back on old tricks. And they didn't work for him. Not this time."

"This always happens," said Una, "when you're around." The smell was sickening her. "Poor Sebby."

"He'll pop up again. You'll see."

"It's sordid."

"He set the rules." Jerry was unrepentant. "Everything else led from there."

"How can you say that? You sound like some bloody Palestinian. You fought beside him in the Irgum Tsva'i Leumi. Remember your pledge—to kill every British man, woman or child in Palestine if they wouldn't leave? Does 1947 mean nothing to you?"

Jerry couldn't remember. It was only Una who seemed to worry about keeping track of events. He blinked. "When?"

Catherine was puzzled. "But you were on the other side, weren't you, Una?"

"Somebody has to be. The status quo . . ."

"Ah, of course," said Jerry. "But that's what I'm into, too, Una." He bent to pick up the box. "Are these real diamonds?" He held them to the light. "Look at the facets. Look how they sparkle, Una."

He had won her over. She joined him to stare into the gems.

"He was a self-righteous little bugger, after all."

XII

WIDOW DISAPPEARS FROM AMIN HOSPITAL

A 75-year-old grandmother, Mrs Dora Bloch, has disappeared in Uganda after being caught up in the Entebbe skyjack affair. Her potentially ominous disappearance has led to a diplomatic row between Britain and Uganda. Mr Ted Rowlands, Minister of State, said in the Commons yesterday that it was causing "grave concern". Mr James Hennessy, the British High Commissioner to Kampala who was on leave in Britain, has been ordered to fly to Uganda immediately to seek the release of Mrs Bloch who has dual British-Israeli nationality.
—*Daily Telegraph, 8th July 1976*

"My dear Miss Persson!" Lord Jagged of Canaria, tall and grave in his yellow finery, looking somewhat gaunt, brought the huge swan that was his air-car down over the bluff where she stood supporting her Royal Albert by its saddle and handle-bars. "I received your message and came as soon as I could. Time, you know, presses at present. How beautiful you are." He stepped down beside her and dismissed the swan. He bowed. He kissed her hand. He was irresistible, bearing, as he did, the nobler characteristics of his large family. "You came earlier?"

"Briefly." She smiled. "You are weary?"

"Less so, now that we meet." A movement of a power ring and he provided their picnic. There were salads, meats, champagnes.

She lowered her bicycle and sat down beside the cloth. He joined her. Another kiss. This time to the cheek. Another, gently, to the lips. "Una."

"My darling Jagged." It was impossible for them to keep a liaison for more than an hour or two at a time. The chronic megaflow denied them anything but that.

"I've little gossip for you today," he said. He reached for an avocado. "My own affairs take me away from society. But I heard that the Duke of Queens fought a duel, recently."

"A duel? Here?"

"A droll episode."

"Someone was killed?"

"In a sense." He began to speak of the affair, but it was evident that he made an effort. When he had finished she did not press him for details. "And you?" he enquired. "Are you active, still? And fulfilled?"

For his sake she was bright. "In general, yes."

"Generalities," he said, almost to himself, "are all we have, of course, at the End of Time. I envy you your specifics."

"They blur. Everything blurs."

"Perhaps that is Time's most attractive function, eh?" He seized a tiny melon, then a nectarine. The shadow of his circling swan fell across the meal.

"Soon," he murmured, "I must leave."

"Your experiments? Are they successful?"

"They are interesting. I dare not say more."

"I'll wish you luck, though, I think."

He inclined his head.

"So the Duke of Queens continues to encourage Romance at the End of Time."

"This is a world of Romance." He laughed. "Of generalities, as I said. Sometimes I envy you your realities."

"They are no less romantic, I suppose."

"Everything is a matter of attitudes, in the long run. Of interpretation."

The shadow returned. He stood up. "You have eaten enough?"

She nodded.

He dissipated the picnic. He sighed. The swan descended. Fingers touched, lips were joined. "I will get a message to you," he told her, "if I am successful."

"To the Time Centre," she said. "You can always reach me here, I hope."

"Very well." He had boarded the swan. It swung upwards into dark blue air.

Una was smiling as he departed. She stooped to recover her bicycle, bouncing it on its tyres to rid it of the dust. She glanced at her wrist. Her instruments were giving stable readings for the moment. She did not mount her machine immediately, but strolled with it along the edge of the bluff, looking out over the brilliant gold, scarlet and blue of the plain below. The patterns were mysterious and it was impossible to guess what the creator of the design had planned.

She swung her leg and seated herself on her saddle. She began to pedal, making adjustments to the dials on the handle-bars. Soon she was on her way through Time again, pursuing her lonely, optimistic explorations; searching for one world where tolerance and intelligence were paramount and where they existed by design rather than by accident.

The End of Time fell away behind her, closed, and all the Earth's history opened up before her as she rode, singing, along the megaflow:

"Oh, it's up the trope I go, up I go
It's up the trope I go, up I go
It's up the trope I go—
And the crowd all down below
Sez—girl, we told you so!
God damn their eyes!
God blast their souls!
To bloody hell!"

Ladbroke Grove
July 1976

MARS

Hesitating at the edge of the beautiful ghost town Morgan watched red rust run like a river over a smashed Cerum screen. From below came the uncertain vibration of some abandoned atmosphere plant, its echo murmuring through endless catacombs where the majority of Martians preferred to survive. Only a few like Morgan chose to live beneath the pale wash of the planet's pastel skies and breathe dusty air smelling of licorice, lilac and the sweet old Earth of childhood.

Morgan was sixteen when the community congregated within pink brick Gothic arches to watch an accelerator picture bloom on the viewing wall. Earth, then Neptune, had quietly vanished from the solar system. "A great experiment." Gran had seemed regretful. Scientists who had issued warnings of just such dramatic results were vindicated, but since the colonies were self-sufficient it merely meant the end of innocence, not of civilisation. This was to be a period of forgetting.

Mars had already developed a consciously introspective culture. To them the idea of Earth's departure was more interesting than the fact. Symbolism offered at once a larger and less involving reality.

Morgan reached through the thin, fast-flowing dust to pick up an old paperback lying on the fused clay beneath. It was obsolete and the expensive machines to play it belonged only to collectors, but the cover was interesting. Even after so much exposure the holograms were garish, crude, ungraduated. A figure in a red-and-purple smock threatened another with some sort of weapon and the calligraphy was so complicated it was almost impossible for Morgan, trained on the spare alphabets once fashionable in Morocco, to decipher. It was clearly from Earth. Had the whole planet been so loud? To Morgan's ears much of the music had the same unsubtle quality; it was brutal, almost alarming, though some Martians thought it vivid, possessed of a primitive vitality they had lost.

"We're too cultured for our own good," Wren had said the other day. "It's Mars. At this rate we'll go the way of the other civilisations."

Mars has seen at least nine major cultures thrive and fade. The youngest had lived in the deepest caverns of all before dying out as peacefully and as mysteriously as all the rest. "Mars was never meant to support life. Mars represents the tranquillity of death. Perhaps you should have gone to Venus while you had the chance?"

Once, aged eleven, Morgan had visited Venus and found the elegant landscaping, the elaborately geometrical gardens, the tastefully arranged forests, far too classical. Because her surface had hardly been worth altering, Mars remained much as she had been when the first Earth settlers arrived, her limitless deserts and worn mountains, her craters and her shallow valleys relieved only by occasional bands of low vegetation marking the existence of subterranean rivers and oceans serving those twilight countries whose original architecture had been so carefully adapted and utilised by the latest Martians. At least two previous civilisations had been humanoid and one of them had certainly been a colonising culture, either from another system or possibly even marooned here from another space-time. There was a theory that Mars herself had not originally been part of this system. Fragments of old machines suggested attempts to use the whole planet as a means of transportation. The remains of what were evidently spaceships could have brought visitors to Mars or had perhaps been built in a failed attempt to leave the planet. Only one culture—the huge four-armed tusked bipeds—had apparently succeeded in travelling on.

"They come to Mars to die," Wren had said. "Or they leave. We have no intention of leaving. Mars lets us grow old gracefully."

Nothing in Morgan could easily resist the idea. Few babies had ever been born on Mars and in spite of all efforts fewer still had reached healthy adulthood. Regenerations maintained the race.

"Mars rejects children." Wren's voice had contained a certain depth of satisfaction. "She rejects everything which isn't already mature. She's a planet for people who've grown tired not of life but of exploration. You, Morgan, are in an uneasy position here, for you were almost an adult when you arrived and you never expected to stay. Do you miss your parents?"

Morgan's grandparents had always seemed much closer. They had settled on Mars as part of a scheme offered on Earth to encourage early retirement, but their parents had been born here, to the first real settlers who built the surface towns and the Cerum screens.

"Mars has no secrets from those who love her." Wren had smiled and, in a gesture of sad regret, caressed Morgan's hand.

But Morgan loved Mars. Possibly Morgan's love contained too much passion for the planet to bear. Mars's mysteries were everywhere and were part of her fascination. Morgan enjoyed curiosity for its own sake and was rarely disappointed by unanswered questions.

The paperback replaced in the river bed, Morgan moved towards ochre walls; some old public buildings in the Second Arabian style. Adding water to Martian clay produced a cement as strong as stone. The cheapness of their materials had always allowed the Martians more fanciful and elaborate structures than the Venusians or Ganymedians. Dust could be moulded into baroque splendour and some mock-Versailles raised from the desert in days. It never rained on Mars so only the action of the winds affected these fantastical towns whose architecture recorded the history of Earth's finest periods. Impossible to combine with tints, the towns were the same pale oranges, yellows, browns, pinks and rusty reds as their surroundings, the subtle skies which never quite formed clouds. Attempts to vary the colours by raising holograms and even 2D billboards, by using the picture facilities of the Cerum screens whenever possible, had produced tones too bright for eyes grown accustomed to subtler shades and before their exodus to reinhabit the prehistoric cities few Martians had desired anything but the planet's familiar spectrum. On arriving, Morgan, at first unable to distinguish easily between colours, had thought the place sinister. Even the people had a faded quality, their voices like whisperings in a graveyard. Though they were robust enough, it had been easy to believe in grandparents over two hundred years old.

Morgan's grandparents' generation still tended to call the planet "Pacifica", from the first colonial advertisements. While it bore a closer relationship to the landscapes, the name was hollow to Morgan. Mars had not been associated in anyone's mind with a Roman war god for centuries. What had been "martial" to Morgan's ancestors meant almost its opposite now. To Morgan the word Mars had always been a synonym for peace.

Profoundly opposed to any return to the surface, for weeks Morgan's grandparents had spoken of nothing but the danger. Cheap generators and equipment from Earth factories were no longer available to maintain meteor beams or control dust-storms. Morgan and the others had tried to explain how these unpredictable elements were part of the reason for going back.

Familiar with defeat but not reconciled to it, Morgan had on that occasion persevered, eventually winning the agreement of the community. A year ago twenty-eight people, mostly of Morgan's generation, had set themselves up in Egg City, close to the Little Crack, a dust-river which coursed without interruption across half the planet before joining Main Run near the equator.

Used to solitary lives, the majority gradually went their separate ways until only Morgan and Wren were left in Egg. Faad was furthest away, on the Back Line, some three thousand kilometres from Egg. Faad had travelled on an ancient dust-coaster brought from underground. They were dangerous, inclined to capsize, but you could ride the dust-tides down the deep cracks and cover an enormous distance. Faad had the whole of Whistler to live in. This was the most elaborately fanciful of all Martian cities, with replicas of almost every monumental building Earth had ever raised, from the Taj Mahal to the Empire State to the Gibraltar Berber Mosque, though the location let the winds erode them into extraordinary versions of their originals.

Morgan had not lost any love for the underworld's beauty, the great plumes of atmosphere rising from the hydros in the morning, and shafts of sunlight cutting down from a mile above to strike water which glowed like copper; the pewter caverns, the carved gold-green stalactites whose disturbingly alien faces bore expressions of unguessable sorrow. Or was it sorrow at all? What did humanity really know of any alien entity? Once it was realised that dead aliens offered no threat they were forgotten by everyone save a few academics, as if people refused to consider the implications, the fact that not one race, no matter how perfectly adapted, had continued to exist on Mars for more than eleven or twelve millennia?

Along the banks of frozen rivers and lakes, wonderfully symmetrical structures had been erected, side by side with crazily angular buildings, clearly the productions of two different races who at one time had shared the planet equably. One race had been humanoid, the other avarian but flightless.

An earlier species resembling fine-featured Oriental cats had left statues to themselves all over Mars and Morgan had become almost as familiar with their culture as with Earth's. Their celebrations had all seemed to concern enormous failures. They seemed a race addicted to defeat. Morgan believed in the power of habit, of rituals maintaining patterns of behaviour which had long since lost their psychic or practical usefulness. Humans were the same, especially around power or powerlessness. For millennia, when gender had been a class definition, half the race had seemed addicted to power and half to powerlessness, producing profound philosophies and art forms, religions and sciences out of their addictions.

To Morgan much of what those ancestors had valued seemed trivial or debased and it was only possible to hold faint distaste for so barbaric a past. With Earth's disappearance had gone the reminders of their shame, while the reminders of their glories lived on as magnificent Martian ghosts.

If Earth had contained the descendants of those addicted to power, then Mars sheltered a people who made a virtue of powerlessness; this remained the element in Martian culture which caused Morgan greatest unease. There was no nobility in surviving for the sake of surviving—unless a virus or an amoeba were instrinsically noble—but neither was there any particular moral purity in reconciling oneself to extinction.

Sometimes Wren said that every single piece of architecture on the planet was nothing more than an elaborate tombstone. Wren's ideas were easily understood when, alone, you looked out across red dunes towards eroded cliffs and a sky turned to smoky yellow streaked with orange; but they were too easy, Morgan had decided. Mars was not dead and her people were not dying. It would be a million years before anyone needed to consider the notion.

Morgan got back on the brog and hovered a few feet above the surface before moving forward. There was a good chance of reaching Egg before twilight, though there was no urgency. Any of the old cities were capable of giving temporary shelter. Morgan's vehicle offered electronic intimacies as it calculated distances and speeds, warming the cabin to compensate for Mars's slow, wonderful sunset. Wren waited in Egg and Morgan was nervous of returning, wary of a new relationship which, no matter how perfect, might interfere with this abiding love-affair with Mars, this sense of coming to know profoundly the identity of an entire planet, the nature of her history, the qualities which made her unique among the planets.

Already Wren had introduced a note of scepticism. "You're not exploring Mars. You're exploring yourself, Morgan. That's surely all anyone does? That's what Mars makes you do. That's what Mars gives you. And in turn you learn how to explore and understand others. You're the youngest of us but I always trusted you, most of all, to realise that."

"Mars isn't me," Morgan had said. "I'm not greatly interested in myself."

This statement was so contrary to fundamental Martian belief that Wren's only possible response had been laughter. "Your Mars is you!" Then Wren had dropped the subject. Wren was in love with Morgan, whose pale skin and black hair were strikingly similar to Wren's own. It was the epitome of the Martian ideal of beauty.

Morgan's fascination with Wren had something to do with narcissism but was also a wish to retain emotional contact with another human being, as if that in itself were some sort of safety-line. Aware of Wren's stronger infatuation, Morgan knew it did not matter if a day or two went by before returning to Egg. Wren would almost certainly be waiting. Martians were not encouraged to form intense relationships. Wren would probably expect no more of Morgan and it was not for Morgan to speculate about and respond to Wren's possible or unstated feelings.

Deliberately slowing the brog, Morgan rode beside a line of

ridges that were probably an old crater rim. The sun continued its tranquil descent. Delighted by the almost imperceptible alternation of shades, Morgan next reordered the magnetics to let the vehicle drift off towards Rose de la Paix where once spaceships had come and gone in such numbers.

Just before dark, when the main constellations shone a greenish blue in the depths of the sky, Morgan reached the old port's outskirts, surprised to see that someone had changed its familiar silhouette. Morgan was sure a new building had been added since Faad had driven them here when Isutep and Katchga left for Venus.

Finding a cocoon-bay, Morgan prepared for the night, welcoming the positive security and comfort of the coffin-shaped survival box. In the morning it would be interesting to investigate the new additon to Rose, perhaps one of those random sculptures erected by the Caziz siblings, Mars's leading artists and a constant source of irritation to the underworlders.

An hour or so after dawn Morgan watched fragile sunlight fragment into red and gold bands layering the horizon like geological strata. There was, indeed, an addition to the port, sitting half on a launch-disc which shone like polished lead, a massive thing of ornate brass curves, silver loops and sinuously interwoven tubes seemingly partly metallic and partly organic, its function impossible to guess. But it was clearly not by the Cazizes. There were no materials like it on Mars. Morgan decided it must surely be a vessel, its occupants recognising a spaceship port. Was this the vanguard of the next wave of colonists?

The vessel's colours had now become predominantly greens and dark rich blues, with some glittering reds and almost jarring metal pinks. Morgan could not look at it for any length of time without developing a mild headache. Searching amongst the miscellaneous stuff in the back of the brog, Morgan found an antiglare mask and put this on. The ship now appeared to shift very slowly back and forth through the spectrum, an unexpected effect which gradually stabilised. After some minutes there was a kind of flickering passage across part of the lower latticework of the ship and two indistinct figures stood almost gingerly on the gleaming disc.

Morgan eventually realised they were moving. They were bipeds, chunky in outline but at the same time ethereal. A further flicker in the air and heads were revealed. To Morgan the creatures, almost without necks, with flat features and dramatically deepset eyes, were not immediately attractive. When one of them spoke, it was like a distantly heard harp, the notes drawn out and indistinct, yet Morgan understood a few words. '. . . *unpeace . . . targettable . . . apologisation . . . unfamiliarian . . . intraspaced . . . relationates . . . upset-forthuns . . . plastmuritum . . .*'

Clearly the aliens had learned from Earth broadcasts, for this was spaceship patois and technonlex, which Morgan could speak a little. Replying in the same mixture, Morgan asked them if they had travelled far. They did not understand initially, but after several attempts, lasting almost until noon, they responded, each word drawn out so that it took them hours to deliver their information.

They had come intraspacially and picked up the megaflow which brought them most of the way. Believing themselves in danger, they needed, Morgan thought they said, to contact a ship-controller so they could be buried.

Were they pursued? Morgan asked, and it was almost dark before he began to understand their reply. Probably not. They were being cautious and wanted to hide their ship. There had been home planet "beleaguerments". Considerable "unpeace". The newcomers seemed chiefly concerned for the safety of their fellows. They seemed to be advance scouts or else were already the sole survivors of some catastrophe. They referred sometimes in technonlex and sometimes in English to a place called Erdorig or Three. When Morgan asked them the name of their planet they hesitated until just before dawn the next day and then said "Earth", which Morgan thought a fairly useless piece of translation.

Morgan tried to explain the need to sleep and eventually simply returned to the cocoon for a few hours. On Morgan's coming back to the disc they reappeared before him, ready to continue. Morgan was bewildered by their mixture of terrible urgency and unreal tranquillity. The way the aliens spoke and moved perhaps reflected a radical difference in the texture of their home space. They would pause sometimes for quarter-of-an-hour between words, clearly from need and habit, not because they were seeking the appropriate phrase. Morgan wondered if in their language silences of a particular kind were in fact a form of communication. Their exchange could still take over an hour and still prove meaningless. Morgan maintained this intercourse for almost two more days with little sleep before deciding that Wren must be brought here. Wren was better qualified to continue the dialogue, having a background in semantics and anthropology.

Privately joking that the journey from Rose to Egg and back could probably be completed before the aliens finished their next observation, Morgan assured them they were welcome and that he went to seek others who might help them better. Morgan raced the brog back to Egg, the red dust shrieking and spiralling as it reacted to the vehicle's overtaxed magnetics.

As usual, only Wren was in Egg, sitting in the main square on the steps of a sandstone Los Angeles City Hall watching old newscasts. As Morgan drove in Wren folded the viewer and smiled. "I knew you'd be late. It's all right."

Before Wren spoke Morgan had been full of the event, but now felt a great reluctance to say anything at all, let alone the half-lie which emerged. "I was delayed in Rose."

"Something happening?" Clearly Wren was torn between relief at seeing Morgan and irritation for having been made to speculate.

"Nothing really." Climbing down from the brog, Morgan took a rag and began removing a layer of bronze-brown dust from the side. "I'm glad you weren't disturbed."

"I'm a Martian. We're never disturbed."

Morgan failed to detect Wren's irony and instead looked back towards Rose. "There's a new ship on one of the launch discs."

"Going to Venus? From Venus?"

"Alien. From sideways I'd guess. They're not quite in focus, if you know what I mean. I've been with them most of the time. I can't find out what they're here for. They speak a form of technon-lex, bits of other Earth languages, ship's patois."

"Two days and they haven't told you why they're here?" Wren began to walk towards the slender triple towers where they always stayed when in Egg City. "Not what I'd call communication, Morgan. What are they hiding?"

"They seem to fade out—physically, I mean. Then they'll become so solid and immovable I think they're turning into statues before my eyes. You'd have to see it, Wren."

Wren paused, the anger and frustration dissipating. "What?"

"It's the oddest thing I've ever experienced. It's as if they're fluctuating between maximum stability and maximum entropy. They probably have means of controlling the space they occupy. They're very nearly human. Superficially."

"Remember Faad's joke?" Wren was sceptical.

"This isn't like Faad's joke. It's very easy to tell. These people are frightened. Or angry. I don't know."

"Frightened of you?"

"Maybe. Perhaps of something they've left behind. You should come out to Rose, Wren. You know all those versions of technonlex. You're trained for this. It might be the only real chance you ever get to make use of that prolonged education."

In a newly-relaxed face Wren's smile was beautiful. It was their running game. Wren came striding back to embrace Morgan who beamed with the pleasure of reconciliation. "I can't be everything you'd like, Wren. But I love you."

"Yes," said Wren. "That's what makes it painful. We're fools, we Martians. Is all of this imposed? Is it just the stupid, useless rationalisations of the early settlers? Shouldn't we be trying to change how we look at things? I was considering all that stuff we talked about the other day . . ."

Already Wren was moving the conversation towards abstraction. Morgan could see this typically Martian trait objectively, but Wren was almost entirely unaware of it.

"This is a real event, Wren. These people seem desperate. Do you want to help them?"

"Why not? Can the brog stand a return trip?"

"We'll take the spare. I got careless. Do you need anything?"

"Some food. Some reference stuff. You fetch the brog and I'll be ready."

Suddenly enjoying Wren's companionship, Morgan drove them back directly towards Egg, sailing up over smaller obstacles, gracefully curving around cliffs.

"You seem happy," said Wren. "I mean happier. Is it the excitement?"

"I like doing things with you, Wren, better than I like having conversations. People talk too much for me."

"That's Mars." Wren again unconsciously refused any reason for action or change. "Good old Mars. She does that."

"Well, these people might need something more than talk." Morgan grinned at this. "If there's time."

"You're goony today." Wren enjoyed Morgan's mood, sitting closer and offering an affectionate hug. "You're like a kid. I suppose you are our kid, really. What can we offer the visitors? Or are you just being rhetorical?"

"Help." Morgan shrugged, keeping an eye firmly on the forward terrain, for the automatics were off in order to achieve greater speed. "I think that's why they're here."

"They're not would-be colonists, then? I thought everyone wanted to settle on Mars. Have you ever wondered why such a barren place is so attractive to so many different races?"

"You're sliding off the point again, Wren."

Wren was amiably baffled. "I didn't know there was one. They're emissaries? Are they?"

"That's why I need you, Wren."

Clearly flattered by this, Wren settled more comfortably in the seat. "I like a good problem."

"We might have to start solving this one as rapidly as possible."

"I'll try not to disappoint you, Morgan." Head shaking in amusement, Wren studied the copper-coloured mossy South Dales in the distance. The light caught a sheen of tiny stems so that the entire landscape resembled a vast jewelled snake warming its body beneath the sun. "Oh, this is so good, Morgan. Don't you love Mars?"

Soon Morgan saw Rose coming up on the horizon: fractured skyscrapers, rusted geometries of disused instruments and signals, eroded control towers, domes the colour of pale chocolate and bleached strawberries, ruined customs buildings, a silted quarantine enclosure and, beyond, the Art Hazardos splendours of the Mannaheim Apartments, raised in the days before the fashion for imitation became the ruling aesthetic and gave Martian cities their characteristic appearance of bizarre monuments to a lost planet.

"Awful," said Wren without thinking. Like most Martians, Wren believed any style not previously seen on Earth was vulgar and simply lacking in any beauty. To Morgan the buildings were only hard to read, almost like the spaceship which now came into view and made Wren exclaim noisily about its oddness. "This is stranger than anything we have already. They won't shoot me or anything, will they?"

The two aliens had not moved very far from their original spot. Currently they were so utterly solid, standing firmly on the faintly reflective disc, that almost everything surrounding them seemed a little unreal.

"Well, first things first," said Wren, raising a hand in a sign which no real logic accepted as a universal gesture of peace. Yet the salute was eventually answered, awkwardly, as if the aliens were trying to recall forgotten briefings. Their stolid, ugly faces stared with considerable alertness from massive hairless heads wearing some kind of transparent, protective covering, possibly a membrane or thin bone. "Could you tell me your names? I'm Wren. This is Morgan."

Morgan felt foolish for not having considered this simple first step. Yet the aliens were bewildered until Wren, growing a little more sober, tried a whole series of technonlex versions. The process was as slow as it had been earlier, but at last Wren turned to Morgan with some information. "They're Directed Beings from the Pastoral Choice, they say, and are called Sendes-endes-Ah and Luuk Shenpehr, as far as I can tell. Directed Beings, I think, are people who choose physical work and the Pastoral Choice is probably the nearest thing to a country—a province, maybe. What are they? Farm labourers? There'll be a long way to go before we have a true notion of how they live. But that's all we need for the moment." Wren had become unusually engaged. "Now I'll try to find out a bit more as to why they came here."

A little disturbed by Wren's brusque, almost proprietorial tone, Morgan knew a protective pang. "They must be exhausted. Should we offer them food?"

Wren shrugged, as if finding this question unnecessary, but nonetheless addressed the aliens and after less than twenty minutes discovered that they had taken nourishment while Morgan was away. "I think I embarrassed them." Wren grinned. There was, indeed, a great deal of fading in and out and both aliens had changed from pasty white to a kind of lime green. Now they resumed their solidity and original colouring.

Unhappy with the anthropologist's lighthearted attitude to the aliens, Morgan felt Wren should display more respect. But the aliens were almost certainly unaware of any nuances and Wren was making far greater progress with them. By the following morning the aliens retired to their spaceship while Wren and Morgan, occupying some old crew's quarters not far away, had pieced together a large part of the basic story.

"They were coming back." Wren frowned. "They're sure of that. They've said it every possible way. They were coming back, hoping to find help or escape. They seem to be saying they're Martians, Morgan. Yet there's nothing like them anywhere on Mars. Were they the original inhabitants, so long ago no trace remains?" Wren looked out at the ship. "Their own planet, which either has no name or a name which sounds very much like Earth, is no longer inhabitable. A new species has attacked? Possibly a disease? Their knowledge of technonlex is excellent but it's a version I've never come across. There are gaps, in other words. They want to hide their ship. We should humour them in that, I think."

"Humour them?" Again Morgan was unhappy with Wren's choice of phrase.

"Respect their wishes, then. Don't those pads lower into the ground? They'll have to make a more precise landing, though. They're funny-looking creatures. Old, old people would be my guess. I asked how many inhabitants of their race were left on the planet and they said twelve. But it might have have been twelve hundred, twelve thousand—technonlex won't do it, so far. We'll have to consult with the community. I told them. They seem a worthy enough pair, if a bit boring and ugly." Wren laughed. "Sorry, Morgan. But have you considered this could be a clever trick on their part. What if they're the conquering bully-boys?"

They looked up and saw the air flush with a yellowish red, then the spaceship grew insubstantial for a few seconds. When it regained its solidity it stood dead-centre on the disc. Emerging again, the two aliens settled themselves in front of Wren and Morgan, ready for the next day's conversation. The first thing they did was repeat, rapidly in their terms, that the ship must be hidden.

"We'll need permission from the rest." Wren was clearly impressed. "You'd better go and ask, Morgan. Find your grandparents. I'll carry on here."

Though reluctant to leave and even more reluctant to confront the underworlders, Morgan responded to the urgency and took the brog over to Rose's nearest shaft-gate, driving down into the cool half-light of the hollow world below.

When Morgan returned, having once again earned some subtle kind of disapproval for a failure, as the underworlders saw it, of courtesy, Wren was sitting on the ground with hands in the air and looking at one of the aliens who, perhaps aggressively, brandished what might have been a weapon.

Obviously afraid, Wren looked back at Morgan. "I made a serious gaff, Morgan. I've asked them not to shoot me, but I'm not sure their technonlex has a word for mercy." Wren's mouth was dry. "We made some progress. Maybe too much. They're from Earth, Morgan. Old Earth which went off with Neptune, sideways through the multiverse—not deliberately, you'll recall—and now they're a million or two years in our future. Well, you know more about physics than I do." Wren was talking from panic rather than enthusiasm. "These are the descendants of our original ancestors. They *were* 'coming back'—not to their home planet but to their home star-system. They knew about Mars. Morgan, they were coming home to die! I was right. Everyone comes to Mars to die! Even me, it seems."

Frowning, Morgan stared uncertainly from what appeared to be the weapon in Luuk Shenpehr's hands to the seated, frightened Wren. "To live," said Morgan firmly. "They're here because they're trying to find a way to survive. Surely that's more logical? How did you offend them, Wren?"

"Maybe I got a bit noisy when I realised the truth. Obviously their space-time is now radically different to this one and that explains their apparent slowness and the occasional insubstantiality—which incidentally they seem in the process of correcting . . ." Wren paused. "Don't let them shoot me, Morgan. They like you."

"They said that?"

"They're not pointing a gun at you." This irritating tendency to trivialise even in such circumstances almost made Morgan want to abandon Wren to whatever fate was in store.

"But they were looking for help." Morgan did not want to believe in any reverse.

"The interpretations are tricky. They say they're seeking transformation—resolution?—this is their technonlex, maybe hundreds of years ahead of ours, maybe more."

Earth unpeace . . . Sendes-endes-Ah spoke again in a voice like the distant song of a harp, but stronger, less hesitant. Still Morgan could only understand the one phrase. Was it some kind of ultimatum?

"They won't respond to me." Wren was shaking now. "Please intercede."

"They're not being attacked?" Morgan's voice was faint.

"They are being 'pushed down', they said. Another force is simply occupying their planet as if they don't exist. Morgan!"

Morgan moved cautiously forward. Behind the alien ship the Martian sun had risen like an angel's armour, proclaiming some unspecific glory. The old, red hills began to pulse. The smell of orange blossom crystals sweetened the thin air and made it magical.

"But, Wren, you haven't explained how you angered them."

"Perhaps I was facetious. I couldn't believe they hadn't resisted the invaders. They say they're fewer than twelve now." Wren took deep breaths, trying to control panic. "A civil war? Oh, Morgan." The gun moved in Luuk Shenpehr's hand. The risen sun made it blossom with sudden colour. Then, in a second of inspiration, Morgan stepped forward and took it from the alien. There was no resistance.

Shaking with relief, Wren stood up, while Morgan held the thing to the light. Wren began to smile sheepishly, but Morgan's features had grown profoundly sad. Morgan understood the object's function.

"I think you saved my life." Wren was anxious to fill in the silence.

Morgan's head moved in a tiny gesture of contradiction.

Stretching towards the blazing, complicated thing, Wren asked: "How does it fire?"

"It doesn't," said Morgan, sighting along it. "It can't." There were no moving parts.

"It's clearly a gun. I've seen stuff like it in paperbacks."

Morgan turned the object this way and that to let the sun's rays play on its awkward curves and peculiar angles, this icon, perhaps created in desperation from insubstantial data on a race's long dead past. "It's not a gun, Wren."

The dust blew for a moment around their legs while from the Northern Shafts the Martians, masked against the light, were emerging, moving hesitantly towards their Earthling cousins. At last Morgan handed the object to a still baffled Wren.

"It's only the memory of a gun."

London
April 1988

THE LAST CALL

Champion! Champion!
    In those spaces between waking and sleeping I heard them. Dimly at first. I heard their voices. They were calling. They were distant. Distant and echoing like breakers in a lonely seacave. Somehow I knew they were calling me.

Champion!

I could not bear it.

"No!" I screamed. "No! I cannot—I will not—I dare not hear you!"

But they were relentless.

Champion!

"Begone!" I cried. "Begone! I have done too much. There is nothing left of me to serve!"

Champion!

I lay face down. I could not open my eyes. I had the sensation of something wet against my cheek. Had I been weeping? I caught a smell—acrid, bitter and yet also sweet, familiar . . .

. . . your last orders!

"I'll take no further orders. I have fulfilled my destiny. There is nothing left for me . . ."

One more! One more!

"No! I cannot!"

I felt sick. I felt a strange dizziness. My whole body seemed to heave and tremble. And still I could not lift my head. Still I could not speak.

. . . time! Time . . .

"Let me be! Let me lie in space. I have no more to give. And there is nothing more that I can take!"

Champion!

With enormous effort I raised my head, but it was impossible to open my eyes.

Champion!

I could not remember how I had come here. What I had been doing. I could scarcely remember my own name. What was it? I had had so many names, so many faces, so many identities. Why should it be possible for me to know which was which?

We must win. This time we must win. We have the men, we have the experience. All we need is leadership . . .

There is no-one . . .

Only one and he is . . .

There is no way to beat them this year . . .

Only if we can find . . .

Fragments of conversation, of some sort of religious litany. Angry voices. Desperate voices. Defensive voices. Who were they? What did they need? Were they calling me? Or were they calling someone else? Were they calling at all?

Again I raised my head up and tried to open my eyes. For a second I caught a glimpse of a rank of figures, all men, lined before me. They wore strange flat headgear and each one held in his hand a vessel. They were turned, all of them, towards a shining light above their heads. It was bright enough to blind me. It illuminated their faces, but still I could make out no clear features, no details of their garb. I shuddered. There was something about them which filled me not so much with fear as with a disturbing, miserable ennui, a sense that I had come to a place where everyone was dead, where everyone waited, frozen, for something to breathe life into them. Was it me they wanted? Was I to give them life? I could not tell.

I tried to speak. But no words would come.

Champion!

The sickly, bitter-sweet smell increased. I reached out a hand towards the figures.

"Where am I?"

None heard me. Every face was turned to the source of the light. It seemed to me that it changed, that the colours changed, that dim shapes moved in it.

Had they brought me here? Was it all to begin again? The awful struggle? The voices raised in anger? The perpetual fighting? The hideous violence? The savagery? The waves of human flesh pouring over the green earth, turning it to bloody mud? The high screams of the young as their bodies were broken? The tears of the women?

"No! No! I want no more of it. I can stand nothing further. Free me from this. I beg you! Free me! Free me!"

Now at last the heads began to turn. Not many. But still the majority of them were intent on the source of the light, on the vessels they clutched in their fists—vessels full of some reddish, translucent liquid—liquid which foamed. And it was this which gave off the stench which clogged my nostrils and made my stomach heave.

"No!"

Quiet! one brusque voice ordered. But the others continued to observe the flickering light.

Champion!

Magic!

We're bound to win now!

"Please," I begged. "Please tell me. Where is this place? I must know. What do you want? What do you want?"

Another head turned. A bloated, half-human face regarded me. I shuddered. Had I fallen amongst the creatures of Chaos once more? Was I forever doomed to find myself in such circumstances? I had thought I was free from my fate at last. But this was worse than anything I had experienced before.

"Please. What do you call this place?"

Why, lad; what canst tha mean?

The voice was rough in timbre but almost kindly. The figure broke away from the rank of its fellows and approached me. It still held the vessel in its right hand. The liquid was almost gone from it, yet still it foamed a little.

"Who are you? And where am I now?"

Ee, lad, tha's had one too many by the look o' yer. You know me. You must know me. Everyone knows Old Enry . . .

"How was I brought here? By what means? What do you call this place?"

By Eck, lad, there's only one way you could 'a come here if tha didn't walk. By the Number Eighty. 'Tis all that passes The Six Jolly Dragoons nowadays, since the privatisation.

I tried to ask more of him, but his attention was fading, his head was turned back to the source of the light. He was mesmerised almost as badly as the others. What was this evil which possessed them all?

Come on, lads. Time! Time! Drink up, please.

There came a murmur of protest. Discontented grunts. Then a sudden cheer.

"What is it?" I cried, trying to rise and failing. I fell to my knees. My head was pounding. My mouth felt suddenly dry. My stomach still heaved. "What is it?"

'Tis two one. Old Enry turned his head. *There's no way they can win now.*

"So you don't need me?"

Why, lad, you're no use to anyone in that state.

"I can go?" An enormous wave of relief came over me. I began to weep. I was free. I was allowed to leave that dreadful place. I was no longer doomed to be part of their struggle.

Old Enry moved towards me. He put a hand under my arm and helped me to my feet. *Come, lad. Where d'you live? I'll get thee 'ome.*

I tried to remember. I recalled a number. A name. I tried to speak. Slowly the two of us moved away from the ranked men. Suddenly the light went out and they turned, staring after us.

It were a great game, that, Enry, said one as he waved farewell.

A huge door swung open and cool air struck my face. I began to feel that I might be able to walk again unaided. I straightened my back.

Aye, said Old Enry, as he signalled goodbye to his compatriots, *it were champion.*

Blackness lay ahead of me. Wet and howling. But anything was preferable to what I had just witnessed. I pulled myself together as best I could and began, with Old Enry at my side, to walk with slow painful steps into the bleak, mysterious dark. Behind me still came the cries of those I had believed summoned me. Then, one by one, the voices died, the lights dimmed and were extinguished.

I gave myself up to the Chaos which heaved within me.

Munich
March 1987

NON-FICTION

CONTENTS

INTRODUCTION

Recently, much has been written on the subject of free speech and pornography. Many, it seemed, who talked most about free speech in defence of pornography all too readily edited and changed what they didn't like, or took out expensive law-suits in order to keep someone quiet.

An early and minor example of this for me was *Playboy* magazine, the first publication I ever saw which specifically printed "rewrite sheets" onto which accepted material was retyped in order to conform with editorial policies. While one could see the point of this in *Reader's Digest*, it hardly fitted the image *Playboy* tried to promote in the '60s as a champion of freedom. It was for this reason, originally, that I refused to let my work be submitted to *Playboy*. Now on principle I won't accept commissions or submit work to any magazine deriving its income from pornography nor any magazine, like *Omni*, which as well as being a stablemate of *Penthouse*, frequently publishes its own share of gynaephobic material.

I have no record of paranoia and I'm inclined to think the best of people's motives, but when the *Guardian* undercut the point of my piece on *Porn Gold* by illustrating it with a large soft-porn photograph from the Pirelli Calendar, I was by no means the only person to object. The *Guardian*, honourably, ran an apology, albeit some two months later.

I suspect the *Sunday Telegraph Magazine*, which commissioned but didn't use *The Case Against Pornography*, didn't like my arguments. I suspect the same was true of *The Times Literary Supplement* who paid me for *What Feminism Has Done For Me* and whose excuse for not running it was that, because I had mentioned Andrea Dworkin briefly, it was essentially the same piece that had appeared in the *New Statesman* a week or two earlier. My regard for the *TLS* was never very high. Now I'd put it on a level with the *Literary Review*.

Years ago, my determination to keep NEW WORLDS going was fuelled by a disgust for much of the literary world where these days principle seems to play an even smaller part and the level of nepotism alone seems to have reached epidemic proportions.

I felt less angry with the *Daily Telegraph*. By and large you know where you are with that newspaper and it was foolish of me to think I could air my political views in it (and perhaps a bit naïve of them to expect an old polemicist to keep his mouth shut). Both pieces from the *Telegraph* reprinted here have the *Telegraph* cuts printed in italics. These cuts are reminiscent of a censor's cuts all over the world and are the kind that would begin to appear more often if Mrs Thatcher's demands for increased State censorship are granted.

In Orwell's *1984* the State was happy to produce and disseminate pornography while exercising absolute political censorship. People who confuse free speech with pornography might do well to think about that particular idea as we face the prospect of even more repression in our society.

London
January 1989

SCRATCHING A LIVING

It once occurred to me that if Henry Luce II, having axed *Life* in the interest of economic efficiency, had taken over this particular journal, its staff might now be clocking in at Time-Punch Inc. I thought of this because a couple of weeks ago I was described by *Time* as "a British writing machine". Flattered though I was to be condensed and, as it were, cleaned up for mass market presentation, I was also a little stunned to be so characterised by one who as far as I know never met me, let alone spent a few days at my home.

If I'm any sort of machine, then I'm more on the lines of the engine which took *The African Queen* up-river than the astonishing device which gave lift-off to *Jupiter One*. I'm far better at sighing, wheezing, clanking, covering myself with warm grease and mysteriously losing pressure in midstream than I am at purring unostentatiously into sophisticated drive mode and carrying a mighty creative tonnage to safe harbour on the other side of some imaginative universe.

It's not a fact I'm particularly proud of, but I feel obliged to record—not only am I baffled by the very notion of word processors, I have been known to write whole novels with the aid of nothing more than a couple of exercise books, a leaking Osmiroid and a bottle of Quink.

When interviewed about my working day I generally say I do a regular nine to five shift, take an hour off for lunch and keep weekends free. Actually, when everything's going particularly well I manage a routine which approximates to this. I believe an author has no special right to temperamental fits or an erratic lifestyle which discommodes family and friends.

My image of a really grown-up writer is someone I'd guess

nourishing breakfast you disappear discreetly to your study. Emerging for lunch you glance through papers and mail, exchanging a polite word or two with spouse and whatever children are knocking about, returning to work until six or so, when you appear again ready to relax with friends and loved ones.

In the early stages of a book perhaps you rise around dawn. Disturbing no one, you take your setters for a long stroll. Your keen eye misses nothing of the world around you. With one of those thin gold propelling pencils and neat leatherbound notebooks you record your thoughts and observations before returning home. While consuming your yoghurt and orange juice, you write, in a clear yet idiosyncratic hand, a few pages of your journal. It's true you might be a trifle abstracted. You apologise for this; you make a little joke about it. Your affectionate family, respectful of your creative processes, goes about its business with the minimum of noise or bustle.

In other words a thoroughly humane, well-balanced, civilised sort of working day. All one really needs, I'd guess, if one wants to start aiming for it, is a house roughly the size of Tara, a bunch of servants as cheerful and loyal as the cast of *Upstairs, Downstairs*, a soulmate who is a cross between Albert Schweitzer and St Thérèse, an agent who is to you what Joan of Arc was to the Dauphin, and offspring combining the decency and virtue of *Little Women's* Jo and Beth with the resourcefulness of *The Railway Children*. Not much to ask for, all in all, one thinks as one sits blearily picking one's feet and watching the IBA Test Card at 11.45 a.m. while, elsewhere in the house someone, with the ruthless self-absorption of Caligula, clatters dishes in the sink and demands your attention in the matter of your preferences for that evening's supper. Is it any wonder you haven't got further than typing *Chapter One. I am born*, and it's now three weeks since your contract stipulated you had to turn in an "acceptably finished manuscript"? Who would not feel profoundly wounded?

The fact is that like most people I have several sorts of working day. When all's well it's up at seven, feed the cats, make the tea, check the news, get into the shower, and by 8.30 sit down to the previous day's output before rolling another sheet into the typewriter. A break for lunch—soup, some crackers—and by six I'm ready to unwind. That's when I'm fairly well into a book, with a good idea who the characters are and what they're doing. Although sometimes scarcely aware of my surroundings I'm otherwise cheerful, a reasonably tolerable companion. If there's a domestic crisis, I spring to meet it. With loved ones I'm solicitous. These are the days most closely approaching my sense of what is proper.

There are other days, however, when I rise determinedly at seven, feed the cats etc. etc. By 8.30, having arranged notebooks and pens to hand, I switch on breakfast TV for the news. By 9.30, when all news is over, I catch the weather and headlines on Teletext. This done I look up my Stars on Oracle, road conditions in England and Wales, the value of the zloty against the yen, air traffic movements at Heathrow, by which time I'm ready for *Advanced Urdu*, *A-Level Mathematics* or *Scandinavian Reindeer Breeding*. As an example of my iron discipline I must say I draw the line at *Cartoon Time*, *Postman Pat*, *Playschool* and, by and large, *Pebble Mill At One*. If questioned on the matter ("I thought you said you had a lot of work to do") I explain as patiently as possible when dealing with philistine simpletons that this is, of course, research.

When Schools programmes finish I switch off the TV (I can honestly claim never to have seen a full episode of *Grange Hill*) and go out for a breather before beginning work. I might do a little crucial shopping (five old picture frames, a full set of plastic funnels, a *Roy Rogers Annual* for 1954) or visit the library for essential reference (*Do It Yourself Winegrowing*; *That Most Urgent Agony: The Creative Process in Crisis 1975–79*; *First Steps in Urdu*; *More About Reindeer Breeding*). Naturally when I get home I note the living-room floor needs Hoovering and that I've forgotten to clean the paint brushes I used just before Christmas. These tasks done I pick up my notebook and retire to bed, saying I'll work as soon as I'm refreshed. By the time I rise again it's close to dinner, so I decide to start after I've eaten. When I've washed up and put the dishes away it's far too late to do much so I watch TV until bedtime. At bedtime I begin to work furiously for fifteen minutes until I fall into an exhausted slumber. At 3.30 a.m. I wake in a sweat of anxious confusion wondering at my weakness of character and the plight of my finances. I resolve to get up earlier tomorrow for a proper start. Let the reader's cynicism determine how long they think this cycle lasts.

At least such working days don't much involve anyone else in my private horror. There are some days, however, when reason and humanity desert me completely. I become a monster of egomania, self-pity, psychosomnia, vicious complaint and paranoia. There was a time, long ago, when the local glazier used to estimate his annual budget based on my regular custom (we had glass doors then). It's still fair to admit that the occasional cup or lighter item of furniture is not altogether safe during such working days as these. I'm not greatly given to physical violence but whatever creative gift I possess becomes wholly devoted to the art of accusatory rhetoric. Stalin condemning counter-revolutionaries in the Comintern or Hitler on the subject of International Zionism are as nothing when I take on, for instance, *The Shocking Discovery of Saboteurs and Traitors in My Own Home*.

Perhaps this is why I've become fascinated with the private lives of the great dictators. There's a familiar echo both in their technique and the general drift of their subject matter. I suppose we should all be grateful I never seriously considered going into conventional politics and that sustaining a singular line of argument is not my strong point. I think on the whole I prefer a working day involving a *blitzkrieg* on a ream of A4 while issuing belligerent communiqués to the cats, rather than one devoted to dividing up Poland or invading Abyssinia. However, on such days it's admittedly a fine difference for those in my immediate vicinity whether I'm getting on with *Chapter Two: My Schooling*, or invading the Sudetenland.

When it comes right down to it the only important distinction between your war machine and your average writing machine is that the latter is marginally more interested in other people's points of view.

MERVYN PEAKE

Everything Mervyn Peake did, he did with a passion controlled and channelled so delicately it was almost frightening to experience—like a violent Glaswegian stevedore washing a new-born baby with that gentleness possessed only by the very strong. His control of line, as a draughtsman, remains unrivalled by any contemporary; his control of the structure of his great *Titus Groan* trilogy was astonishingly disciplined—the remorselessness of the apparently inevitable plot becomes a fundamental part of the book's attraction, as it is, for instance, in Conrad's *Victory*.

Peake was a conscious artist who protected his privacy with an exterior and perfectly natural amiability; he was a true dandy in an age which had elevated the uniform, the proclamation, the mani-festo, above subtler human values; a true Romantic, who believed in the wonder of human aspiration in all its aspects, who saw human relationships as the fundamental subject matter of art, no matter how superficially "grotesque" it might be. His artist's eye could no more judge this character a "villain" and that a "saint" than could his poet's tongue invent a sentimental (or cynical) lie. His truth was tempered with the gentlest irony, couched in the most powerful images; so much so that it made some of his less imaginative and less intelligent contemporaries (many young critics today, even) afraid, self-conscious, baffled by it unable to accept its generosity—for to the unimaginative mind everything is "exaggeration".

It is this search for the controlled expression of a rich, romantic imagination which is one of the underlying themes of *Peake's Progress*. Self-discipline, a tolerant understanding of those who do not possess the particular gift of romantic creativity, and enormous patience are among the qualities such a person must encourage within himself particularly if, like Peake, he is also a teacher.

113

Peake taught a good many people to draw well and his small book on the subject, *The Craft of the Lead Pencil*, remains one of the most inspiring of its kind.

That Peake was no naïf is very evident from this book which describes his progress from youthful talent to the mature genius of his last writing. I have not asked Maeve Gilmore (his widow) if she intended the book to be a kind of complementary volume to John Watney's recent biography of Peake or an amplification of her own moving memoir *A World Away*, but for me this is how the book functions best. The early work—from Peake's boyhood and youth—shows above-average talent, but it is familiar enough and derivative enough to be the work (both the writing such as *The White Chief of the Umzimbooboo Kaffirs* and the earlier drawings) of almost any boy possessing similar gifts. The fascination of *Peake's Progress* is chiefly in the splendid way one is able to witness the development of an artist, the sudden improvements, the leaps from easy skill to idiosyncratic technique, the instinctive intelligence which learns to mould and select the material. All the early drawings are "imaginative" or "grotesque", but by his twenties Peake had trained hand to respond to eye in drawing what the eye saw, without self-consciousness. By his thirties he was selecting his subject matter (his Belsen drawings are both moving and objective) and was able to write and draw in almost any medium he selected. His early nonsense verse is followed by moving, "middle-period" poetry, by the passionate quiet lyrical poems of his manhood, by the *deliberate* choice of deceptively simple or direct forms in which he chose to work.

His was the difficulty of a person of many talents and an abundance of artistic gifts ("I am too rich already," he wrote in a poem, "for my eyes mint gold") which he often used casually to entertain and delight his wife, his children and his friends. His "minor" work—his children's books, his nonsense verse, some of his illustrations—was done with the same generosity and spirit, but was often done simply because he was able to sell it, whereas his more important work was, until relatively recently, always difficult for him to sell and has only become available to a large public since his death. He indulged the requirements of publishers, he cheerfully indulged his family and friends, but he never indulged himself as an artist. This meant that he never made very much money from his work (he drew, painted far too little—his painting is underrated in my view—designed stage sets, wrote prose, poetry and plays). It was through his plays that he hoped to find commercial success. The splendidly performable *Wit to Woo* is reproduced here in full; it is an actor's delight, but it was "unfashionable" when it was written; we were entering that awful age of "realism" and reductionism characterised by the work of Amis, Braine and Osborne. Peake was not a great playwright, any more than Faulkner was a great film-script writer, but his work here bears all the same hallmarks of an artist restraining exuberance and imagination in the understanding that the "full-strength" stuff is unfashionable, not with the public (which can accept and applaud far more than most critics or producers), but with the impresarios who at that time controlled our theatre so meanly and so cautiously they almost destroyed it.

The most difficult thing in the world for an imaginative artist to imagine is an unimaginative person. Peake made the effort, but I don't think he could quite believe that, for some, "too little" is always better than "enough". The act of writing plays was as much an act of faith as anything else he did; it is to his credit that he would know despair but he would never allow himself to be betrayed by cynicism. And he was trying to make a living in that drab age of cynicism, the 1950s. By the end of the Fifties, of course, he was horribly ill, suffering from the encephalitis which would kill him, after a prolonged decline, by 1968, just when a new, predominantly young, audience was arising which was vociferously renouncing the cynicism of the "low-profile" lads in their nostalgaesic macs and bicycle clips, and looking for contemporary literary and artistic heroes who would affirm their own faith in tolerance, kindness and the fullest possible exploration of the human heart and mind. He appealed to many of the artists of this generation not because his images were exaggerated but because his control and his humanity in handling those images showed that it was possible for a mid- or late-twentieth century artist to take risks without giving in to the demands of self-consciousness or egomania which had possessed so many since the War. He described what his eyes and his mind observed and if anyone still thinks that his imagination was "merely grotesque", exaggerated, "Dickensian", I suggest that they look again at our recent history, or at any average day in their nearest Crown Court. Peake was an artist of wit, intelligence, humanity, boundless creative gifts and a deliberately conscious, almost aggressive simplicity, who renounced all attempts to involve him in movements once he had realised what damage membership of "groups" can do to artistic spontaneity: that direct communication of the creative imagination (disciplined and shaped, to be sure) to its audience.

Peake's Progress can be enjoyed in conjunction with the excellently-conceived but rather poorly-produced *Mervyn Peake, Writings and Drawings* (1974), as well as the memoir and biography. It is a celebration and an affirmation and worth more to the aspiring writer or artist than any number of Arts Council bursaries or courses. If offers hope. Maeve Gilmore's selection is both sensitive and intelligent (as one would expect from so fine a painter) and publishes a great deal of work (including a partially-executed memoir by Peake himself) which has not previously appeared in book-form.

For me, this book is the best possible representation of the "whole" Peake. He was my friend, inspiration, model: a man of amiable generosity who died too soon—before his talent had reached full flowering, perhaps; certainly before his potentially large audience had discovered him. Peake's progress was halted by illness and death, by the cruellest of ironies—but his journey had already led him further and deeper than most of us can ever expect to go.

London
April 1979

HARLAN ELLISON

It could be argued that Harlan Ellison possesses the romantic imagination without quite enough of the romantic discipline. Instead he substitutes *performance*: Keep it fast, keep it funny, keep 'em fazed. And this is why in my opinion his work is so uneven, often within the same story. I don't think any other writer pleads his own cases so often or at such length. This phenomenon supports my theory. His stories are usually buried in their own weight of introductions, prefaces, and running commentaries because each collection is a set (in the musical sense); this nonfiction is the patter designed to link material for the main numbers. Each story is an act—a performance—and almost has to be judged as a theatrical or musical improvisation around a theme. The idea of working in public, in a shop window, is anathema to me and most other writers—to Harlan Ellison it is a natural extension of his writing methods.

As with jazz, he'll use a rubato technique to catch up on himself, get to his original drift (tune or phrase) often after very long digressions. His best stories are scarcely stories at all: they are images, emotions, characters, collages. They are often at their worst when they try to fit genre conventions and dash themselves to fragments against the edges and walls of the form. "A Boy and His Dog" (1969) is an excellent piece of work and only bad when it tries to become a run-of-the-mill SF story (the underground scenes). "Eggsucker" (the "prequel" written some years later, in 1977) is better because it doesn't try to be anything more than an anecdote (and paradoxically is more of a well-made short story than much of Ellison's work). "Imagist" writers don't need to worry too much about plots—witness Stevenson's best short stories—and can destroy their own conceptions by conscientious attempts to fit them into conventional shapes. This is often the case with Ellison whose plots can distort the "real" information in his short stories. Ellison's information is no more in his plots than is, say, J. G. Ballard's in his—or Poe's or Sterne's in theirs. The information is in his images, characters, his pyrotechnic highly oral method of *performing* a piece.

Flashes of autobiography, of self-revelation, are usually immediately disguised or obscured (for all he claims to tell us exactly how it is). Trente, he says, in "Paingod" (1964), had reached a Now in which he could no longer support his acts. If Trente is Ego naked and at large, we know whose ego he represents. In this story everything works fine while the images are coming—the trip through the universes, the skid row scenes and so on—while the characters are being described—but when we are given "plot" it is a letdown. The story part—a pretty banal statement about there being no pleasure without pain—could easily be discarded without the essence of the piece being harmed at all. How much of this is Ellison's fault and how much the fault of SF magazine editors (most of whom have probably done more to ruin the flowering of imaginative talent than any other single group) is hard to say.

In his introduction to "'Repent, Harlequin!' Said the Ticktockman" (1965) he admits the fact that he is always late. (A fact—as someone who's almost always early and an anxiety neurotic who's terrified of missing deadlines—I can vouch for. It is a hideous experience watching Harlan limbering up for a deadline whose date has already passed.) This, too, is a trait more often associated with a performer who needs to give so much of himself to his act that he is always vaguely reluctant to begin until the last possible moment, always exhausted afterwards. I have met more people like Harlan when I've been performing with rock and roll bands than I have met at writers' conferences. It is worth noting, I think, that he has worked as a stand-up comedian and a singer in his time and is always in demand as a speaker when he never fails to give a complete performance. His personal life is much closer to the personal life of, say, Al Jolson than it is to John Updike and I'm sure he prides himself on the fact. He is by no means the only writer to work and live as he does, but he could be one of the first to draw on performing rather than dramatic and literary disciplines to aid him to shape his writing. Byron and Shelley, Swinburne and

Rossetti (these two latter are probably better examples) had poetic meter to control and give shape to their imaginations; similarly a writer like Ballard has chosen to use literary methods to control the flow of his creation. In America there is more of a tradition of what could be called pseudo-oral writing (Twain to Vonnegut) and Harlan Ellison's best work is in this tradition, of course. But films, radio, comic strips have taught him more technique than, I suspect, have books. In this he breaks more thoroughly with tradition than he does in his subject matter which is fairly conventional. He is conscious that he is *competing* with visual forms and so he seeks perpetually for immediacy—for the immediacy offered by popular entertainment, by newspapers, by rock music, by the performers from George Burns to Lenny Bruce whom he so admires. It is no accident that he finds himself spiritually at ease in Hollywood, that he blossoms on a podium, that he takes naturally to TV appearances, that he shows on occasions a somewhat wary attitude to the more staid gatherings of writers and critics where performance is not expected of him.

High above the third level of the city, he crouched on the humming aluminum-frame platform of the air-boat (foof! air-boat, indeed! swizzleskid is what it was, with a tow-rack jerry-rigged) and stared down at the neat Mondrian arrangement of the buildings.

Harlan Ellison speaks about fifteen languages, all of them English. This gift is derived from a natural relish for words which enables him to make use of them far better than most of his contemporaries. It also enables him to work an audience. If he could produce his stories in front of about 2000 people at Circus Circus, Las Vegas, I think he would probably be in his element. The trouble with writing is that it is still a somewhat slow process, still essentially a solitary activity, and Harlan Ellison is still trying to beat those particular problems.

Almost all the characters in these stories are, of course, Harlan Ellison. Harlequin the gadfly is an idealised Ellison, justifying his penchant for practical jokes, giving it a social function (one can also see him as a "good" version of Batman's adversary, The Joker). This particular story is one of the most successful of

Ellison's 60s performances, for all that its ending tends to be a trifle ordinary and it reveals, to me at any rate, some of his own associations—"childishness" with "freedom" and "parsimoniousness" with "social responsibility"—at their crudest (he is far too intelligent and subtle a man to make such associations in any terms but those of metaphor, I should add). The story is in many ways a thematic rerun of the earlier "The Crackpots" (1956).

That he is capable of producing an SF story quite as ordinary and dull as the average SF story he demonstrated in 1974 with the publication of "Sleeping Dogs" which slipped naturally into the pages of *Analog*, a magazine which since 1940 or so seems to have devoted itself specifically to the curtailment and even destruction of the creative imagination. He seems to have gone into this enterprise with much the same spirit of a skilled high-wire monocyclist who for some reason wishes to show the world that he is as good at pushing an ordinary bike along an ordinary sidewalk as anyone else:

A moment later, a new sun lit the sky as the dreadnought *Descartes* was strangled with its own weapon. It flared suddenly, blossomed . . . and was gone.

"Bright Eyes" (1965) was improvised around an existing illustration in response to a challenge by that remarkable editor Cele Lalli, whose editorship of *Amazing* and *Fantastic* in the 60s did so much to encourage the best writers of what came to be known as the US "new wave"—Disch, Zelazny and so on. Here we see Ellison responding to a sympathetic audience (in the shape of Lalli) with a far better story that is still on a familiar theme (the central character is typically "alienated", another version of "the artist") and which I suspect presents us with more original images than appeared in the illustration. The image of the bleeding birds is particularly good. Again we find a fairly conventional "story" element, but all in all "Bright Eyes" is a successful performance if not a spectacularly ambitious one. "The Discarded" (also from *Fantastic*, but six years earlier) repeats the alienation theme and is about as unremarkable a story as "Sleeping Dogs". Ellison was here still translating his social rejects into people like the mutants in this story (and presenting arguments about the social usefulness of such rejects all but identical to his current arguments). Although he had written documentary fiction about actual social rejects (New York street gangs) he did not yet seem to have made the realisation that greater "immediacy", more effective surgery, could be gained by discarding conventional SF ideas and using his own experience. The familiar trappings of SF, the familiar "optimism" of pulp stories, can be seen completely obscuring any individual idea or language in the second earliest story reprinted here, "Wanted in Surgery" (1957). Like me, Ellison is a pretty lousy science fiction writer.

Possibly because we are both lousy science fiction writers we independently picked on similar themes for our early work. Ellison wrote "The Beast that Shouted Love at the Heart of the World" (1968) at about the time I wrote a story called "The Lovebeast". He wrote "Deeper than the Darkness" (1957) at about the time I wrote a story called "Consuming Passion". All I can say about the latter is that they were both run-of-the-mill stories. I'm not sure, however, that I could call my own "pyro" story a "tone-poem". . . .

Like Ellison I was regarded for some years as a pretty ordinary kind of SF writer. Then we began winning prizes for work which the average *Analog* reader would dismiss as mere "borderline" SF, or worse, "fantasy". Certainly, in "I Have No Mouth, and I Must Scream" (1967) there are appropriate SF terms—computer is one of them—but essentially Ellison has learned to use the imagery and terminology of SF as metaphor—he has ceased to be dominated by the conventions of the genre and is making use of them. Compare that story to "Big Sam Was My Friend" (1958), a perfectly reasonable SF story which had appeared nearly ten years earlier. The storytelling method is much the same. The 1958 story is a well enough put together collection of fairly familiar SF images and ideas and the sentimental conventions of the ending are pretty mawkish. By 1967, however, Ellison had learned how to communicate his anger at the manifest ways in which the human spirit is debased, warped, robbed of its dignity by the stupidity and unimaginativeness of our social institutions. (He has always reflected his times but happily the 60s were more radical years and they made a far better mirror for his temperament.) He is still capable, occasionally, of sentimentality or (the opposite side of the same coin) obvious cynicism, but he has learned to check it not so much by standard literary "distancing" techniques or by the kind of irony found, say, in Ballard or Disch, as by an almost frenetic oral style which balances off one view against another. In a performer (a comedian of Bruce's stature for instance) it would emerge as "Oh, so ya don't like that version, eh? Then how about this one, then?" Like all of us he is aiming to please his audience. Like some of us he is aiming to please it without flattering it, without appealing to universal middle-class assumptions about life, without distorting the fundamental subject, without wiping out the ambiguities and paradoxes which are the "truth" he is trying to make us see. Because he equates the cooler ironies of acceptable literary style with an unwillingness on the part of the author to "involve" himself in life (and often, naturally, he is right) he has sought and found his own peculiar, sometimes bizarre methods of storytelling. These can involve an attack on syntax and grammar which only a fool would find offensive, a wild mixing of metaphors and a rapid bringing together of associated images done not necessarily to achieve ironic effect, but done in an ironic "careless" spirit which again I tend to identify with the rapid, scatological delivery of a superb comedian (which Ellison, incidentally, is). My only regret is that Ellison doesn't, in fact, make the final transference from fantasy to comedy in his fiction (he has written far too little comic fiction)—for, as one of his heroes Gerald Kersh consistently proved, comedy can be an even better method of intensifying and "exaggerating" incident and imagery than fantasy.

"Eyes of Dust" (1959) is still too early a story to show anything more than the theme, yet again, of Individuality Destroyed. it lacks resonance. And "World of the Myth" (1964) seems to me to lack any saving irony to make it more than a conventional idea expressed in fairly conventional images, whereas "Lonelyache" (1964) is almost completely its opposite in intensity of imagination and feeling. And here in the introduction we receive another clue to Ellison's methods—performance as a kind of therapy in which the performer reaches for catharsis and in turn transmits it to the audience: a potentially self-destructive working method. It is the only way to play the blues, but it is a dangerous and sometimes unsuccessful game which can ruin a human personality when "vitality" is equated too much with "art" and reading a story like this makes me worry, as I sometimes worry when I watch David Bowie giving himself, like some latter-day Piaf, to his audience, if Ellison isn't exhausting himself too quickly. Such greedy drawing on the world of dreams requires enormous restitution unless we are to find ourselves living in a waking dream, a reality which lacks the texture of those deeper, semiconscious worlds of sleep: for we are using the fundamental stuff of our inner selves, which needs particular forms of contemplative tranquillity (too easily translated as "death") in order to replenish its reserves. In that sense, then, this particular story is the most frightening in the collection, for it describes a familiar (to me) suicide equation.

I read Ellison's introduction "Delusion for a Dragon Slayer" (1966) after I conceived my "performance" theory. The style itself is scarcely "experimental", but the form is much more free than most of those he had used up to that time and, in my view, much more satisfying as a result. The interesting thing is that he says of it that he wanted "a density of images, a veritable darkness of language, comparable in narrative to what saxophonist John Coltrane blows in his 'sheets of sound' style". In this story he is able to display most of his virtues and few of his vices and it is a story which carries for me almost the emotional intensity of my favourite Ellison imaginative story, "Croatoan" (1975).

And in the introduction to "Pretty Maggie Moneyeyes" (1967) we find a further confirmation of Ellison's frustration with the written word, with his looking to the techniques of the film (and possibly the record) for his models. "I scream," he says, "helplessly at the inadequacies of the lineal medium. There is a section herein in which I try to convey a sense of impression of the moment of death. In films I could use effects. In type-on-paper it comes down to the enormously ineffectual italics, type tricks, staccato sentences and spacings of a man groping to expand his medium. Bear with me. It is experimentation, and unless typesetters and editors somehow develop the miracle talent of letting writers tear the form apart and reassemble it in their individual ways, the best I'll be able to do in terms of freedom of impact is what I got away with here . . ."

Impact could be the key word in that statement. A good many writers—particularly those who accept and enjoy the world about them—are conscious of their rivals in films and tv and even newspapers where virtually nothing is demanded of the audience but that they sit and be "entertained". Like me, like Ballard, like Disch and like, I suspect, most of us, Ellison watched a lot of television (witness *The Glass Teat*) and from time to time he probably lost the will, habit or impulse to read a book thoroughly. He knows that his impatience with the printed word is reflected in the majority of his potential audience. In seeking ways of challenging the rivalry of screens and stereos he is taking part in a movement which began almost with the century and assimilates and develops subject matter, images and dramatic techniques which periodically revive, expand and enrich that most flexible medium of all—the medium of printed fiction.

Ironically, of course, it is in this medium that Ellison—who has tried his hand at most other forms—excels, and stimulates many other writers, particularly the young. He has done a lot more for American imaginative fiction than many of those currently praised by a cautious literary establishment. For one thing, his performances are considerably tighter than those who appear to have set out to produce the fictional equivalent of "Tubular Bells", (1973) in which one four-bar phrase is repeated over and over again on a variety of instruments, and in which every musical vice is combined (tautology as an art form?). It would probably be enough if Ellison simply rocked on. But, happily, he does rather more than that, whilst retaining the virtues of a "vulgarity" which in history is always looked back on as legitimate and enviable expression of the romantic spirit.

He is, as I have said elsewhere, a brave little beast, this dwarfish Jew, this Midwestern Byron, this persuasive spieler who has been able to make me produce the first critical introduction to a book by an individual I have written in 12 years. Like all the finest performers, he uses his charm almost unconsciously. And because he is such a good and generous performer, it is extremely hard not to forgive him virtually anything.

Which, of course, must be another reason why he writes so many introductions and at such length.

*

A FIERCER HEN

Even more than the world of publishers, the world of professional SF writers and fans is notoriously timid and conservative. In the last ten years, as the popularity of this genre has grown, the number of writers supplying it has risen accordingly. Now, like battery hens, they produce regularly and reliably and what they produce is virtually without flavour or value of any kind. The label on these eggs is a bald lie; this "imaginative fiction" is a series of well-established tropes and commercial fiction conventions designed not to frighten off a public now established in publishers' minds as a "market".

In the United States (where the logic of category publishing flourishes even more than here) since the mid-sixties Harlan Ellison has adopted the role of fox to the SF hen-coop, and while many of the inmates believe he is merely after their blood and flesh and the ultimate destruction of the coop, others argue that his activities will produce a brighter, fiercer hen, with improved survival characteristics, laying a tastier, more nourishing egg. Ellison has been stirring things up with a series of speeches, television appearances, personal confrontations, letters, stories and anthologies designed to provoke the complacent and to stimulate the despondent into producing genuinely radical stories in a popular genre whose practitioners range from a majority of hacks like Heinlein turning out naive and reactionary "mechaporn" to a minority who, like Disch or Ballard, have created their own sophisticated, highly idiosyncratic styles.

A little ironically, the latter writers are represented in *Again, Dangerous Visions* by rather tame stuff, whereas some of the old hardliners have been goaded into producing lively and untypical stories. There are to be three volumes in the series of anthologies which began with *Dangerous Visions*, and will end with *Last Dangerous Visions*, yet to go to press. The second book is much better than the first, for there are now many more promising writers in SF, due partly to Ellison's own efforts (*Dangerous Visions* is an SF bestseller in paperback in the US and is widely used as a teaching text). The quality of contents varies greatly. Some of the voices often seem to be shouting too loudly—but it could be argued that a few of the quieter voices are far too quiet;

mumbling self-consciously because they don't want people to confuse them with the rowdy, rather embarrassing crowd with whom they're forced to associate. But individual quality isn't important. A good anthology should be, as this is, a work of synthesis in which the contributions form parts of a mosaic of the editor's creation.

Again, Dangerous Visions is vulgar, brash, sometimes silly; but it is alive and optimistic in a way we can expect from few books of any kind these days. There is no point here in attempting to deal with individual stories (there are 46, each with a foreword by Ellison and an afterword by the author). I can, however, recommend the collection. Ellison's enthusiasm is infectious, his involvement is admirable, his own judgement eccentric and his taste questionable. In an introduction, he admits that he turned down a Disch submission out of personal dislike for the author; he berates himself for his foolishness, relates how he came to like and respect Disch, how they became friends, and how he insisted Disch be included in this volume.

He leaves himself open to every sort of cynical response from his critics—and this is his real strength both as a writer and as an anthologist. He reports private conversations, describes the characters of his contributors, sometimes with sentimentality, sometimes with contempt, and gives us a book which, for all that it was published in the US four years ago, retains an energy, a liveliness which refuses to fade. More cautious rivals might cultivate a well-bred tone, select their contents with cooler judgement and better taste, but none of them will contribute as much to the genre or last as long. This monster stands as a monument to the SF genre at a time when it is in a state of metamorphosis, when writers are excited about what they are doing. No other popular genre has such a monument, possibly because messianism is an integral part of the SF writer's temperament.

Reflecting this temperament, a collection of Harlan Ellison's own stories is also published in what I gather is a planned uniform edition of his work (which includes documentary novels from the time he joined a New York street gang and the incisive articles on the visual media written for *The Los Angeles Free Press*—Ellison's main income is from script-writing). This collection includes stories originally published between 1957 and 1969 and show far less development in technique than they do in subject matter. The many Ellison enthusiasts here will be glad to have these stories available at last. The collection includes a longer, revised version of the Nebula-winning "A Boy and his Dog", first published in England after being turned down by editors in the US. All the stories are written with an almost maniacal energy, but if they have a drawback for me it is probably because they still contain far too much SF and not nearly enough Ellison. He is a brave and lively little beast, who makes a great show of himself to the hounds, but remains far too wary ever to lead them to his real lair.

London
June 1976/January 1977

ANGUS WILSON

M ost people don't think of writers as outdoor workers, dependent like farmers and grave diggers on the vagaries of the weather, yet part of the reason Sir Angus Wilson looks so healthy at 70 must be that his books have largely been written in the sunshine. "I only started to write when I was just on 40," he says, and he remains perhaps a little thrilled by good fortune other writers often take for granted. He still enjoys the luxury of being his own master, able to work in the garden of his East Anglian cottage or, when abroad, the grounds of boarding houses and hotels.

After leaving Oxford in 1936, he worked in the British Museum Library, served in Intelligence during the Second World War, then returned to the Museum with the job of replacing 300,000 volumes destroyed during the bombing. The crunch came in the late 1940s; a breakdown, the idea of writing stories as therapy, the discovery of a remarkable talent for fiction. His first collections of short stories—*Such Darling Dodos*, *The Wrong Set*, *A Bit off the Map*—brought him immediate recognition and his novels have established him, in the opinion of many, as the leading English writer. His books display a consistently expanding range of technique and subject, yet always remain highly readable while rigorously exploring his moral and social themes. "I'm against deceit—especially self-deceit. I've always been a liberal-radical, and yet many of the people who are attacked in my early work are rich people who propose themselves as socialists."

Many of his characters are people who find themselves in crisis, beginning to realise the extent of their own self-deceptions. His first novel, *Hemlock and After*, dealt with an eminent novelist, a married man who discovers he is homosexual. *Anglo-Saxon*

Attitudes is about the rationalisations of academics buildings up their own miniature empires at a university; *The Middle Age of Mrs Eliot* concerns a privileged woman who, on the death of her husband, is forced to re-examine preconceptions which all her life she's taken for granted.

When *The Old Men at the Zoo* first appeared, many critics were unsure what to make of this remarkable departure from his earlier territory: a social and political satire set in the near future. He was consciously expanding his range. With *Late Call* he had a hard-working, self-possessed woman, forced to live with her obnoxious headmaster son in a new town; and then with *No Laughing Matter* he drew on his own background to tell the story of a somewhat bohemian family from the turn of the century more or less to the present. "My family were people who lived, most of them, an absurd and mocking life, almost a pantomime. My mother, a Christian Scientist, was given to social pretence I'm afraid. My father was always spending both his and her money very rapidly and we lived in boarding houses—private hotels they were called. Once a year, because it would look bad if we never seemed to go away, we would 'go abroad', to Boulogne. But on the boat coming back my mother would say: 'Angus dear, you know that place where the Prince of Wales stays; it's called Le Touquet, and I think the people in the hotel would find it more interesting if you said that's where we were.' I've always had a hatred of that sort of social deceit, I find it terribly destructive." *No Laughing Matter* combines a variety of 19th- and 20th-century literary techniques to tell of the consequences of such social- and self-deceit.

In *As If By Magic* he again consciously expanded, this time to deal with a much broader geographical canvas, chiefly in the Far East, while *Setting the World on Fire* is almost a single location. Tothill House, the aesthetic and idealistic focus of two brothers. This book is also an attack on the unimaginative cruelties of blind terrorism. All very different books, all united by a relentless examination of personal and social evils, a tremendous sense of comedy and a hatred of sentimental and moralistic sham exemplified by the ludicrous yet sinister Blanchard-White of *The Old Men at the Zoo*.

"I live in a world of danger. For a modern novelist I do have a strong sense of evil—perhaps because I was brought up a Christian

Scientist and we simply pretended that sin, sickness and death didn't exist. I do detest the voice of sweetness. I'm suspicious of people who merely try to make life lovely without seeing what they're doing. Like that woman at the beginning of *Late Call* who comes to the farm and teaches the little girl 'life is lovely dear, you must enjoy it', then has nothing to offer when the girl, in hot weather, takes her clothes off and the father beats her; the woman can do nothing but withdraw in horror."

When not travelling, Angus Wilson lives quietly in the country, either writing in his garden or working on it (experience he used for his autobiographical essay *The Wild Garden*). I interviewed him in his small flat near Regent's Park Zoo. He's a member of the Royal Zoological Society and believes firmly that "one can't engage with people unless one engages with the rest of the natural world". He realised this consciously with *The Old Men at the Zoo*, he thinks. Simon Carter, the hero, has a great talent for natural observation which is obscured by his other talent for administration which ultimately leads him astray. "He's based very much on someone I knew, a very able man. The watching of the badgers is what he 'should be doing' as it were, but he's also got a way of coping with people, though it's not his own real feeling. That's his acting."

Much of the book was drawn from his own experience of the late 30s. "I had the job of taking valuables from the Museum down to Aberystwyth on the train, where they put a lot of them in caves. I was one of the first people to go. I'd been demonstrating for two years against Hitler and the Blackshirts, and so on, though I remember feeling we'd never really have a war. But that was the moment, on the train, when I felt that war was going to come."

He has never compromised his principles, which made his knighthood, in 1980, all the more welcome to those who knew him. For years he championed the cause of writers as Chairman of the Arts Council Literature Panel, actively opposed censorship in the arts and all forms of political oppression and bureaucratic stupidity. Yet he believes one can never know how one might have behaved, for instance, if Hitler had succeeded in conquering England. To some extent *The Old Men at the Zoo* is an examination of how decent, well-meaning people might have behaved under the Nazis. Remarkably, the story avoids sensationalism, forces us to examine our own areas of self-deceit and concentrates on the ordinary subtleties of a near-future in which a fascist government gradually assumes power. As in all his books, there are some tremendously funny scenes and it's this mixture of irony, social observation and comedy which makes him such an entertaining writer. He's also a highly entertaining companion, with a gift for accurate mimicry which can make you ache with laughter. "I've always had this talent for mockery, imitation and so on. But I do think that as a substitute for life, mockery is not really quite good enough. So my books, I hope contain reality with mockery all mixed in together."

His enthusiasm for other writers means that he's an excellent and original teacher. He was Professor of English Literature at East Anglia and frequently visits universities, especially in America, to teach. His talent for passing on insights about Richardson, Smollett and Dickens, for instance, as well as about more recent writers (he was an early champion here of Eudora Welty, the Mississippi novelist) has brought him the additional bonus of going abroad for some five months of the year to teach, returning to England via some warmer country (where he's able to write outside). "I'm very fond of Arab countries," he says, in reference to the TV version of *The Old Men at the Zoo* (which substitutes Arabs for Europeans as the "enemy"). He's written on the edge of the Sahara, in the jungles of Sri Lanka, on the African shores of the Mediterranean. Perhaps his love of the sun has something to do with his mother being from South Africa where he spent much of his childhood. This could also explain his special fondness for the Zoo. He used to enjoy lying in bed at his London flat listening to the roaring of the big cats, the trumpeting of the elephants at night, and much of this atmosphere was captured in *The Old Men at the Zoo*. He remains as curious about people as he does about the natural and the created world around him, and this is probably the reason why each new book is so fresh and vital. "I've always led a tremendously full life. I still do."

His books are exceptionally sensual—crammed with sounds, smells, sights, tactile sensations, whether he's writing about an English country garden in full bloom, a barren African desert or a mysterious South-east Asian jungle. For me it's the mark of a good novel if you can recall its scenes vividly after 20 years. I mentioned I was surprised his stories, so easily adaptable to a visual medium, had not been snapped up for TV sooner (*Late Call* has been the only other serial). "I must say I'm a little surprised, too," says Sir Angus. "Still, it's nice that it's happened now."

Energetically he rises from his chair, not at all like an old man, and suggests we walk to the Zoo for lunch.

Oxfordshire
August 1983

ANDREA DWORKIN

Until the publication of *Intercourse* (Arrow, £3.50) last year, most of the left considered Andrea Dworkin a respectably radical feminist; sometimes a little extreme in certain areas, solidly on the side of reform, her books accepted cornerstones of modern feminism. *Our Blood*, *Right-Wing Women* and *Pornography* continued the work of Millett, Firestone and Mitchell, providing us with fresh political ideas, deeper understanding of the fundamental issues, a new hope for sexual equality.

Intercourse, it seems, went too far. Dworkin suggested the political might be altogether too personal. "Traditional" sexuality might have something to do with sexual inequality, she thought.

And there was an outcry, not just from the predictable sources: the plummy El Vino socialists and nervous Chestertonoids, the right-wing women journalists whom one suspects of having been rugger groupies in their youth, the hearties of the *Literary Review*, which seems to be the book world's answer to the *Sun*. The left joined in too, devoting, in this country and in the USA, enormous amounts of space condemning Dworkin's proposal that the politics of inequality were reflected in, and maintained by, the way we approach the sexual act itself.

In Minneapolis, the Dworkin/MacKinnon Bill had been passed and for a short while a city law accepted that pornography, as defined by the Bill, could be a direct as well as indirect cause of sexual crime and sex discrimination. Had not the mayor vetoed it twice, the Bill would have allowed anyone harmed by pornography to bring a case against the pornographer on the basis that pornography contravened their civil rights as citizens. This legislation would have taken the debate away from an obscenity issue to a sex equality issue and made redundant repressive legislation like our own Obscene Publications Act, thus dismantling at least some of the machinery of state censorship.

This radical and clear-sighted approach to pornography as a civil rights issue was attacked by many organisations, including the well-known "*Playboy* lobby", employing ACLU lawyers. The city of Indianapolis was actually sued for passing the Bill. As Dworkin remarks in *Letters from a War Zone*:

> [Feminists] are the ones with different ideas, political ideas, subversive ideas. Yet the energy of the civil liberties lawyers as well as the pornographers . . . has gone into shutting us up. Their argument is that when we address male sexual hegemony as expressed in and perpetuated by pornography . . . we are endangering the speech of others.

The attacks continued, especially from *Playboy*, *Penthouse* and *Hustler*, who began to spend fortunes in attempts to discredit radical feminists in general and Dworkin in particular. This at least was understandable. What's presently baffling me is hearing the left condemn Dworkin as a right-wing pro-censorship activist and criticising her works from that perspective. It is from the left and her traditional allies that she has begun to receive her most savage attacks. Few have read the Dworkin/MacKinnon Bill; few have read the published evidence of the Minneapolis Hearings, *Pornography and Sexual Violence* (Everywoman, £4.95); few have read Dworkin herself on the subject. Reports, frequently from people describing themselves as feminists, referred to her efforts to "ban" porn and represented her as a misanthropic "anti-obscenity" biological determinist when the truth is very much the opposite.

"With pornography we're talking about the Left defending commodity capitalism in all of its forms so that when you defend free speech, what it means in this country is that you're defending the right of people who have money, who have been able to buy speech, over the rights of people who have been disenfranchised from the system," Dworkin said in a recent interview in *On The Issues*.

Dworkin says her books are not prescriptive but descriptive. While continuing to expand the boundaries of feminist dialectic, she argues from a humanistic and idealistic perspective both intellectually stunning and stylistically eloquent. In her reluctance to remain within the defensive walls of accepted liberal wisdom she shares something with Orwell, who so angered the left with his own refusal to repeat the comforting reassurances of conventional socialist thinking. She attacks male supremacy, male injustice, male cruelty, but she has no belief in any biologically inherited wickedness. Her own father was loving and tender and it shocked her to find that not all men were like him. She still believes that most men could be both just and sensitive, that men and women are socialised into their roles and that legal reform and enlightened education together can change society, ridding us of inequality, providing genuine liberation for women and, incidentally, for men. All her arguments are founded in this belief.

In *Intercourse* she devotes much of the book to discussions of male writers she admires. In *Letters from a War Zone*, she says where she has benefited from identifying with male writers. What she fights against, in everything she writes and does, is male refusal to acknowledge sexual inequality, male hatred of women, male contempt for women, male power. And it is when she addresses these issues that she is impressive in her anger, her articulation, her perceptions. Gloria Steinem has referred to Dworkin as the women's movement's Old Testament prophet. But Dworkin is more than a visionary; she is an analyst, a polemicist, a political force whose influence on the politics of liberation many radicals already acknowledge as seminal. Moreover, Dworkin is not an ivory-tower feminist; she remains an active speaker and organiser throughout the West and a powerful voice for working-class women:

Pornography is an issue that has mobilised poor women; the kind of women who have been in pornography or prostitution, the women who have been incest victims or homeless. Women . . . who make the $60,000 a year also control the media in the Women's Movement. They are the ones who are saying "Shut up, we really don't want the stigma of this issue on us." Whereas the poor women are saying, we have no escape from the impact of what pornography means in our lives. It's a real rich/poor issue.

Perhaps this is why Dworkin has lately become such an object of hatred to the middle-class left. Certainly it continues to misrepresent her to an astonishing degree, discussing her anti-pornography campaigning as an issue of censorship rather than an issue of civil rights and seeing her as attacking female sexuality, when in fact she is passionate in her vision of a world in which human sensuality is not only heightened but qualitatively improved by changes in the way we perceive and experience it:

> It's amazing to me how little attraction the word "equality" really has for people. How they so deeply get their pleasure from forms of inequality of all kinds. It seems to me that if a society had real equality, the forms of sensuality that would exist between people would be deeper and richer and more various, less fetishized and alienated.

Scarcely the words of a puritan. But then Dworkin is only puritanical in the zeal with which she is currently keeping the flame of radical feminism alive.

These are bad times for social reform. In the present economic and social climate, allies are deserting the left on almost every issue. Surely the few of us with the courage and capacity to fight on should be supported not condemned? It would seem that the least we could do is to read and understand such writers, before allowing ourselves to be talked into passivity by interests currently using the debased slogans of an earlier liberalism to ensure their own commercial security. Dworkin is not the first genuine radical to be pilloried by the left. Neither would she be the first free spirit to be silenced in the name of free speech.

London
May 1988

MAEVE GILMORE

I was a teenager when she first invited me to tea one September Sunday, to the mock-Gothic suburban house full of books and paintings and stuffed birds, and I think she was amused by me. I was probably pretty naïve and my references to the Sexton Blake Library and the various children's magazines I worked for at the time must have seemed very peculiar. But she invited me back and began a friendship between her family and me which has lasted over thirty years.

I attended most of her openings and saw her paintings become more and more substantial, increasingly complex and technically adventurous. I own several, including a coloured drawing—a kind of harlequin and harlequina, one of a series in which she represented her relationship with her husband, sometimes celebrating, sometimes mourning, for he was hopelessly ill for the last ten years of his life.

Maeve was a beautiful woman. She had honey-blonde hair and hazel eyes ("wasp-coloured" in the words of one of the many poems written for her) and her complexion was like ivory, warm in the gentle sun. The quiet dignity of her manner, the apparent serenity which reflected a shy self-respect, made her more romantic admirers, like Dylan Thomas, compare her to a goddess. But since she was so rarely able to disguise her feelings about people, her face, revealing her thoughts, even when she attempted to be non-committal, was always supremely human. She remained fundamentally shy, but learned to present a confident face to a world which became increasingly demanding.

She was born in 1919; one of a large and rather strict Roman Catholic family, educated at a convent and then, as a concession to her talents, allowed to attend the Westminster School of Art, studying sculpture. It was there on her first day that she met her husband, a young teacher already beginning to make a name for himself as a painter and whose eccentric wit and magical personality captured her imagination.

It is impossible to say now which of the two was the more talented or whether Maeve, rather than taking the role of wife, mother and, later, manager of her husband's affairs, would have become as famous as he was. Her own work, sometimes delicate, sometimes raw, was of a different kind, interpretative where his best-known work was more aggressively impositional. She never regretted that role and she recalled marvellous, fulfilling, happy times in Kent, on Sark, in London and Surrey, with her husband and their three children. She felt her first twenty years or so of marriage were frequently idyllic, a life which even a World War could not seriously threaten.

When I met Maeve, the best years were almost over, though that became obvious only as her husband's disease worsened and surgery exacerbated his condition. We now know that he had a disease akin to Alzheimer's, but in the late 50s there was much less discovered about such things. Maeve still had about her the air of the "unworldly" young woman who had lived an almost fairytale life with her family, painting side by side with her husband, raising children who spent much of their early lives in a rural paradise. I don't think it too melodramatic to say that she went from heaven into hell in a relatively short space of time, and it was a tribute to her character that she adapted to the change with unusual courage.

Maeve did everything she could to keep her husband at home and help him to work. Her own work suffered, of course, and it was not until she at last admitted the impossibility of his remaining at home, even with a full-time nurse, that she eventually began work again. She had taken charge of all financial and publishing affairs, she cared for her growing children in their sometimes baffled distress, she helped organise exhibitions of her husband's drawings and, finally, she began to produce paintings of extraordinary power.

Her work became darker, angrier and more intense. Agonised figures stared helplessly from useless bodies; female forms supported male forms frequently crucified or tortured; terrified lovers embraced. All of Maeve's thoughts and feelings emerged in those canvasses which were so powerful, so directly a record of the horror of what was happening, that the galleries which had earlier taken an interest in her work now began to recoil, virtually demanding that she return to a more modest or delicate style, something perhaps in tune with their preferred image of her as the wounded hand-maiden to Genius.

Maeve was always her own woman. For all the love and extraordinary kindness she exhibited (to my wife Linda, among many others) she was never given to sentimentality. She claimed to dislike babies, yet painted a wonderland of murals in the upstairs rooms of her house, just for the delight of her nine grandchildren. Indeed, the whole of her house in Drayton Gardens, Kensington, was alive with murals—in the kitchen, the hallways, on the stairs —and on the screens she began to paint, originally as an idea for raising much-needed money and later for her own pleasure. There were also knitted dolls—pierrot, columbine and others—which eventually became the characters in her only children's book, *Captain Eustace and the Magic Room*, where there remains a record of the dolls as well as some of the murals, now the only physical trace of that work. When Maeve died, the house had to be sold and the new owner destroyed the murals.

Maeve's other book was an account of her life with her husband, Mervyn Peake. It is called *A World Away* and in its directness, its recollection of happiness, it remains one of the most moving memoirs I have ever read. Life had begun to improve for her, after many years of distress and struggle, during which Mervyn died in 1968, while her arthritis worsened.

In 1983, she went into hospital for a hip replacement and eventually she was told that she had bone cancer. Understanding that she did not have very long to live, she faced this last disaster with the same directness and courage she had faced the others, her concern for her family and close friends as considerable as always.

She was buried in the village churchyard at Burpham, Sussex, beside her husband. At her funeral the vicar praised her for being a wonderful wife and mother and eulogised her husband's gifts.

Mervyn would have been the first to want it made clear that her gifts were as outstanding as his own. Her generosity, her sensitivity, her practicality, her humour and her dignity were just a few of the qualities which, added to her marvelous talent, made her a person whom I still love and who remains vividly alive in my heart. I shall never cease to miss her. She will always be with me.

TAKING THE LIFE OUT OF LONDON

Of the three most recent books of this title, Celina Fox's Londoners is the latest and most disappointing.

The wonderful pictures (currently in the Londoners exhibition at the Museum of London, where Dr Fox is Keeper of Paintings, Prints and Drawings) show a lively population going about its business and pleasure through the capital's centuries, but their vitality is frequently contradicted by a deadness of text ranging from academic sobriety to sheer silliness, some hint of which is given in the picture captions.

A mid-Victorian painting, Maid Descending Stairs, is described as "a variation on the familiar juxtaposition of cats and maids which often had sexual overtones".

David Jones's picture of a maid cleaning a suburban window has "the delicately curvaceous fronds of the trees reaching out like tendrils while the beribboned cat echoing the maid's beribboned bottom provides an amusing sexual pun". The maid's "ribbons" are apron strings.

Maybe it's unfair to complain that an art historian's thesis is dry, that by nature it can hardly fail to codify and distort Londoners' ordinary realities, but the publisher gives no hint of what's offered when we're told on the jacket that we are to get a "vivid and lively recreation of London's past".

Actually we get statistics telling how visual artists responded to Londoners as subjects. For instance we learn that painters were attracted to Pearlies and frequently idealised or mythologised them, but we're told nothing about the real people. Though Rothenstein's Coster Girls is included—"Japanese-inspired composition"—those all girl gangs whose spirited members alarmed Whitechapel in the 1890s aren't even mentioned.

Dr Fox's eye for good pictures is clearly her strength. A writer more familiar with everyday London might have done a better text. You don't have to track down Tube drivers and sewermen to provide prose for these pictures, but it seems daft to rely on other academics' accounts when literature offers so much.

It's as if Defoe, Dickens, Colin MacInnes or less well-known lovers of London like Morrison or Pett Ridge had never existed. What a marvellous chance for someone with a rich knowledge of the city's history, such as Maureen Duffy, to celebrate the people of London! Instead this expensive book seems not much more than a sadly wasted opportunity.

London
April 1987

THE SMELL OF OLD VIENNA

Fin-de-siècle Vienna was a remarkable meeting place of ultra-conservatism and genuine radicalism. By 1899, at the very beginning of *la belle époque*, that brief golden age that lasted until August, 1914, architects like Wagner, Loos, Plecnik and Olbrich had already given Vienna buildings of rich glass, sinuous iron and flowing stonework characteristically *art nouveau*, while the decorative arts of Klimt, Loffler, Friedrich and others were astonishing people with their innovative beauty.

In painting, the Vienna Secession, formed in direct opposition to a powerful academic art establishment, alarmed the bourgeoisie as much as Schoenberg and his followers would attract the violent anger of concert-goers a few years later. Johann Strauss, the Waltz King, had just died, to be succeeded by the "silver era" composers Oscar Strauss, Franz Lehar and Robert Stolz, while Mahler, last and perhaps greatest of the Romantics, had been appointed the Vienna Opera's director by Emperor Franz Joseph, himself a myth as enduring to Middle Europe as Queen Victoria to the English-speaking world.

Here in 1899, the Werkstatte art guild foreshadowed the Bauhaus; soon Trotsky would find asylum to edit Pravda; Theodor Herzl, influential correspondent of the enormously powerful Neue Freie Presse, proposed the idea of Zionism in the pamphlet, "The Jewish State"; anti-Semitic German Nationalist politics were rapidly developing in a city where almost 10% of the population was Jewish in origin, and it would not be long before Hitler arrived and failed to get into art school. Meanwhile, as Larry Wolff frequently tells us in *Postcards From the End of the World*, Freud "anxiously awaited" publication of "The Interpretation of Dreams".

"This Austria is a little world in which the large one is tried out," wrote playwright Christian Hebbel nearly 50 years earlier—an idea even more applicable to Freud's Vienna. In spite of terrible working-class poverty, Vienna attracted artists, intellectuals and politicians from the whole Austro-Hungarian Empire as well as other Slavic and Balkan countries; radical politics were tolerated here perhaps because Franz Joseph's rule seemed monumentally stable, what Stefan Zweig called "the golden age of security".

Italians, Bohemians, Hungarians, Poles, Serbs, Russians and Germans were drawn to a city, the third largest in Europe, to which they attributed the mythical qualities people would later invest in 1920s Paris or 1960s London and Los Angeles. Most great cities function from time to time in this way, and geographically as well as spiritually, Vienna was ideally located to attract a variety of talent. With all the wealth and confidence of a 19th-Century seat of empire, Vienna was as tolerant of nonconformity as London, which had sheltered the likes of Marx and Bakunin. On another level, however, the capital was deeply suspicious of change, and it can be argued that many of its famous citizens, including Freud, were producing sophisticated formulas by which it was possible for people to retain habits and attitudes embraced since the Middle Ages.

Some people now believe that both Freud and Hitler responded to the shock of the new as reactionaries rather than as radicals; Freud with a logic and vocabulary that merely put a gloss on old Judeo-Christian notions of human behaviour (with their marked anti-female overtones) and Hitler providing the German people with political rhetoric encouraging all their atavistic yearning for a simpler, more primitive society in which 20th-Century morality, along with 20th-Century complexity, could be brutally rejected. As the world entered the Machine Age's first decades, witnessing more social upheaval in a few years than in all the preceding centuries, only a few—the Futurists, for instance—welcomed this. In the light of the massive social and psychic changes taking place, Freud's ideas can easily be seen as the banal speculations of a cocaine addict, unquestioningly rooted in an ancient and masculine romantic tradition and borrowing heavily from earlier writers like Arthur Schnitzler, who proposed the concept of the unconscious nearly 10 years before "The Interpretation of Dreams".

This Vienna, in 1899, is the background of Larry Wolff's book, "Postcards From the End of the World", which takes its title from a series of ironic cards published to coincide with the apocalypse many believed must come with the end of the century. The cards were mentioned in the Neue Freie Presse, from which Wolff derives much of his text, having discovered in its files several cases of child murder, two of which involved horrible child abuse and which were reported at length. The first case, written in highly sensational and sentimental terms by Felix Dormann (librettist, seven years later, of Oscar Strauss' popular "Waltz Dream") describes Hedwig Keplinger, who shot herself and her little daughter when her expectations of marriage were dashed. Typical of the time, Dormann's prose reflects both the urge to fictionalise the stark truth of the woman's despair and the strong mood of anti-urbanism, which became an important ingredient in Nazism and in American politics of the interwar years. A second case is that of Anna Hummel, tortured to death by her parents, while a third about the Kutschera children, also written up by Dormann, who were systematically tortured by their parents.

Wolff writes about Freud's studies of the adult-child relationship in the context of these cases to understand Freud's own social notions; to discuss the "modern" conception of the abused child; to show how then, as now, the majority of reports are still slanted to give the impression that physical and sexual violence against women and children (especially girls) is somehow a rare aberration performed not by "ordinary" middle-class men but by sub-human brutes. We are gradually accepting that such abuse is prevalent in our society, where power and the means of interpretation/communication remains largely in male hands, an elite for whom Freud so successfully provided a rationale, where the genuinely radical analyses of writers like Andrea Dworkin, whose "Intercourse" last year caused at least as much of a furor as Freud's first books, remain largely ignored.

As now, child abuse was widely recognised in Freud's Vienna in private, but scarcely admitted publicly; as now, child pornography was widely circulated in private—Felix Salten's pornographic novel "Josefine Mutzenbacher or My 365 Loves", for instance, describes with great relish his heroine's childhood sexual encounters (Salten is best-known as the author of "Bambi"). Wolff most successfully discusses this familiar mixture of sadism and disguising sentimentality, showing how, in this area at least, turn-of-the-century Vienna is clearly a model of our own world. If his book has a flaw it must be that, because it largely accepts established academic and psychoanalytical wisdom, it therefore fails to provide very much fresh light on how to understand and control the enduring cruelties and injustices it catalogues.

Majorca
May 1988

LITERALLY LONDON

The conscientious tourist, not so much interested in chewing the fat (or drinking the warm beer) in a smoky public house as in visiting some impecunious Restoration wit's rustic hideout, around which urban red brick and Portland stone have grown like a healing scab, and looking with awe at a desk similar to the one where, before popping out to keep an assignation with a friend's wife, he dashed off a couple of begging letters, will not be disappointed by Andrew Davies's *Literary London*. It is crammed with famous names. It is not irreverent.

This is the world of literature viewed from an open-topped bus, our guide declaring a pious familiarity with the famous that has a distinctly proprietorial air. This is how he assumes ownership of the dead and their creations. The occasional mistake comes as a welcome stimulant and as the catalogue of names and addresses takes us from the East End (no mention of Pett Ridge or Kersh) to Mayfair (Arlen's not even in the index), we are forced to fantasise to keep ourselves awake.

We long to see the cemeteries of Highgate, Brompton, St Ann's, Soho and Kensal Green burst open and release their hordes of vengeful poets and novelists raging for blood. A year of life would not be too much to pay to witness Lytton Strachey, zombie-biographer, groaning the name of Holroyd as he lurks near the mummy-cases in the British Museum, or the squeaking corpse of H. G. Wells locking its tiny but perfectly formed hands around the throat of the first literary editor to voice some banal convention, some piece of received wisdom, about his "decline", or Ben Jonson in a rotting winding-sheet shoving eighteen inches of best Toledo down the throat of a mewling theatre historian while George Meredith gives brisk chase up Charing Cross Road to the latest publisher to dismiss his best novels as "too difficult" for a modern public.

With deadly dispassion the voice of Mr Davies drones on. We pass Cheyne Walk but don't see Swinburne yelping naked down Rossetti's banisters, to Meredith's dismay, while in Holborn Chatterton dies a mere forger. There is no mention of his providing a mystery which Peter Ackroyd turned into a novel and Wallis (while having Meredith pose as the dead poet on the couch and having it away with Mrs M. in the conservatory) made the subject of a painting. Chelsea, where the modern breed of After Dinner Novelists first met before transferring to Notting Hill, has more to offer us than the fact that Mr and Mrs Carlyle were an argumentative pair or that Oscar Wilde was arrested for sodomy at the Cadogan Hotel. "Liven it up, Davies," we feel like crying. "Let's *hear* the arguments. Let's *see* the sodomy!"

Isn't it enough that Aphra Behn should die in poverty, Keats catch TB or Donne be hauled off to the Fleet without some self-appointed specialist profiting from their despair? Is it the fate of all writers to fall, dead, into such deadly hands? Don't they suffer enough while alive? The Eng. Lit. industry, full of people with degrees in a subject that's notoriously stifled the moment someone conceives a course in it, already populates half the once-decent parts of London, spreading like the plague from Bloomsbury to Hampstead, from Chelsea to Notting Hill.

I know certain authors, including me, who live in stark terror at the prospect of some Yuppie Booker panellist moving into the flat next door. Imagine having an *Observer* reviewer for a neighbour! In my experience, there is only one thing worse than a steel band living and rehearsing next door and that is the distinctive and utterly terrifying sound of a literary dinner party.

London is no longer safe from the Lit. Biz. As publishers merge and grow into media conglomerates, as the creeping blandness of Attenboroughism infects our capital and it becomes harder to distinguish between a Song for Europe and a Book for England, as more and more minor bureaucrats are appointed art-arbiters by a public so lazy, or uncertain or illiterate, it can't even choose its own books from the library, young London writers find themselves rehoused in Bracknell and Uxbridge, forced to inhabit suburbs even Pooter would have derided, denied the heartland which is their heritage and replaced by Lit Biz careerists who, together with others of their dreadful kind, have sanitised Stepney and neutralised Notting Hill to the point where all there is to write about is themselves.

Literary London is now the empty restoration of Michelin's Mausoleum and a characterless Maxwell House, the Johnson Museum, the Dickens Museum, the Carlyle Museum, the William Morris Museum, the Blue Plaque Special Tour. Soho and Chelsea and Fleet Street, even Bloomsbury, and poor gentrified North Kensington, have all gone the way of Hampstead. Could *Little Dorrit* or *Mrs Dalloway* or even a Great Detective be born in these streets today? Can London only now perpetuate the baffled middle-class male egoist blundering and blustering from affair to affair, or the wounded middle-class woman searching for sensibility and understanding in a world only she can afford?

A decadent city is one dedicated to preserving its past and suppressing its future. Where a Victorian bourgeoisie failed, the Thatcherian Yuppie could well succeed. A miasma of conformism threatens to engulf literary London as much as the rest of society. If London wakes one day to discover too late that she's hived off her heart and privatised her soul to sell as a minor tourist attraction to Disney, you can bet your life Mr Davies will be running "Dickens World".

West Kensington
April 1988

PEOPLE OF THE BOOK

Italicised phrases are those cut by *Daily Telegraph*

Fanatic fundamentalism is the religion of the dispossessed, the dispersed and the defeated—the negative remedy when the positive one seems impossible. The Lebanese novelist Amin Maalouf, describing the last years of Arab Granada, shows how fundamentalist response to that crisis accompanied the fall of a liberal and life-loving culture far more attractive than conquering Spain with her political hypocrisies and her Inquisition.

The renaissance of Arab culture, to which the Ayatollah is a reaction, has gone largely unremarked in the West where the odd free-spending millionaire or plane hijacker are the only representations of a civilisation older than our own whose mathematicians laid the foundations for our present technologies.

For those of us who don't know the difference between a caliph and a sultan or a Berber from a Bedouin, Maalouf's *Leo the African* (Quartet, £12.95), translated by Peter Sluglett, is about the most entertaining education we could wish for. Based on the life of Hassan al-Wazzan—baptised "Leo Africanus" by a Medici Pope—whose *Description of Africa* was a standard work for 17th-century geographers, the novel describes Leo's travels in North Africa, the Middle East and Europe at the time of Barbarossa, the Ottoman conquest of Egypt and the bloody occupation of Rome by Lutheran lansquenets.

This was a world in flux. Islam had its rivalries and differences as considerable as those of Christendom; conflicting creeds allowed imperial ambition to spread almost unchecked. Maalouf's procession of places and peoples has a gorgeous Arabian Nights quality which never detracts from the human concerns.

Leo the African is a celebration of the romance and power of the Arab world, its ideals and achievements. *Solitaire* (Quartet, £9.95), an early book by Tahar Ben Jelloun, winner of last year's

Prix Goncourt, shows us the other end of the spectrum. Maalouf's Morocco was independent, confident, thriving, expansive, and remained so for centuries before the French finally succeeded in making it a protectorate and began a familiar process of exploitation and re-education. Ben Jelloun writes about the effects of this colonialism on a single individual, a poor immigrant Moroccan trapped in a cycle of lonely, desperate poverty where even his room is rented to one set of lodgers by day, another by night.

He captures the hopeless humiliation of the Arab divorced from his heritage, baffled by a world despising and deriding his culture and consequently better able to manipulate him. The book, translated by Gareth Stanton and Nick Hindley, is a furious indictment of the attitudes creating such cruel degradation in our wealthy Western cities. The young Arab's bewilderment and shame, his poetic reveries, his fantasies of revenge and triumph as he declines in a Paris slum, are reminiscent of Zola at his angriest.

The last Arabs of Granada, driven from Europe, took little with them but their history and their self-respect. Four hundred years later, their history systematically devalued by conquering colonials, they had almost lost their self-respect. Now, with the Arab literary resurgence, Arab writers are discovering fresh pride in a tradition of art and scholarship which goes back to the golden age of Haroun al-Raschid and before. Tempted today by a new kind of humanity, *an understanding of the political frustrations of women*, it reflects the progressive aspects of Islam *which is only an unchanging and repressive faith in the hands of fanatics, of which Jewry and Christendom also have their share.*

Between them these two very different novels do much to destroy the stereotypical image of the Arab and should, perhaps, be required reading for anyone who goes to North Africa or the Middle East for their holidays.

Oxfordshire
July 1988

LONDON LOST AND FOUND

Italicised passages are those cut by the *Daily Telegraph*.

*I*n *Mrs Thatcher's generous Britain* [in today's generous Britain] the vagrants have become so numerous they are a familiar sight to any Londoner who visits the South Bank or strolls through Lincolns Inn. Tourists heading for *Follies* at the Shaftesbury can't fail to miss the tribe which inhabits the little road island park outside the theatre, while a walk down Oxford Street provides plenty of evidence of that particularly unsavoury aspect of current social policies, the evicting from their asylums of the mentally ill.

It's fashionable to compare our present age with the late Victorian which, in fact, was an age of increasing reform and humanitarianism. We are actually closer in political philosophy to the Second Empire under which the French bourgeousie reclaimed everything the poor had earlier earned. The Gilded Fly sits on a London fast becoming as corrupt, as diseased and as hypocritical as Balzac's or Zola's Paris and perhaps there are lessons to be drawn from these models if we are to rescue ourselves from the illusory prosperity and security so many of us are presently enjoying at the expense of those Londoners who have *learned the lessons of any disenfranchised class, whether modern Muscovites or nineteenth century Parisians, to* become expert beggars, clever prostitutes or successful petty thieves.

These are the people Derek Lambert takes as his main characters in *The Night and the City*—a group of youngsters living on the dole, inhabiting a squat and forever subject to suspicion, both from the well-to-do and the confused poor, from the Law, which increasingly ceases to represent their rights, and from immoral speculators who have discovered the means of making hitherto run-down parts of the city look safe for their yuppie clients *and introducing estate agents' offices where once the corner grocer and the laundromat served a community which, however broke, had at least preserved its self-respect.*

The casual greed of the newly rich is the message of Derek Lambert's novel and, if the book fails in its analysis, it at least shows concern for those Londoners whose identity has been threatened *by the carelessly powerful.* What might lose the book the authority it perhaps deserves is the sketchiness of its experience and the crudeness of its description. Things haven't changed much in the world of English pulp-writing since *I worked on Sexton Blake Library in* the 1950s when this kind of style was favoured by reporters turned thriller-writers. It was, I think, considered poetic or, anyway, lyrical. The attempt, if I'm not mistaken, was to provide a shabby-romantic style for London such as Chandler provided for Los Angeles:

And then it really was spring. Window-boxes bloomed with hyacinth and tulip and in Epping Forest the black fallow deer gambolled prettily and in London Zoo two big cats mated and in the parks young couples kissed and occasionally the dark corners of the city were visited by hope born on questing breezes.

Many popular writers have transcended their genre when writing about the cities which inspire them—Hammett's San Francisco and, of course, Conan Doyle's London. Margery Allingham's powerful postwar London stories like *Tiger in the Smoke* showed how a good detective writer could produce a novel transcending its form, while Gerald Kersh's own *Night and the City* (1946) is a superb evocation of East and West London and his *Fowler's End* remains one of the great comic classics of London life.

Mr Lambert isn't able to affect anything remotely as good as Allingham or Kersh, though his book is bizarrely evocative of their period rather than our own. It has something of the distanced quality of Colin MacInnes's London novels which were essentially the work of a well-meaning spectator rather than participant. Mr Lambert's protagonist is a 19-year-old Liverpudlian, but he's a youth of the 40s. His experience is of Tizer and outdoor toilets, not a 70s world of clubs and avocado bathroom suites. A London cabby calls him "guv", a likeable latter-day Artful Dodger calls him "cully", and 1987 Kings Cross is described as "Gothic", while the young CND demonstrators are, at least spiritually speaking, wearing 1950s duffle-coats. It's like a surreal Doctor Who story where the Intercity trains are contemporary but the upholstery in them is the livery of the LMS. People in their 30s possess, uncannily, the memories of their prewar forebears. Doctor Who would immediately smell a time-slip. Martin Renshaw, journeying South to solve a family mystery and discover himself, is understandably baffled by the world he finds. Anyone dumped from 1950s Liverpool into London of the late 1980s would be. Perhaps that, too, is why he lacks the angry frustration of a modern jobless youngster and fails, as it were, ever to become a real boy.

There is much that needs urgently to be written about London's dispossessed *thousands* and Mr Lambert, who nowadays lives in Spain, has made a worthy stab at exposing the injustices of their situation. His heart seems to be very much in the right place. His body, unfortunately, isn't.

London
September 1988

BUILDING THE NEW JERUSALEM

P rediction has never been my strong point. My vision of
London, since my first unpublished novel in 1957 and the first
Jerry Cornelius novel, "The Final Programme", in 1965, has
tended to be somewhat on the apocalyptic and fanciful side, rather
than the realistic. I'm inclined to regard "2001", for instance, as
one of the dullest films ever made. Much predictive SF has always
seemed to me to be about little utopias and written by littler
Hitlers.

My attitude might have more to do with my past, with its rockets
and bombed sites, than with any immediately likely future. I
thoroughly enjoyed the landscapes of my early childhood and felt a
deep resentment when, after the War, people began to build on the
ruins I had made my own.

What they built, by and large, was ugly, unimaginative and
inhumane. The rejection of all forms of romantic flourish characterised a country recovering from the insane, tacky romanticism of
Nazi grandiosity but it allowed architects and planners to justify
the "clean" lines of their concrete blocks, those machines-for-
existing-in given authority by misusing the theories of Le Corbu-
sier who was never, himself, very happy with urban environments.

Because of the Blitz, further destruction was justified in the
spirit of spartan exigency conditioned by wartime thinking. By the
end of the '50s London was filled with some of the cruellest living
accommodation to be found outside the penal system and some of
the most miserably uninspired public buildings, providing us, in
places with a skyline owing more to Stalin than to Wren or Norman
Shaw, all raised in the name of "the Future", all reflecting a vision
of a sleek, easily-run and uncomplicated city.

But cities *are* complicated.

Cities can neither be simplified nor easily defined. They are hard to interpret. They are the ultimate and natural expression of human evolution, of human dreams and needs; they are as complex as the people who build them, as the planet itself; they have a sensitive ecology. In their architecture and their social organisation they are capable of reflecting the very best in us.

What's more, cities traditionally have liberal, even radical, governments responding to an infinite variety of demands. They tend to oppose conservative or reactionary governments and as a result always come under attack from the Right. The Nazis' hatred of Berlin is well known and was convincingly documented by Speer, their own architect.

Clearly Thatcherites have the same animosity towards London. Simple-minded authoritarians always fear the city's complexity. But when you bring simple rural remedies to the city they have disastrous results. The Arab insurgents in 1918 and the Ukranian and Spanish anarchists rapidly discovered this, while soviet zoning policies helped turn the Russian capital into the bleak non-place travellers find so depressing. Ironically, as opponents of the poll tax have pointed out, such simplifications actually require an ever-increasing bureaucracy to sustain them.

Repressive governments hate cities because their populations are hard to control and frequently impossible to brain-wash. The South East Asian communist remedy of driving citizens piecemeal into the countryside is a clear example of this. As in Savonarola's Florence a hatred of ordinary human ambiguity always characterises the authoritarian. Those who love cities are also inclined to celebrate such ambiguity and subtlety.

While the city represents the best in human nature, the worst is not inevitably represented.

Crime and violence are not necessarily a consequence of large numbers of people coming together. Crime and violence can just as readily be the result of our failure to recognise the city for the organic, living expression of human evolution that it is. If the city fails to provide the best education, the best moral and social experience, the best in humane legislation, it is not the city itself which has failed; any failure could as easily be a failure of vision and understanding on the part of the citizens, their legislators and educators.

Ultimately the best answer to crime is to spend more on improving the quality of life in the city, to reduce tensions resulting from the politics of polarity, to emphasise equality in every possible aspect, to provide real hope, a moral education based on a profound belief in liberty and egalitarianism.

As a great supporter of autonomy in all things, I've often wondered whether there's an ideal population to a city, beyond which it becomes unwieldy, even unworkable.

I was once attracted to the idea of independent cities or city-states of no more than a million or so, yet finally this seemed unrealistic. Now I'd like to live to see London of 20 million or more functioning at its peak. The greater the population, the greater the variety of people and the more stimulus to art and ideas there can be. Possibly, too, more wealth would be generated which could be used to fund all kinds of enlightened social experiment.

This, needless to say, is unlikely to happen to London in another 12 years. Certain predictions can easily be made for the near future; there will be more traffic, there will probably be more crime and increasingly youthful criminals, there will be, given present trends, a greater division than ever between the poor and the rich and, unless there is better and more funding, our social services are likely to be eroded even further.

On one hand the bizarre ruralisation of the city will continue, with Home Counties yuppie colonists confidently flowing in to take over traditional working-class and lower middle-class strongholds; on the other we'll see an increase in the brutalisation resulting from short-sighted unintelligent Thatcherite capitalism.

These policies are not accidental. Just as powerful South Kensington helped polarise and ghettoise North Kensington in the '60s and '70s, so will certain Tories continue with schemes which will produce self-fulfilling prophecies of doom and decay. It's not difficult to achieve when you control the funding.

In spite of all that, I remain optimistic for London, particularly if enough Londoners grow tired of divide-and-rule reactionary policies from both major parties and begin organising their own local groups to represent their own real interests, to resist the erosion of their traditional liberties, the attack on their dignity as citizens, and the greed of the speculators and developers.

Old-fashioned socialism won't do any better than Toryism. It is too bound up with imposed ideological notions, too given to over-simplification and bureaucratic solutions to be able to feel the real pulse of London and find the means of remedying her ills.

Perhaps the reactionary threat will stimulate us to find new ways of resisting those devolutionary tendencies and build street-level organisations actually representing our needs as Londoners. That is the hope of one who loves London and would like to see her grow bigger and better, pushing out her boundaries beyond the Green Belt, possibly even swallowing redundant parts of it, ultimately absorbing Dorking and Guildford and all the smug little stock-brokers who have not yet moved to Stepney or Wapping.

We must repossess our city.

With good modern architecture echoing and amplifying the best of London's existing character and reflecting the return to a more imaginative, flexible and creative phase in our history, by extending the real city into the suburbs, we could, in the twenty-first century, have become a magnificent model for other great cities.

Instead of retreating from the notion of the megametropolis we should have embraced it, celebrated it, grown comfortable with it, equipped it with hospitals, creches, schools, houses set among imaginatively laid-out parks and "wild-gardens", with low-rise assymmetrical buildings designed to blend with and reflect the organic world around them. We should acknowledge and revel in the natural complexity of the London we can create for ourselves.

We should consider the best, most optimistic, possibilities our future offers. To romanticise the worst aspects of the city is to provide ourselves with a formula for doing nothing, solving none of our problems. By accepting the logic and aesthetic of the true city we can produce for ourselves an environment at once civilised, stimulating and secure, a city of equals, sharing equal liberties, equal rights of speech and expression. We should have to work for it, take positive action, determine what we really want for ourselves.

For me London's future could be one representing the true harmony of a highly complex but healthy organism, providing the best social services and transportation, with education and creative life at a peak of excellence, ultimately benefiting Londoners and non-Londoners alike.

Again, this vision can't be imposed on London. It has to be

developed from what already exists, what Londoners actually want. It would mean some disruption, if the existing bleak barracks are to be destroyed and better accommodation built to replace them. Some of the money for this could be levied from those who put virtually nothing back into the city they exploit—those who live in Surrey, for instance, but derive their wealth from London, could pay an extra non-resident's tax, just as people who don't live in countries from which they derive their wealth must pay appropriately higher rates.

This move to increase London's power would not go unresisted. Also we should have to make sure that non-city-dwellers would not be disenfranchised in the way they have helped disenfranchise Londoners. As we reclaim our city, our identity, our power, we should show tolerance to those who prefer the dormitory towns and suburbs, or even the rural life, while remembering our responsibility, which will be to take our civilisation into the next great phase of its evolution.

For Londoners to retrieve control of our city would not be difficult. All it requires is the will to use existing legislation—some of which was actually designed to erode our power—to our advantage. By dismantling a party political structure which has nothing to do with our needs, by using the resources we still have, by supporting those who genuinely represent Londoners' interests, we could see a massive improvement—even by the year 2000!

There's no point in passively bemoaning the dissolution of the GLC and ILEA and blaming all our ills on those awful but not very bright people in Downing Street and Whitehall when we can take advantage of the chances we now have to make positive and optimistic plans for a better, not to say a utopian, London!

We *can* repossess our city. And in doing so we could recover, as early as the year 2000, an important power-base from which to build a brighter and better future for all.

London
May 1988

Pornography turns sex inequality into sexuality and turns male dominance into the sex difference. Put another way, pornography makes inequality into sex, which makes it enjoyable, and into gender, which makes it seem natural. By packaging the resulting product as pictures and words, pornography turns gendered and sexualised inequality into "speech", which has made it a right. Thus does pornography, cloaked as the essence of nature and the index of freedom, turn the inequality between women and men into those twin icons of male supremacy, sex and speech, and a practice of sex discrimination into a legal entitlement.

Catharine A. MacKinnon, *Feminism Unmodified*

WHO'S REALLY COVERING UP?

What on earth will most women make of this pernicious book which, in its every attitude, displays an astonishing lack of interest in the hundreds of thousands of women whose bodies, and possibly spirits, are the basic collateral of the pornography trade? It contains no hint that women's sexual identities are anything but what men define. The only women quoted are those who, for whatever reasons, are happy to accept that definition. *Porn Gold* is like a 19th century examination of the slave trade where the pros and cons of the business are comfortably discussed, quoting only slave-owners or those slaves who (on American plantations, for instance) told interviewers they would be miserable if freed.

Hebditch and Anning, the authors, state they take no moral view; that theirs is the first "investigative" book on the porn trade, but make no mention of important books readily available—among them Dworkin's *Pornography*, Kappeler's *Pornography of Representation*, the entirely factual *Pornography and Sexual Violence*—and blithely dismiss those women directly harmed by pornography as "moral crusaders", "radical feminists" or as indulging in a "retrospective process of self-justification" (i.e. porn models who state they were coerced into performances).

Most of this book is filled with information from direct interviews with the "porn barons", men and women who make the most money from the £3 billion international porn trade. These affable rogues reassure the authors, just as South African officials cheerfully reassure journalists every day, that everything is done on an amiable voluntary basis with nobody suffering: Of course you get the occasional alleged "victim" whining about violence, the odd "moralist" pretending there's some sort of harm in the system, but surely that's the sort of criticism every enterprise must endure?

Content to swallow these lies (and they are lies, I know) the authors retail them to a middle-class audience, reassuring it in turn that there's nothing to worry about, the status quo is unthreatened and "nobody ever died from an overdose of pornography".

Because of their sloppiness of method, their hypocrisy, because they can't admit to their evident bias, the authors of *Porn Gold* have produced a piece of "investigation" about as effective as Mary Whitehouse's. They begin by asking a series of questions: Where is porn made and by whom? Do pornographers seduce people into appearing in porn productions through drugs, blackmail or physical coercion? Does porn cause an increase in sex-crime? Does porn degrade women? Can porn be stopped by legislation? and so on. They conclude by assuring us that pornographers don't force people into porn which doesn't cause an increase in sex-crime, which doesn't degrade women and which can't be stopped by legislation! Their "evidence" comes largely from statements made by the pornographers. They ignore or dismiss evidence from most other sources, or support their arguments by reference to notoriously biased reports like the Meese Commission's. Nowhere are women opposed to porn (such as Linda "Lovelace" Marciano, who has published considerably on the subject) quoted directly. The only question they answer—the only worth this book has—is roughly who makes hard porn and where. Soft porn—*Playboy*, *Penthouse*, Paul Raymond's operations—isn't investigated.

While claiming not to take a moral view, the authors display more outrage about British porn-users being deceived by unscrupulous dealers into buying soft porn disguised as hard than about the trade in child-pornography which they suggest goes on mainly in Thailand!

This removal of the unavoidable truth to a far-away place (i.e. the highly publicised "kiddy-porn" rings revealed in London aren't even mentioned) seems typical. Indeed the only real piece of "investigation" concerns a minor figure in the Thai child-porn trade and is taken entirely from US police files.

The self-contradiction in this book is considerable. It's accepted that coercion is prevalent in non-Western countries but denies it exists here. It denies that drugs are used in "seduction" but admits that drugs are used freely by participants. It denies that organised crime has interests in porn but suggests Mafia involvement.

Even as a reassurance to those of us who'd rather not face the issues, it's ramshackle and lazy. Those prepared to accept its "evidence" must be as thoroughly dedicated to the preservation of the status quo as any who believe that the silencing of Nelson Mandela is justifiable.

As usual "free speech" remains the province of the power elite and its servants. Those refusing to take the appropriate line are mocked, shocked or brutalised into silence. This book is pernicious because it conspires in maintaining their silence.

London
June 1988

WHAT FEMINISM HAS DONE FOR ME

Feminism has had a profound and increasing effect on my life since, I suppose, Kate Millett's *Sexual Politics* was published in 1959. Feminism's first direct influence on my work was probably in a book I published in 1975, *The Adventures of Una Persson and Catherine Cornelius in the 20th Century*, a fumbling attempt at a feminist perspective. Since then I found myself increasingly attracted to the use of women central characters, though I couldn't say that feminism, *per se*, was the cause of this.

Kate Millett, Shulamith Firestone, Robin Morgan, Juliet Mitchell and, in particular, Andrea Dworkin have had an enormous influence on my political thinking. The great feminist writers have done more to reveal and explore the boundaries between art and politics than anyone; they have provided me with a political philosophy which is in no way at odds with my writing because feminist politics is always about people. By definition it can't easily be anything else. The easy abstractions of socialism, say, are simply not possible in feminism. For me, feminism is the only real political hope for the future; the subtleties of its analyses, the humanity of its remedies, the intelligence of its dialectic, makes all current party politics redundant. I believe as passionately, if perhaps not as urgently, in Women's Liberation as Millett or Dworkin. For me, it's the only positive way forward, out of our present decline, our rejection of humane social reform, our horrible embracing of the mores and attitudes of the Second Empire, of "Thatcherism".

What presently disturbs me is the increasing rejection by the Left of the politics of Women's Liberation. This has recently been shown in high profile by much of the response to Andrea Dworkin's latest books. She is a genuinely egalitarian writer. What seems to annoy people is the power with which she presents her arguments, the relentless refusal to compromise, to ignore the injustices and cruelties of male power. Her novel, *Ice and Fire*, makes me weep whenever I read it. Her insights and the precision of her intellect are marvellous to me and she never fails to stimulate me.

Feminism reminds me not simply of my humanity but also of my anger: and it is anger, of course, which frequently fuels the creative process. Dworkin's recent essay on *Wuthering Heights* had the effect on me that Leavis at his most incisive once had, to inspire me to do my very best as a novelist. Dworkin takes literature seriously and in this age of slight ambition, of cautious retrospection, she demands of the novelist a dedication and a moral commitment which I find admirable and cheering.

For me, feminism describes problems and answers questions which once baffled me and for which I could find no adequate descriptions or answers in socialist polemics or, say, conventional psychology. Kate Millett was a revelation to me. Robin Morgan has been an inspiration, together with less well-known feminists like Susanne Kappeler, whose *The Pornography of Representation* is one of several marvellous books to emerge from the British Women's Movement in the past decade.

What I continue to find baffling is the refusal of men and women, who represent themselves as liberals, reformists, radicals or simply as people of principle, to accept the logic of writers like Millett or Dworkin. Perhaps more predictable is the reaction of powerful men who make their incomes wholly or in part from the sale of pornography—people like Paul Raymond, Simon Hornby or Hugh Hefner— and who respond with pained dismay, fear or anger to the accusations of those they help exploit. Hugh Hefner has told his staff that "these chicks [radical feminists] are our natural enemy. It is time to do battle with them . . . What I want is a devastating piece that takes the militant feminists apart" (sadly he found people, including women, to do it), while Paul Raymond declared recently that he would put Clare Short in the stocks because if her Page 3 Bill goes through "then the freedom of the Press has gone." Simon Hornby sees no hypocrisy in his firm, W. H. Smith, promoting Feminist Book Fortnight and continuing to sell and distribute pornographic magazines and books which encourage the brutalisation and humiliation of women. Yet women are constantly and systematically silenced by men, by male-dominated society; and when they object to the means by which that silence is maintained they are told they are trying to censor free speech. It would be wonderful if those powerful interests who accuse women of this felt so strongly about free speech that they spent the same kind of money they spend defending pornography in promoting the cause, for instance, of Nelson Mandela and Zephania Mothopeng. The extent and the level of such hypocrisy continues to amaze me.

Feminist writers still have a long way to go before their ideas affect and ultimately do away with such attitudes, before we can hope to see a genuinely equal society. I'm proud to be one of an increasing number of men who look to Women's Liberation as their own hope for the future and see their worth not in terms of the power they can wield but in terms of the power they are prepared to relinquish to women.

London
April 1988

CAUGHT UP IN REALITY

Introducing BIRD OF PREY by Tasane and Dreyfuss

Child abuse is about the exploitation of the weak by the strong. It's about the theft of innocence and the destruction of trust. It's about stealing someone's future, making them profoundly confused and depriving them of their ordinary options in society. It's an act of despicable cowardice.

No language is too strong to describe child abuse. No anger is too great. The act itself is not "misguided" or "weak" or "pathetic" or "unimaginable" or "unfortunate" or "desperate" or even "disgusting". It is an act which strikes at the heart of our system of ideals as surely as the Nazi Holocaust: and in some ways it is even more terrifying, for it is cynical brutality conducted in secret by trusted relatives and friends. Frequently the victims do not even understand that they are victims. Frequently it is they who feel the guilt.

God alone knows how many millions of children are dehumanised, robbed of honest joy, of the beauty of their sexuality, of their ability to love and accept love, sometimes of their lives. Those thousands of children who are injured by adults, usually parents, and are every year taken into care might be considered the lucky ones. The child abuser is protected by a world that would rather not know what is going on. It is a common, if depressing, characteristic of our society. Again, the experience of Nazi Germany stands as an eloquent symbol of people's positive will towards ignorance: a will exemplified by the Press, including the so-called "quality" Press, which frequently does everything in its power to shout down, silence and discredit those few who try to tell the world the extent of the crime.

Millions of children every year—most of them girls—are to one degree or another educated in a vocabulary of violence, self-hatred and lies, frequently disguised in expressions of the lushest sentimentality. A vocabulary which, in its daily application, frequently condemns them to seek out or repeat the forms of violence, or versions of them, previously perpetrated on them. Our bodies learn this language quickly, as Pavlov's dogs learned; our minds are conditioned by it. When terror and cynicism consume us, terror and cynicism become our only form of communication. We are taught it. We teach it.

We teach what we are taught. We extend the vocabulary. Some of us work to refine it. To many it is the only language they know. We seek out those who speak it. As human beings we are drawn to the familiar. Frequently this "recognition" is mistaken for love. We doom ourselves to repeat the trauma over and over again.

To break that cycle takes considerable courage, a great deal of help and a lot of time. This book offers hope. To many, it could well offer a signpost to freedom.

What I am saying is glaringly obvious, especially to the hundreds and thousands of adults in this country who have known abuse as children. I am lucky. I had no experience of abuse as a child and for years the notion was inconceivable. Twenty years ago I would have regarded the act of child sexual abuse to be that of a rare and singularly wicked pervert. Experience—and especially the experiences of those who know directly how common a crime it is—has taken that innocent misconception away from me. In writing about child abuse I feel inadequate. I lack the authority of those who know all too thoroughly what is involved.

This book offers the authority which I lack. By presenting the evidence in the form of a play and a novel, Dreyfuss and Tasane cope with the complexity of the subject in a way which few factual texts could.

The sexual abuse of children is practised chiefly on girls and by men. Overwhelmingly, statistics show that men are the brutalisers and girls the brutalised. The almost gleeful way in which the popular press celebrates the occasional female abuser (or attempts to make a man's terrified female partner equally to blame), the outrage with which it usually treats the rape of a boy as opposed to a girl, is a sure and depressing measure of male or male-influenced attitudes to the crime. Not only is the abuser telling the victim that she has no value save in her ability to gratify his needs—society (certainly in the form of the Media) is constantly confirming his message.

It is the secret message of a Barbara Cartland romance. It is the explicit message of all pornography. And that is why this novel is so important, for it isolates the deep lie which our society so consistently propagates and which allows brutes to convince themselves that there is "no harm" in what they do. There is "no harm" to the victim because the victim has no value. Therefore she cannot be a victim. Therefore she is wrong to feel hurt. It is her fault. Woman-batterers are confirmed in their actions by women conditioned to believe that somehow they are the cause of their own pain, terror and brutalisation.

Graphically and movingly, this novel presents an unwelcome truth. Men in particular do not want to hear it. In the play Steve Tasane took the part of Danielle, the victim of sexual abuse as a child. A man took the part of a woman in order to give authority to that woman's voice. So that men would listen, because men are conditioned to believe that what women say is not important, not real, not true. Because he did not wish the play to be dismissed as some kind of "feminist rant". Because a woman would not be taken seriously, no matter how terrible her experience.

A man played a woman in order to give authority to "Danielle's" experience, to try to make that experience "real" and "important" and "true" to an audience which, he believed, would become irritated and uncaring if a woman played the role. To me, this is as accurate a reflection of the casual brutality our society accepts as familiar, traditional, "normal", as any I have ever come across. It's as if a Gentile had to play the part of a Jew in order to convince an audience that six million were actually killed in the Nazi camps!

I'm sure Steve Tasane, whose courage and concern I respect, has now discovered another unpleasant fact of day-to-day life in modern Britain—that a man "siding" with women may make some impression on those men already aware that something is badly amiss with our system, but he will also feel himself subtly losing his familiar everyday sense of power. Such experience reveals how much power a man takes for granted, how little a woman takes for granted. Those "ordinary blokes" the man seeks to address on the subject will dismiss what he has to say as, at best, misguided sentimentality. They are anxious to defend the power they do not even admit they possess. Such experiences are worthwhile. They prove so easily how thoroughly the status quo is maintained, how thoroughly men work to keep women as second-class citizens or as no citizens at all.

Which is not to say that there is no point in men trying to address other men on this issue. It means that any man who cares about an obscene injustice is morally bound to speak against it. It should not require too much courage. Not the amount of courage it took Steve Tasane, with no experience of the stage, to go before an audience and represent Danielle. Somewhat less courage, for instance, than it takes the average woman to walk a few yards down a badly lit street.

This book is in itself an act of courage. I can hardly begin to imagine the kind of integrity required to examine the subject, especially if it is one's own experience. Moreover Dreyfuss and Tasane have also created a work of fiction which displays genuine talent.

I don't want to discuss *Bird Of Prey* here but to recommend it. I think it is an excellent novel. It is a genuinely realistic novel. I think it speaks brilliantly for itself. It addresses one of the crucial issues of our time, an issue which must strenuously be attacked if we are to improve the quality of our society and give ourselves any kind of worthwhile future. It is a humane book and it is, after all it reveals and describes, an affirmative book.

"Luke and Danielle," write the authors towards the end of this novel, "Were caught up in reality . . ."

Bird Of Prey describes a reality which anyone with any claim at all to a social conscience should confront and confront urgently. It is a reality being experienced, as you read this, by thousands of children. It is a reality which hundreds of thousands of adults have inherited. Some of those adults will try to pass on their brutal legacy or even seek to recreate it in their adult lives. This book will help make sure that some of them, at least, will fail.

It is an immensely valuable book. I am grateful to the authors for writing it.

Oxfordshire
April 1989

ANTI-PERSONNEL CAPABILITY

GETTING MUSCLE TO THE FRONT

The USAF/McDonnell Douglas YC-15 is a tactical STOL transport prototype. It can fly 40% faster than the C-130 it is designed to replace. It can take off or land on short unimproved combat airstrips with typical payloads of:

6 cargo pallets and 40 troops at one time.
Or, a 203 mm (8-inch) self-propelled howitzer.
Or, a 175 mm self-propelled gun.
Or, a M113A1 armored personnel carrier, an M551 armored recon/airborne assault vehicle, and a jeep.
Or, 8 jeeps.
Its mission? To help the U.S. Army get muscle when and where it needs it.
At the front.

The porn emporia of Tottenham Court Road, Princes Street, Praed Street and Bayswater stand side by side with the electronics shops. The same introverted faces, the same hunched shoulders in raincoats or sports jackets, move from one window to the next, studying the stock with the same peculiar mixture of passivity and intensity; specification manuals full of glossy photographs, chrome and black vinyl, written in a sensual, technical rhetoric so formalised as to have lost all real meaning, are carried home for private study. It is no coincidence that dirty book shops almost invariably put a few sf titles in their windows in a bid for respectability (mine are always popular . . .), or that girlie magazines publish an above-average percentage of anthropomorphic sf stories, and have done since the early days of *Playboy*. In 1946

Steve Frances was a founder of *New Worlds SF*. He later became better known as Hank Janson. Years later the publishers of the Hank Janson series bought *New Worlds* primarily because they thought it would give them enough respectability to get them accepted by W. H. Smith . . . Hugo Gernsback of *Popular Mechanics*, founder of the first specialised sf magazine *Amazing Stories*, ended his days as the editor/publisher of *Sexology*. It is also no coincidence that the majority of J. G. Ballard's moral fables study the relationship between technology and neurotic sexuality.

In private Cessna executive jets, in the first-class section of Boeing 747s, business men and military bureaucrats carry copies of *Penthouse* and *Interavia (World Reviev of Aviation, Astronautics, Avionics)* in silver-trimmed black leather brief-cases. They are, as it were, the top end of the market. Written well, the language of technology in its romantic intensity, its poetry, can teach us almost as much as Browning about how to handle complex ideas in a concentrated, lyrical form. The language found in *Interavia* is as specialised and as baffling to the lay reader as the language of the sex magazines, and usually has as little to do with most people's experience of reality. In this case both languages are potent shorthand, distancing rather than defining those terrors and power-fulfilment fantasies in some way affecting our lives, whether or not we share the obsessions. As in the girlie magazines one occasionally comes across good writing. But since the publications are primarily advertising media it is this aspect which is most striking. The advertising tells us most about the publishers and their audience.

Interavia's advertising is just as disturbing as *Penthouse*'s. The girlie magazines will offer us specialised sex films and photographs, masturbation aids and methods of attracting desired sexual partners or countering impotence: sexual security. *Interavia* advertises civil aircraft and electronics, but predominantly we are promised security in the form of weapons systems, missiles, fighters, rocket guidance systems, bombers, tanks. As ordinary human emotions are disqualified subject-matter in the majority of sex magazines, and words like "grief", "tenderness" or "love" are rarely found in their true context, so words like "death", "kill", or "war" are abolished from *Interavia* advertising and related editorial copy. Here is another (and rather mild) fragment of advertising:

AIR POWER

IAI's combat-proven technologies enable us to offer a wide range of systems and components that put you in command in the air. KFIR C-2—a Mach 2.3+ single seat multimission combat aircraft: interceptor, fighter and ground attack, with rapid mission conversion. KFIR C-2 has twin internal 30mm cannon, and can carry a large and varied payload of offensive and defensive air-to-air and air-to-ground ordnance. Its highly developed aerodynamic design provides outstanding performance throughout the flight envelope . . .
At your command from IAI

Israel Aircraft Industries Ltd.

People are either "passengers" or "personnel". At best they are "pilots" and "crew". Machines designed to kill them have "anti-personnel capability". A daring copy-writer might refer to "conflict areas". This is specialised language reduced to the level of quasi-scientific euphemism. The vocabulary is abused in order to give a spurious ring of authority to aggressively cynical ideas. The copy-writers know very well what they are really talking about. They often know far more than they're saying. Arms salesmen are skilled Newspeakers with a jargon fundamentally identical to that of high-class pimps murmuring confidentially of "studs" and "eager" ladies. As in the brothel business, fear and guilt are subdued, but at a huge cost to the human spirit.

Any publication, whether it be technological, political or literary, which places individuals in emblematic roles must, it seems to me, be in some sense vicious. Soldiers, policemen and physicists, politicians, thieves and whores will assure us, with reasonable truth, that not all generals love the game of war, that not all policemen are euphoric about their power, that most physicists are humane and humorous, that politicians believe in individual justice, that thieves are often the kindest of creatures and that there is many a whore with a heart of gold. In common with other rational people I want to believe this. What distresses me and stretches my credulity, however, is when the soldiers, businessmen, journalists or whores are discovered persisting in their use of a debased and simplified jargon to dehumanise themselves and those they serve. Their self-deceiving contempt, born of protective cynicism, is possibly a more dangerous threat to liberal democracy than any opposing totalitarianism, the fear of which is constantly exploited by *Interavia*'s advertising.

Interavia also fulfils a straightforward demand for technical information; no doubt its editors and publishers would be offended by any suggestion that their magazine catered to some of the least attractive human vices. And that is why I shall continue to be a terrified, fascinated reader of every issue. In a world of shifting polarities one needs sophisticated guidance systems. With *Business Week*, *Interavia* remains among the best and cheapest available.

Ladbroke Grove
November 1977

THE CASE AGAINST PORNOGRAPHY

For most of my adult life I have worked actively against censorship. I have edited and written for magazines which were constantly threatened by some authority attempting to silence them. I am profoundly opposed to the Obscene Publications Act and believe British public life would be enormously improved by a Freedom of Information Act allowing us to inspect among other things our own medical, educational, employment and financial records. I am shocked by the way in which the Official Secrets Act is used to silence the Press.

Over the past twenty years I have also seen evidence which has convinced me that pornography of all kinds is directly harmful to those who use it and the women who frequently become its victims. I found that I was faced with a problem shared by many who desire an egalitarian society in which personal liberty within the Law is of paramount importance. The dilemma, in other words, was "how can we get rid of pornography without increasing censorship?". Until recently this dilemma seemed unsolvable.

During the 1960s a magazine I worked for was taken over by a publisher whose chief business was the production and distribution of pornographic books and magazines. Though their porn was not "hard core" they had the occasional run-in with the police who nonetheless took a friendly attitude towards them and occasionally even socialised with the firm's bosses. In those days I shared a view in common with many of my friends that "soft porn", at any rate, was harmless and acted more as a release mechanism than any sort of stimulant to violence. It didn't take me long to realise, however, that this simply wasn't what was happening.

Two things helped change my mind. The first was the cynical attitude of the photographers towards their subjects: during sessions they were cajoling and friendly, afterwards, in conversation with other men, they could be shockingly brutal and crude. The second, and perhaps most persuasive, was the letters sent in by readers.

The letters published by the magazines were often bad enough. The letters which the magazines could not publish were sickening. They were usually written in response to photographs and frequently would name which group of photographs they had liked best. Sometimes they discussed in cold and terrifying detail how the picture could be "improved" or "made stronger" (i.e. more blatantly obscene).

They frequently reflected an obsessive hatred of women while at the same time describing what the writers did to their wives and girl-friends in scenarios directly taken from the magazine features.

They could also be accusatory—complaining that the women known to the writers were "holding back" by refusing to take part in "fun" clearly enjoyed by the women in the photos. ("Fun Books" is a familiar trade term, incidentally, for porn magazines). Why won't she do it for me? was a familiar theme. I made her do it. I know she'll enjoy it once she tries it. I bet she does it for him. I showed her the pictures so she could see what to do. She's basically "fun-loving" and likes to look at the pictures with me, then I make her . . .

A small percentage of the letters were astonishing in that they openly admitted to acts of intercourse with their own children or neighbour's children and asked for "stronger" material which they claimed stimulated the children's interest. These letters did not, to my knowledge, contain addresses. More frequently they expressed the writer's interest in bondage, leather and rubber, rape and forced sex of every description. There were requests for features depicting bestiality, rape and women being mutilated in one way or another.

The editorial staff responded to these letters with amusement and then proceeded to use them to plan future issues. Whereas they could only hint at some things, they angled their features and photosessions to pander to the writers' demands. Bondage and sadism were the easiest because they actually fell more easily within the guidelines about the degree of nudity and intercourse permitted by the authorities. Whereas pictures of an erotic or educational kind between consenting men and women were deemed obscene, pictures of women hanging by their ankles from poles, chained to chairs, struck by flails and encased in bizarre bondage paraphernalia were "acceptable". These met with considerable reader approval.

In letters which were neither markedly illiterate nor sub-normal men would write in offering suggestions about how to "improve" future issues further. They wanted more shots of, say, Suzie tied up with ropes but needed clearer pictures of the knots to copy and complained that the welts on her buttocks looked as if they had been emphasised by lipstick.

It was not then possible to publish most of those letters and I'm reluctant to quote anything further. Once you have been exposed to pornography and its users you are, in my view, infected for life whether your response is one of fascination or disgust. I have come to believe that pornography is a drug at least as harmful to society as heroin and far more widely spread.

In spite of my convictions I remained opposed to the likes of Mary Whitehouse who want to ban whatever they happen to find offensive. I believe that the Obscene Publications Act with its vague wording about proof being needed that something has a "tendency to deprave and corrupt" is both ineffectual at controlling pornography and dangerous in that depravity and corruption are, after all, a matter of opinion. Whoever happens to be in power can decide what constitutes those tendencies. Thus books like Joyce's *Ulysses*, Hall's *The Well of Loneliness*, Forster's *Maurice*, Lawrence's *Lady Chatterley's Lover* can be, and often have been, prosecuted under such legislation. All kinds of political, social and sexual material can, and have, been defined as harmful under this definition. The activities of people like James Anderton in Manchester, whose police force were responsible for jailing a friend of mine for selling novels which had been on public sale in this country for ten years, is a case in point. And that is frequently why people who hate pornography and understand the damage it does, especially to women, have in the past been reluctant to use the Act to bring cases against the pornographers.

For me and many like me the dilemma was resolved in the mid-1980s when two women in the USA, both involved with Civil Rights activities, proposed a radical new way of fighting pornography.

They argued that the bulk of pornography depicted women in humiliating, degrading and brutalised postures. Essentially this was propaganda promoting and encouraging the continuing dehumanisation and subjugation of women and specifically led to crimes of sexual violence being committed against women. Therefore the pornography question became not a question of defining what was and what was not obscene but a question of defining what clearly promoted the degradation and brutalisation of women. Since the Law already agrees, for instance, that publications promoting the degradation and brutalisation of people of colour are socially harmful and an incitement of racial hatred and, since we also have Sex Equality legislation which allows people to bring cases of sexual harassment and discrimination before the Courts, it should be possible to introduce legislation accepting that pornography which clearly shows women being hurt and degraded should also be prosecuted. Obviously a clear definition of this pornography would be required. I believe the blueprint for this definition and for the legislation itself exists in the Bill proposed by Catharine MacKinnon and Andrea Dworkin in the United States. That others believe this is obvious for in the US at least two City Councils asked MacKinnon and Dworkin to help them gather evidence of the links between pornography and sexual violence with a view to passing legislation on the lines proposed.

The first of these Councils was Minneapolis, which had a history of humane and egalitarian legislation. In December 1983 began an historic series of Public Hearings in which the organisers set out to prove that pornography was discrimination against women. This evidence was conclusive enough to convince the Council and the majority of voters present. The evidence was given over a period of two days and came from academics, public servants (including policemen and prison workers) and, perhaps most tellingly, those who were the victims of pornographers. Linda "Lovelace" Marciano, star of *Deep Throat*, offered convincing testimony of the techniques of fear, torture and humiliation used to force her to take part in pornographic scenarios and pretend to enjoy them. One scenario, she said, took place at Hugh Hefner's *Playboy* mansion and involved an animal. Rape victims described how they had been forced by their attackers to act out scenes displayed to them in magazines and on videos. A woman described how, as a girl scout, she had been raped by three hunters who referred to the pornography they had been reading when they caught her. Psychologists, sociologists and academics described studies proving over and over again ("a weight of evidence far more overwhelming than that proving the links between smoking and lung cancer") that exposure to pornography made men more callous and brutal towards women and far less sympathetic to rape victims. When asked if they would rape a woman if they felt sure they could get away with it a shocking percentage replied that they would. Many, after being exposed to pornography for several days, had come to believe that women "enjoyed" rape. The photo-scenarios they had seen, the videos they had watched, proved it, they said.

Soon after the evidence was heard the multi-million dollar porn industry began marshalling its forces in attempts to block the legislation which followed. So far they have been successful. Pictures of women being flayed, raped by animals, brutalised and physically injured in magazines like *Hustler* have so far been accepted as examples of Free Speech in the US. *Pornography and Sexual Violence*, the complete record of the public hearings in Minneapolis, never, however, found a US publisher. Free speech, it seemed, was the domain only of those powerful enough to define it. It was not until February 1988 that the book was published. It was published in Britain by *Everywoman* with help from the Cadbury Trust, thanks to efforts by among others Cathy Itzin, of The Campaign Against Pornography and Censorship, and Clare Short, MP. *Pornography and Sexual Violence* provides all the evidence that absorbing pornography can lead directly to sexual violence, that it is a drug which requires stronger and stronger doses to stimulate the user, that many men are encouraged by pornography to commit sexual crimes, including incest, child molestation and rape and that they in turn use the pornography as a means of "teaching" their victims what they are supposed to do. My own experiences meant that I needed no convincing of this but I am grateful for the confirmation. And I am certain that thousands and thousands of women will welcome this confirmation— "ordinary" women as well as the photographic models, prostitutes and molested girls whose experience has proven only too frequently how little "release" and how much incitement is contained in the magazines regularly displayed and sold by newsagents and book-sellers in every British High Street.

Currently I am part of a group planning to fight pornography as a Sex Discrimination and not a censorship issue. Meetings and campaigns are planned in the UK with the object of recruiting women and men of all political, religious and philosophical persuasions to work together to discover legal means of persuading the book and magazine trade to stop producing, distributing and selling pornography and to convince the public that pornography is directly responsible for all types of sexual crimes, primarily against women and children. In my view the widespread acceptance of pornography has led directly to the vast increase in sexual crime. *Pornography and Sexual Violence* offers the evidence. I hope this campaign will ultimately help create a safer, more dignified and genuinely egalitarian society from a world which at present remains for so many women an intolerable nightmare.

London
February 1988

FICTION

CONTENTS

GOLD DIGGERS OF 1977

(TEN CLAIMS THAT WON OUR HEARTS)

For Glen Matlock,
Siouxsie Sue, Nik Turner
and everyone else who was never reduced to this. . .

INTRODUCTION

ADDING TO THE LEGEND

*G*old Diggers of 1977 was originally written and published in about two weeks to coincide with the release of *The Great Rock 'n' Roll Swindle*, a reasonably competent film featuring The Sex Pistols, a rock and roll band which revived a number of fashions in the late Seventies, rode high (though maybe not very happily) on a variety of publicity stunts (most of which were banal and most of which, of course, worked) and eventually broke up. A fairly typical set of recriminations and antagonisms between band-members, management, record-companies, culminated in a miser-able tragedy in The Chelsea Hotel, New York, when Sid Vicious, accused of knifing his girlfriend to death, died of a drug overdose.

A great deal of sentimental publicity followed Sid's death—as it seems to follow the death of any rock figure—and another young martyr was added to contemporary popular mythology.

The music press, feeding on its own fictions, characteristically compounded the myth while at the same time appearing to deny it. Like all mass-circulation periodicals, they first inflate someone to larger-than-life proportions and then attempt, often by the cheapest kind of mockery, to deflate the idols they have helped create. Their ugly criticisms of Elvis Presley just before he died were matched in intensity only by the exaggerated tributes follow-ing his death. People seem to need heroes desperately and resent any signs of ordinary humanity in them—to the point, on occa-sions, of assassinating them if they refuse to conform or respond to the dreams of their loonier fans.

When Virgin asked me to write a book to go with the film I agreed (after I'd watched the film) because it fitted in with one of my own obsessions (see for instance "A Dead Singer") and because I'd always seen Irene Handl as Mrs Cornelius. The third reason was that "Anarchy in the UK" introduced a lot of people to the idea of anarchism and presumably led at least a few to Kropotkin and other anarchist theorists whose work is gaining increasing attention. For me, Nestor Makhno is the spirit of romantic, active anarchism, and although he might have been a trifle naïve in some of his hopes, I have a considerable soft spot for him. He, too, died young, of consumption, in poverty and some despair, in Paris in 1936. This story is as much dedicated to his memory as it is to the memory of Sid Vicious and all those others who have, in one way or another, been destroyed by their own simple dreams.

Ingleton
Yorkshire
June 1982

CLAIM ONE:

MAGGIE ALL SET FOR VICTORY

Designed by Huber & Pirsson, The Chelsea Hotel was opened in 1884 as one of the City's earliest co-operative apartment houses. It became a hotel about 1905. The florid cast iron balconies were made by the firm of J. B. & J. M. Cornell. Artists and writers who have lived here include Arthur B. Davies, James T. Farrell, Robert Flaherty, O. Henry, John Sloan, Dylan Thomas, Thomas Wolfe and Sid Vicious.
—*Plaque, The Chelsea Hotel, NY.*

"Well, it's not what I bloody corl a picture." Mrs Cornelius waded across the foyer on old, flat feet and lowered her tray of Lyons Maids and Kia-Oras to the counter. "I mean, in my day it was love an' adventure an' that, wannit."

Lifting a crazed eye from behind the hotdog warmer Sergeant Alvarez opened his disturbed mouth.

"Who . . . ?" he began. But his attention was already wandering.

"Now it's all vomit an' screwin'," she continued. "I wouldn't mind if it was Clark Gable doin' it. *An'* there's no bloody adventure, Sarge. Wot you grinnin' at?"

"Who?"

"Oh, shut up, you pore littel bugger. It's that Mrs Vicious I feel sorry for."

"Killed . . . ?" said Sergeant Alvarez.

"Too right." Mrs C. heaved her tray around. "Oh, well. Back into the effin' fray."

As Time Goes By
On the screen an old robber, desperately clinging to the last vestiges of publicity (which he confused with dignity) pretended to play a guitar and wondered about the money. Something in his eyes showed that he really knew his credibility in South London was going down the drain.

"Then who the hell did get any satisfaction out of it?" Mo Collier felt about in his crotch for the popcorn he'd dropped.

"You got a complaint?" Maggy's voice was muffled.

Mo sighed. "Now's a fine time to start asking."

Robbers cavorted on beaches. Robbers limbered up. Robbers made publishing deals and wondered why their victims went crazy.

Mo looked away from the screen. He sniffed. "There's sulphate in the air-conditioning."

"Is jussa keepa way," said Maggy.

"What?"

She raised her head again, impatiently. "It's just to keep you awake."

"Oh."

The popcorn was running out.

A kilted figure came on screen and began to rationalise his own and others' despair. It was called hindsight.

"I think I'd better try to see what happened to it." Mo hated political movies.

"What? The money?"

"Call it that, if you like. Unless you have a plot, see, you can't have the paranoia."

Maggy rested her head on his thigh. "I don't think it *is* sulphate. It's something else." She tasted the air. "Is this an EMI cinema?"

But Jerry was already backtracking.

New Recruits in the Psychic Wars

"As long as we all believe in the New Jerusalem," said Mitzi Beesley, having trouble with her Knickerbocker Glory, "we stay together. And as long as we stay together, we can all believe the same thing. And if we can all believe the same thing long enough, we can believe for a while that we've made it come true. We all have to be a bit over the top. But when some silly bastard goes well over the top, that rocks the boat. The trouble with Johnny, for instance, was that he wouldn't bloody well stay in uniform. And after Malcolm had gone to all that bother, too."

"I wouldn't know abart any o' that, love." Mrs Cornelius waved away the offer of a bit of jelly and icecream on a long spoon. "Can't stand the stuff. I 'ave ter carry it arahnd orl bleedin' day, don't I?"

They sat together on red vinyl and chrome stools at the bar.

Behind them was a big plate glass window. Behind that was the traffic; the Beautiful People of the Kings Road in their elegant bondagerie. Dandyism always degenerated into fashion.

Little Mitzi was having trouble getting to the bottom of her Glory. Her arms were too short. Mrs C. tilted the glass. "Pore fing. There you go." She laughed. "Didn't mean ter interfere, love." She glanced out of the window.

From the direction of Sloane Square a mob was moving. It was difficult to make out what it consisted of.

"Skinheads," said Mrs C. "Or Mods, is it? Or them Rude Boys? Or is that ther same?"

"Divide and Rule," said Mitzi. "My dad always thinks. And *that's* the first lesson in the management of rock and roll bands."

"Oh, well, they all do that, don't they." Mrs C. squinted up the street. "Blimey, it's a load of effin' actors. Innit?"

The mob was dressed in 17th century costumes. "Pirates?"

"Nostalgia hasn't been such a positive force since the Romantic Revival."

"'Ippies, yer mean?"

"The Past and the Future—they'll get you every time."

"I know wot you mean, love." Mrs C. picked up her handbag. "Stick to ther Present. I orlways said so, an' I bloody orlways will. I've met some funny bastards in me time. Lookin' backwards; lookin' bloody forwards. It's un'ealthy. Nar. Ther future's orl we fuckin' got, innit?"

"And it doesn't do you any harm."

The mob was carrying effigies of four young men. Over loud-speakers came the sound of Malcolm McLaren singing *You Need Hands.* The mob began to growl in unison.

"I've seen 'em come an' I've seen 'em go." Mrs C. shook her head. "An' it'll end in tears every time. Wot good does it do?"

"It stops you getting bored," said Mitzi. "Some of the time, anyway."

The effigies were being tossed on a tide of angry shoulders.

"You can get 'em attackin' anyfink, carn't yer." Mrs C. was amused. "Give 'em a slipper ter worry 'an they won't bovver *you*."

"The Sex Pistols were the best thing that ever happened for British politics at a very dodgy moment in their career." Mitzi reached her money up to the girl at the till. "Or so we like to think. But no bloody B.O.s or whatever they are for them. Divide and Rule, Mrs C. And up goes your Ego."

"I 'ope this doesn't mean they've stopped ther bloody buses again." Mrs Cornelius looked at the clock over the bar. "I'm due for work at one."

"They still showin' that picture?"

"It's really good business."

"I think Malcolm McLaren is the Sir Robert Boothby of his generation, don't you?" Helen got to the exit first and pushed on one of the doors.

"Well, 'e's no bloody Svengali, an' that's for sure."

"He did identify with the product . . ."

"'E should 'ave bought an Alsatian. They're easier ter train."

A youngish man in a trilby and a dark trenchcoat went past them in a hurry.

"That's Jerry." Mitzi pulled on her jacket. "He still thinks there's a solution to all this. Or at least a resolution."

"It's one o' ther nice fings abart 'im." Mrs C. directed a look of tolerant pity at her retreating son.

"The trouble with messed up love affairs," said Mitzi "is that you waste so much time going to the source of the pain and asking it to make you better."

"'E'll learn. You on'y got yerself ter blame in the end." Mrs Cornelius saw that the mob had parted to allow a convoy of No. 11 buses through. "I'd better 'op on one o' these while I've still got ther chance."

"The ultimate business of management is not just to divide your group but to divide their minds. The more you fuck with their judgement, the more you control them. It's like being married, really." Mitzi waved to Mrs C's lumbering figure as it launched itself towards the bus.

"Don't let 'em piss on yer, dear." Mrs C. reached the platform. "Just becos yore short."

"You can only manage what you create yourself. The trouble with people is that they will keep breaking out."

The mob was beginning to split up. Fights were starting between different factions. Cocked hats flew.

"After all," said Mitzi shadowing Jerry, "someone has to take the blame. But you can bet your chains we won't have anarchy in the UK in our lifetime. Just the usual bloody chaos."

What Do You Need?

"Role models make Rolls Royces. Kids pay for heroes. But it doesn't do to let either the audiences or the artists get out of control—or you stand to lose the profit. It's true in all forms of showbusiness, but it's particularly important in the record industry."

Frank Cornelius lay back in his Executive Comfort Mark VI leather swiveller and wondered if it would be going too far if he waved his unlit cigar.

"What can I do for you, Mo?" His eyes, wasted by a thousand indulgences, moved like worms in his skull.

"I was wondering what happened to the money." Mo unbuttoned his trenchcoat, looking around at the images of rock singers in various classic poses, emulating the stars of Westerns and War films except they had guitars instead of rifles.

"It hardly existed." Frank put his cigar to his awful lips. "Well, I mean, it's real enough in the *mind*. And I suppose that's the main thing. What are you selling me, Mo? Thinking of going solo? This company's small, but it's keen. We really identify with the kids. Can you play your guitar yet? Don't worry if you can't. It's one of the easiest skills in the world to learn."

"What happened to the money, Frank."

"Don't look at me. Malcolm had it."

"He says you had it."

"I haven't made a penny, personally, in six months. It's all gone on expenses. Do you know how much it costs to keep an act on the road?"

"Where's the money?" Mo was beginning to lose his own thread. Frank's responses were too familiar to keep anyone's attention for long.

"Gone in advances, probably. Ask Malcolm, not me. I only became a director towards the end. For legal reasons."

"Where's Malcolm?"

"Who knows where Malcolm is. Does Malcolm know where Malcolm is? Is he Malcolm? What is Malcolm, anyway?"

Mo frowned. "Give me an address, Frank."

"You're not kipping on my floor again. Not with your habits. Haven't you got a squat to go to?" Frank glared in distaste at his brother's ex-friend.

"Where?"

"You're too heavily into bread. That's your problem. You've really sold out, haven't you? I remember you when you didn't give a shit about money or anything else. What are you really after? Mummy and Daddy, is it? If you don't like the heat, you should stay out of the kitchen. I look after a lot of people, but I can't look after you all the time. It's killing me. I have to deal with the hassles, cool out the managements of the venues, pay for the damage . . ."

He raised a suede arm. "I haven't had more than twelve hours sleep in a week. Profits? Do you think there are any profits in this business? If so, where are they? Show them to me?"

"They're up your nose, Frankie."

There came a noise from Frank's throat like the sound of an angry baby. Mo recognised it. It was called The Management Wail. It was time to leave.

Public Image

Identity Manipulation Associates (IMA = Whatever You Want Me To Be) had taken over the old Soho offices. Mo was beginning to feel a little flakey around the edges. He'd started off thinking this was a caper: a time-filler. Now, what with one thing and another, it was beginning to smell like an obsession.

"I've had enough of obsessions." He felt the old call to retreat, to get some air. "On the other hand, this might not be one. It could just be ordinary."

He opened the door and went into the lobby. A young woman looked up at him from threatened brown eyes. "Can I help you?"

"I was wondering about the money. Did Malcolm . . . ?"

"We only do identities here. The money comes later."

"Is there anyone I could see?"

"They're all in meetings. Are you a performer?"

"I . . ."

She became sympathetic and far less wary.

Mo was no-one to be afraid of. She spoke softly. "They won't be back this afternoon, love. What do you play?"

"I think it's Scrabble, but I'm not sure."

"Magic!"

He was plodding off again.

Adapted For The Market: Finally It's The Movie

The permanently depressed tones of Malcolm McLaren, doing his best to make some sense of his impulses, could be heard on the other side of the doors.

Mo pushed his way through. There were no pictures, only a soundtrack. The little room was dark, but somewhere in it lawyers and accountants shuffled and whispered. "Why is everybody so unhappy?"

"Sometimes it's all you've got left of your adolescent enthusiasm," said Mo. He began to giggle.

"Were you ever talented?" Aggressive, self-protecting, attempting condescension, a lawyer spoke.

"Did you deliberately set out to shock?"

"I don't know," said Mo. "I don't read the papers any more."

"Have you just come from Highgate?"

"That's an idea."

"It's the image that's important, isn't it?" This was an upper-class woman's voice. Lady D?

"So they say."

Bodies were coming closer. "Well, ta ta."

"Ta ta."

Swallowing Your Own Bullshit

Mo waded into the mud. He was not quite certain what lay on the other side of the vast building site. He wasn't sure why he was trying to get to South London. A helicopter came in low seeming to be observing him. He looked up. "Mum?"

A voice began to sing *My Way* through a loud hailer.

It was beginning to feel like victimisation, or a haunting. That energy was going. Or maybe it had already gone and that was what he was looking for.

All he'd wanted was a bit of this and that. Some peace and quiet. Some fun. Everybody was going crazy. He hated the lot of them. Why couldn't they leave him alone? Why couldn't he leave them alone?

He was dying for a crap.

He cast about for an anchor. Five feet away the back wheel of a new Honda could be seen, sticking out of the mud, as if the rider had tried to make it across this no-man's-land and failed.

Mo blinked. "Sid?"

What the hell did it matter anyway?

Sulphate Heaven

The room was full of heavy metal. In one corner about fifteen old hippies were wondering where it had all gone, while in the opposite corner fifteen punks were wondering where it was all going.

Mo stood in the middle.

"Anybody want a fight?"

A few eyes flickered, then faded again. Wired faces tried to move.

It was a musician's graveyard. They existed as far apart as Streatham and Kensal Rise. They had served their turn. Many of them had even shown a profit.

Mitzi came in. "Blimey." She rattled her box.

"Line-up, lads," said Mo. "The lady's got the blues."

"Been to Highgate yet?" she asked him.

"Is there any point?"

"Not a lot."

"I'm on my way," he said.

CLAIM TWO:

WE HAVE A GOOD REASON

Johnny Rotten, the angelically malevolent Scaramouche, is a third-generation son of rock 'n' roll—the galvanic lead singer of the Sex Pistols. His band play at a hard heart-attacking, frantic pace. And they sing anti-love songs, cynical songs about suburbia and songs about repression, hate and aggression. They have shocked many people. But the band's music has always been true to life as they see it. Which is why they are so wildly popular. The fans love the Sex Pistols and identify with their songs because they know they are about their lives too.
—*Virgin Records Publicity, 1977*

"Sex and aggro are the best-selling commodities in the world. Everybody's frustrated or angry about something, particularly adolescents."

Frank was having his hair redone to fit in with current trends. "Easy on the Vic, Maggy. We don't want to go too far, do we?"

The phone rang. Maggy picked it up. Her hand stank of camphor. "Popcorn."

She listened for a moment and giggled. She turned back to Frank. "It's your mum."

"Tell her I'm dead."

"You're about the only one who isn't."

Frank took the greasy receiver.

"Hello, mum. How are you? What can I do for you, then?" He was patronising.

He listened for a while, his expression becoming devoutly earnest. "Yeah."

Maggy began to pluck at his locks again, but he stopped her. "Okay, mum."

He frowned.

"Okay, mum. Yes. Yes. Look after yourself." He handed the phone back to Maggy. "Well, well," he said.

197

From the other side of his office door his dogs, a mixed pack of Irish Wolfhounds and Alsatians, began to scratch and whine. He sometimes felt they were his only real security. Moved by some impulse he couldn't define, he placed a reluctant hand on Maggy's bum.

Sentimental Journeys: The Other Side of the Coin

Mo had managed to reach Tooting. Autumn leaves fell onto the common. In the distance was what looked like a ruined Swimming Baths. He dipped into his tub of Sweet and Sour Pork and Chips. His fingers were already stained bright orange, as was his entire lower face. Over to his right the road was up. Drills were hammering. He was beginning to feel more relaxed. It was when they put you in the real country that you went to pieces.

Jimi was waiting for him behind a large plane tree. "I shouldn't really be talking to you, you bastard."

"Divide and Rule," said Mo. "Aren't we part of the same faction any more?"

"What does Malcolm say?"

"Haven't seen him."

"Or the Record Company."

"They haven't released anything."

"Then it could be okay."

"It could be." Mo offered Jimi the tub. The guitarist began to eat with eager, twitching fingers.

"I've been trying to make this deal with the devil all day," he complained. "Not a whisper. What you up to then, you bastard?"

"Very little, my son."

"Got any money?"

Mo shook his head. "How long you got to stay down here?"

"Another six months. Then I might get remission."

"Play your cards right."

"A bit of spit never hurt anybody. Are you in Tooting just to see me?"

"No. I'm looking for a train robber."

"They're difficult to fence, trains."

"You have to have a buyer set up already."

"Things were simpler in the fifties, you know. The poor were poor and the rich were bloody rich. People knew where they stood I blame it all on rock and roll. Now we're back where we started."

"It was the only way out. That doesn't work any more. You think it does. But it doesn't."

"The music goes round and round." Jimi farted. "And it comes out here."

Rock Around the Clock

Mrs Cornelius flashed her torch around the cinema. "It's filthy in 'ere. You fink they'd do somefing abart it."

Customers began to complain at her. She switched off the torch. "Please yerselves."

She went back into the foyer.

With intense concentration, Alvarez was dissecting a hot dog.

"Found anyfink?" she asked.

"Not a sausage."

"Anybody ring fer me?"

"Ring?"

"Never mind."

She'd done her best to warn Frank. Now it was up to him. Three guardsmen in heavy khaki and caps whose visors hid their eyes marched into the cinema and bought tickets. "This had better be good," said one of them threateningly to Alvarez.

"You can't go wrong with sex and pistols." His mate began to guffaw. They had that smell of stale sweat and over-controlled violence common to most soldiers and policemen. It was probably something in the uniform.

Sonic Attack

"A little vomit is a dangerous thing." Miss Brunner tried to smooth a lump in her satin trousers. Her thin hands were agitated, irritable. "There's no point in going for that. Not unless you mean to do it properly. Vomit has to have some meaning, you know."

"What about gobbing," said her eager assistant, Clive. "Should that stay?"

"Well, it is associated with the band, after all." She sniggered. "Disgusting, really."

"But we have to get into disgust, don't we? Disgust equals the Pistols. Ugly times. You know? But will people be disgusted enough?" This was the constant worry of the publicity department at the moment. "I mean, it's important to associate Sex Pistols with nastiness. They should be synonymous in the public's view."

"True." Miss Brunner touched a finger to a blackened lid. "Should we emphasise the urine angle?"

"Piss-stools." Clive laughed a high-pitched, artificial laugh. "Rebels with bladder problems?"

"Now you're being facetious. It won't do, Clive. This is serious. We want the name in every paper by Thursday."

"But the record isn't mixed yet."

"The record, dear, is the least of our problems. We want the front page of *The Sun*. And the rest of them, if possible."

Clive put a pencil to his post-office lips. "Well, we'd better get busy, eh."

"Our first problem," said Miss Brunner, "is to find a nicer word for gob."

And Now, The Sex Pistols Controversy

Mo came out of Balham station and walked into the High Street. DIY shops and take-aways stretched in both directions.

"Nobody ever really hates you," said Mitzi. "It's more that they enjoy being threatened. You know, like throwing a baby up to the ceiling. You couldn't lose. It's just that you expected a different reaction. It's all fantasy. It happens every time."

"You could kick 'em in the balls and they'd keep coming back for more. You've got to feel contempt for people like that." Mo was down.

"I don't know why. They're only enjoying themselves. That's what they pay for. Better than fun fairs. What you're asking them to do is to take you seriously, to believe you're real. But you're not real. You're a performer."

They reached a high, corrugated-iron fence.

"Here we are," she took a key from her pocket and undid a padlock, pushing open the creaking door.

It was a junkyard. Piled on top of one another were dodgem cars, waltzers, chairoplanes, wooden horses and cockerels, roller coaster cars.

"See what I mean," she said.

"What's the point of being here?"

"There's a fortune in scrap, Jerry."

Sex Chaos

Frank Cornelius zipped himself into his leather jacket while Maggy added a few touches to his make-up. "Why is everybody flying South?" he said.

"It's the way the band-waggon's going. Balham, Brazil, Brighton."

"Get the car out. I'm heading for Highgate."

As they went down the stairs, he said: "What we need is a few more novelty acts. They only have to think they're new, that's the main thing. As long as you *think* you're new, you *are* new. And the punters will think you're new, too. There's nothing new under the old limelights, Mag."

"What about the spirit?"

"You mean the blood?"

He began to laugh. It was a hideous, strangled sound. "New equals good. It's been going on for at least a hundred years. The New Woman and all that. New equals vitality. New equals hope. One thing's for sure, Maggy. New very rarely equals profit. Not at first, anyway. It has to be modified and represented before anyone will buy it in a hurry. That's the secret of the process. But it takes so much energy just to get a little bit of something happening that there are bound to be casualties. Look at poor Brian Epstein. It was the writing on the wall for management. It had to become us or them. We didn't want another manager coughing it, did we? How many A&R men do you know who've killed themselves recently?"

"I dunno."

"None. It's the survival side of the business, my love."

They arrived at the street. Ladbroke Grove was full of beaten-up American cars. Maggy went round the corner to the mews to get Frank's Mercedes.

"It really is time we moved away from this neighbourhood," he said. "But it's where I've got my roots, you know."

C'mon Everybody

"Your mistake was in cocking a snoot at the Queen, my lad." Bishop Beesley unwrapped a Mars Bar and, like an overweight pigeon, began to peck at it.

"Well, we took things more seriously at the time. We needed something." Mo sat down in a battered dodgem. "Do you really own all this?"

"Every bit. You must have a lot of money stashed away. How would you like to invest?" The Bishop wiped his pudgy hands on his greasy black jacket. "Americans buy it, you know. And people from Kensington and Chelsea. It's decorative. It's nostalgic. It's fun. Good times remembered."

"If not exactly relived," said Mitzi.

"You can't have everything, my dear. Junk, after all, has many functions and takes many forms. None of us is getting any younger."

"Speak for yourself," said Mo. "This is an investigation."

"Into what, my boy?"

"We haven't decided yet."

"Anybody dead?" His chocolate-soaked eyes became speculative.

"You thinking of buying in?"

"I have an excellent wrecking crew, if you're interested. And we specialise in salvage, too. I mean salvation." He grimaced and sought in his pockets for another Mars Bar. "We could be mutually useful to one another."

Mo got up. A pile of Tunnel of Love boats began to creak and sway.

"We'll be in touch," said Mitzi.

From somewhere within the stacks came the sound of heavy breathing.

Bishop Beesley went back into his hut and locked the door.

Amateur Night at the Moscow Odeon

It was a mock-Gothic complex. Frank signed in at the gatehouse and Maggy drove through. The gates were electronically controlled and shut automatically behind them. Surrounding them were tall brick walls topped with iron spikes. At intervals was a series of buildings once used to house Victorian painters. Now they were used for recording purposes.

The largest of the buildings was at the far end of the square. Maggy parked in front of it.

Wheezing a little Frank got out of the car. "I should never have had that last bottle of amyl."

He mounted the steps and pressed a buzzer. A bouncer in a torn red T-shirt let him in. He descended to the basement.

The studio was deserted. In the booth a shadowy figure in a rubber bondage suit sat smoking a cigarette through an enema tube.

Frank said: "Mr Big sent for me."

"Not 'Big', stupid. 'Bug'." The voice was mysterious, slurred.

"Are you Mr Bug?"

"I represent his interests."

"Somebody's on to us."

"What's new?"

"My mother just told me."

"So?"

"Hadn't we better start worrying?"

"Worrying? We're just about to make the real money."

Frank was nervous. "I can't see how . . ."

Mr Bug's representative began to unzip the front of his suit. "In exposure, you fool. What do you think *The News of the World* is for?"

"I'm not entirely happy," said Frank.

"That's the secret of success, isn't it?"

Frank began to sink.

The voice grew sympathetic.

"Come here, you poor old thing, and have a nibble on this."

Frank crawled towards the booth.

Wotcha Gonna Do About It?

The train from Balham was stuck on the bridge over the Thames. The bridge seemed to be swaying a lot. Mo felt tired. In the far corner of the compartment, Mitzi Beesley had curled herself on a seat and was asleep. Elsewhere came the sound of desultory vandalism, as if weary priests were performing a ritual whose point had been long-since forgotten.

The train quivered and began to hum.

In the sunset, the Houses of Parliament looked as if they were on fire. But it was only an illusion. The structure remained. A little graffiti on the sides made no real difference.

"Who's got the money?" Mo asked again.

Mitzi opened her eyes. "The people who had it in the first place. That's where it comes from and that's where it goes. How much did you spend at the pub last year?"

"About thirty thousand pounds."

"Exactly."

"What are you trying to say?"

She shook her head. "What the bloody hell did you ever know about Anarchy in the UK, Mo. You gave all the power back, just like that. You gave all the money back, just as if you'd found it in the street and returned it to the police station."

"Bollocks!"

She shrugged and closed her eyes again. "What's in a name?"

From the luggage rack above them an old hippy said: "Words are magic, man. They have power, you know."

Mitzi glanced up at him. "You've got to walk the walk as well as talking the talk, man."

"I blame it all on nuclear energy," he said.

"Well, you've got to blame something. It saves you a lot of worry."

At the train began to move again Mitzi sang to the tune of *Woodstock*.

"We are wet; we are droopy
And we simply love Peanuts and Snoopy . . ."

Hundreds of drab back-gardens began to fill the windows. The train made a moaning noise.

Mo slid towards the door.

"A pose is a pose is a pose," said the hippy.

CLAIM THREE:

LABOUR OR TORY? THE OLD DOUBLE CROSS

Cries of "Anarchy!" have always been associated with bored, middle class students who followed each other like sheep.

But the Pistols are spearheading, or hoping to, a backstreet backlash of working class kids who have never really had it hard, but are still put down.

"They try to ruin you from the start. They take away your soul. They destroy you. 'Be a bank clerk' or 'Join the Army' is what they give you at school.

"And if you do what they say you'll end up like the moron they want you to be. You have got to fight back or die.

"You have no future, nothing. You are made unequal. Most of the time the kids who fight back don't use their brains and it's wasted. Join a band is one way, or teach yourself is another. It doesn't take very much."
—*Record Mirror, December 11, 1976*

Nestor Makhno, anarchist hero of the Ukraine, took another glass of absinthe and looked out onto the deserted Rue Bonaparte. "As far as I'm concerned," he said, "I died in the mid-thirties. But you can't believe anything you hear, can you?"

"I know what you mean," said Sid.

Things were quiet, that evening, at the Café Hendrix. The romantic dead were feeling generally low; though there was always a certain atmosphere of satisfaction when another young hero or heroine bit the dust.

"Besides," said Brian Jones, "there are these second and third generation copycat deaths, aren't there, these days? You're not even sure if some of these people really are martyrs to the Cause."

"What Cause is that?" Sid helped himself to a slice of pie.

"You know—Beautiful Losers—Dead Underdogs—Byronic Tragic figures. All that." Jones was vague. It had been a long time since he had thought about it.

Sid was under the impression that Jones was simply upset. Maybe he thought his thunder had been stolen.

James Dean limped in and put his Michelob on the table. "It's all bullshit. Boredom is what brought us to this, my friends. And little else."

"That isn't what the fans say. They think we died for them."

"Because of them, more likely." One of the oldest inhabitants of the Café Hendrix (if this timeless gathering place could be said to have an oldest inhabitant), Jesus Christ, offered them a twisted grin. "Dead people are easier to believe in than live people. As soon as you're dead you can't stop the myth. That's what I found. They *want* you to die, mate."

Several heads nodded. Several hands lifted drinks to pale lips.

"You always wind up doing what the public wants," said Keith Moon, "even if you don't do it deliberately. They expect violence, you give 'em violence. They expect a tragic death, well . . . Here we are."

"That's showbusiness," said Makhno. "The pressures get on top of you. You're carrying so many people's dreams. And all you wanted in the first place was a better life."

"They expect you to do the same for them."

Makhno was dispproving. "That isn't anarchism. You can scream at them for years not to follow leaders and they'll say 'Isn't he wonderful. He's right. Don't follow leaders.' Then they come round and ask you what they should do with their lives."

'They think anarchism means impulse or something. They don't realise it means self-determination, self-discipline and all of that. 'Neither master nor slave.' It serves us right for becoming heroes." Michael Bakunin was on his usual hobby horse.

"Don't say you never liked it," Makhno refilled his glass.

"Only sometimes. Anyway, how do you stop it once it starts?"

"Go into hiding and lead an unnatural life," said Jesus. "I wish to God I had. It wasn't any fun for me, I can tell you."

"You didn't have so many bloody journalists in your day," said Sid. "And you had a high opinion of yourself. Admit it."

"Well nobody was calling you the bloody Son of God." Jesus tried to justify himself, but they could tell he was embarrassed.

"They called me the Antichrist," said Makhno with some pride.

"Johnny called *himself* that," said Sid.

Jesus sighed. "It's all my damn fault."

"You should be such a big man, to take the whole blame." Brian Epstein sipped his orange juice. "Do you think we're in Hell?"

"It was all a bloody con." Marc Bolan adjusted his silk shirt. He was sulking again. Albert Camus, from behind his back, winked at the others.

"We just try to make death seem worth something. Like saying good comes out of pain. You can't blame people. And that's our job."

"Dying young?" said Sid. He was still pretty new to the Café Hendrix.

"Making death seem romantic and noble." Byron began to cough. "How they can think that of me I don't know. Death is rotten and we shouldn't have to put up with it."

In a far, dark corner of the café, Gene Vincent began to cry.

Nestor Makhno lifted his glass. "Ah well, here's to another boring evening in Eternity."

"Fuck this," said Sid. He went to the door and tried to open it.

"I'm afraid it's stuck, old chap," said Chatterton.

Sub-Mission

"Self-hatred makes excellent idealists. You tolerate yourself and you get to be able to tolerate almost anything. I suppose there's some good in that." Mitzi stood on Mo's shoulders and climbed over the gate of the Gothic studios. "What do you want me to say to him?"

"Just that I need to see him about me wages."

"All right." She scurried off into the darkness.

"I wish she'd stop bloody talking," said Mo. He turned up the collar of his trenchcoat and lit a cigarette. "This whole thing is ridiculous."

A few lights went on in the farthest building. Then they went off again. He heard a car start up.

The gates opened outwards, forcing him backwards.

A Mercedes droned past. In it were Frank Cornelius, Maggy and, trying to hide from him, Mitzi Beesley.

Mo shrugged and got through the gates before they closed again. He would do his own dirty work.

We're So Pretty

"You always think you must be in control," said Frank, as the car turned towards Hampstead Heath, "but it's usually other people's desperation that's operating for you. As soon as their desperation disappears, the scam stops working. You have to keep as many people as desperate as possible. Look at me. I know what bloody desperation *means*."

"But you should never let anyone know that," said Mitzi. "That's where you went wrong, Frank."

"You were too honest," said Maggy.

"I couldn't keep all the balls in the air. When you drop one, you drop the lot." Frank wiped his lips. "Still, there's always tomorrow. I'm not finished, yet. Lick a few arses and you're back on the strength again in no time."

"You should have been rude to him," said Maggy.

"My morale's weak. After what mum said."

"Mum's'll do it to you every time," said Mitzi. "Are you sure Mo will be all right in there?"

"He'll be better off than you or me," said Frank. "Little wanker. He deserves all he gets."

I'm A Lonely Boy

"Every business is a compromise. You get into the business, you get into a compromise." Mr Bug's representative stroked Mo's frightened head. The old assassin lay spreadeagled across a twenty-four track desk, his wrists and ankles secured by red leather bondage bracelets. Everything stank of warm rubber.

"Now what can I do for you, Mo?"

"Not this."

"You know you like it really. And you've got to do something for the money. Are you ticklish."

"Blimey," said Mo as the feather mop connected with his testicles. He added: "But that's not where I'm dusty."

"Are you a virgin, love?" The voice was greasy with sentiment.

"It depends where you mean."

"Enjoy life while you can, darling. This whole place is due to go up in a few hours. Insurance."

"Aren't the tapes all here? Auschwitz?"

"Every single copy, my beauty."

"They must be worth something."

"They're worth more if they're destroyed. Didn't you ever realise that? The harder things are to get, the more valuable they are. If they don't exist at all, they become infinitely valuable."

"Is that a fact. Tee hee."

"There, darling. You *are* ticklish."

"Tee hee."

"Did you want to see Mr Bug?"

"Mr Bug anything like you?"

"I'm only his representative. I'm an amateur compared to him."

"Then I'm not sure I want to see him. Can I go home now?"

"And where's home?"

"I suppose you've got a point." Mo lay back on the desk. He might as well get the most out of this.

Mr Bug's representative's breath hissed within his mask. "Now you're really going to make a record."

He reached for a large jar of vapour rub.

Punk Disc Is Terrible Says EMI Chief

The black flag was flying over the Nashville Rooms. There must have been another temporary seizure of power. Outside in the street groups of hardcore punks, lookalikes for most of the Sex Pistols in their heyday, scrawled A on every available surface. They weren't sure what it meant but they knew they had to do it.

Nestor Makhno rode up in his buggy. He had never been much of a horseman since his foot was wounded. His woolly hat was falling over his eyes. The rest of his anarchist Cossacks looked as worn-out as he did. Their ponies were old and hardly able to stand.

"I think we might be too late." Makhno guided the buggy round to the side entrance. From inside came the sound of chanting. "Is this what we fought Trotsky for?"

One of his lieutenants fired a ghostly pistol into the air. Its sound was faint, and drowned by the noise from within. "Comrades!"

"They can't hear us," said Makhno. "Is this what we all died for?"

"It's an attack on the symptoms, not the disease," cried a Cossack dutifully from the rear. "Comrades, the disease lies within yourself, and so does the cure. Be free!"

With a shrug, Makhno tugged at the reins of the buggy and led his men away. "Ah well. It was worth a try."

"Where to now?" asked one of the Cossacks.

"Camden Town. We'll try The Music Machine."

You Never Listen To A Word I Say

Something was collapsing.

Miss Brunner plucked at her hair and blouse.

"The more childish you are, the more you score. Throw enough tantrums and they'll pay anything to get rid of you."

Frank looked wildly about. "Are you sure this place is safe?"

"Safe enough."

He lay tucked up in bed surrounded by Snow White and the Seven Dwarves wallpaper, Paddington Bear decals, Oz and Rupert books.

"I can hear a sort of breaking up sound. Can't you?"

"It's in your mind," she said. "How much should we invest, do you think, in that new band?"

"We haven't got any money."

"Neither have they."

"Then it's all a bit in the air, isn't it?"

"Big money still exists, in big companies. It just takes a bit of winkling out."

"No," said Frank. "No more. I've been warned off. I'm frightened. The City is involved. They can do things to you."

"Mr Bug has scared the shit out of you, Frank."

"How did you know about the shit?"

I Made an American Squirm

The former Johnny Rotten tried to focus on Nestor Makhno as best he could. The little Ukrainian was almost wholly transparent now.

"Don't you think we can do it through music?"

"Persuade the public," said Makhno thinly. "We had an education train. But do they ever know that the power rests in them?"

"They never seem to want it."

"They don't want responsibility."

"And that's why managers exist."

"I'll be seeing you . . ." said Makhno, fading.

"That's more than I can say for you."

The former Johnny Rotten reached for his Kropotkin. Maybe it could still work. Maybe it was already working on some level.

Over The Top And Under The Bottom

Mo wriggled. "What do you want me to say?"

Mr Bug's representative stroked the fronds of his cat-o'-nine-tails over his own rubber.

"Anything you like, sweetheart. Isn't this the way to relax? No personal responsibilities, no anxieties? Just lie back and enjoy yourself."

"There must be other methods of relaxing."

"Well, dearie, you could always join a rock and roll band."

Mo began to scream.

Rolling In The Ruins

Bishop Beesley bit off half a Crunchie bar. Chocolate, like old blood, already stained his jowls. "Why is everyone suddenly going South?" he asked.

His daughter shook her head. "Maybe it's Winter."

"Winter?" Frank Cornelius looked unblinkingly at the sun which was just visible over the heap of dodgems. "Some winter of the mind, maybe."

"Let's try and steer clear of abstractions, dear boy." The bishop spoke with soft impatience. "I have a meeting with the Prime Minister in just over an hour. What are we going to do about this, if anything? I mean is it a serious threat to authority?"

"I thought we were avoiding abstractions," said Miss Brunner.

From within an abandoned Ghost Train car, Mo's weak voice said: "I told them nothing."

"You've nothing to tell them, you horrible little oik." The bishop sighed. "I think we're in a poor position, Mr Cornelius."

"Somebody turned the power off," said Mo vaguely.

The wind drummed against the hollow metal of the fairground debris.

City Lights

The Cossacks, by now hardly visible even to one another, had reached The Rainbow and were surrounding it. Their black flag had turned to a faint grey. They were getting despondent.

Determinedly, they rode their horses into the venue, able to pass through the audience as if they did not exist. On stage Queen were displaying the virtues of production over talent. Thousands of pounds worth of equipment was manipulated to produce the desired effect. It was a tribute to a wonderful technology.

Makhno cried into the empty megawatts: "Brothers and Sisters! Brothers and Sisters!"

A young man with longish hair and a "No Nukes" T-shirt turned, then raised his fist at the stage.

"Freedom!" he cried.

The volume began to rise.

Will The Sex Pistols Be Tomorrow's Beatles?

Back at the Café Hendrix Nestor Makhno took a long pull on his bottle of absinthe. He was shaking his head.

"Didn't you enjoy any of the gigs?" asked Sid.

"I didn't see anything I liked. At first I'd hoped—you know, the audiences . . ." Makhno fell back in his chair. "But there was nothing there for us to do."

"Don't despair," said Shelley, "there's a rumour the Sex Pistols are going to reform. After all, they're more popular now than they ever were."

CLAIM FOUR:

WE'RE GETTING THERE

Says Johnny Rotten: "Everyone is so fed up with the old way. We were constantly being dictated to by musical old farts out of university who've got rich parents. They look down on us and treat us like fools and expect us to pay POUNDS to see them while we entertain them and not the other way round. And people let it happen! But now they're not. Now there's a hell of a lot of new bands come up with exactly the opposite attitude. It's not condescending any more. It's plain honesty. If you don't like it —that's fine. You're not forced to like it through propaganda. People think we use propaganda. But we don't. We're not trying to be commercial. We're doing exactly what we want to do—what we've always done.

But it hasn't been easy. Sceptics and cynics simply didn't want to believe what was happening. Quite unjustly The Sex Pistols were written off as musical incompetents. They were savagely criticised for daring to criticise society and the rock musician's role in it. They have been crucified by the uncaring national press—ever ready to ferret out a circulation boosting shock/horror story—and branded an unpleasant, highly reprehensible Great Media Hype.
—*Virgin Records Publicity, 1977*

The city was black. Through black smoke shone a dim, orange sun. The canal was still, smeared with flotsam. From Harrow Road came the sound of a single donkey engine, like a dying heartbeat. Overhead, on train bridge and motorway, carriages and trucks were unmoving. It seemed everything had stopped to watch the figure in the dark trenchcoat and trilby who paused beside the canal and peered through the oily water as if through a glass.

A fly, ailing and lost, tried to buzz around his head. Slowly the traffic began to move again. From behind a pillar Mitzi Beesley emerged, hurrying on skinny legs towards him. She was back in Shirley Temple mode.

"You feeling any better, Mo?"

"You let me down, Mitzi."

"I didn't have any choice."

Mo did not resent her. "How's that wanker Frank?"

"Going through a bit of a crisis, I gather."

"He'd better look after his bloody kneecaps."

"That's the least of his worries."

Mo glanced away from the water and back towards the half-built housing estate. "It used to be all slums round here," he said nostalgically. "Now look at it."

"You've got over your own spot of bother, then? You've stopped looking for the money."

"I think so. But I'm still looking, anyway."

"For what?"

"A solution to the mystery."

"The mystery goes on forever. There's never a solution. There isn't even a cure."

"We'll see."

"Why are you here?"

"Ever heard of the Old Survivor?"

"Well, there's a myth . . ."

"I'm seeing him here."

"Lemmy of Motorhead?"

"He's doing me a favour."

"Isn't he an old hippy fart?"

"His hair may be long, but underneath he's a punk, through and through."

"Something's disturbed your brains, Mo. You need a rest."

"I need help."

Down the steps from the pedestrian bridge came a figure in black leather, festooned with silver badges, a bullet belt around his waist. His face, moulded by a thousand psychic adventures, was genial and distant, ageless. The Old Survivor laughed when he saw Mo and Mitzi standing together. "You look fucking miserable. What's the matter?"

"I didn't think you'd come." Mo made an antique sign.

"Neither did I. But I was passing. On my way home. So here I am."

"You're probably the only one left who can help me." Mo was embarrassed.

"I haven't got any drugs," said Lemmy.

"It's not that. But you'd know about the legend. Whether there's any truth in it or not."

Lemmy frowned. "I didn't realise you were a nutter."

"I'm not. Well, I don't think I am. I'm desperate. Have you ever . . . ?" Mo's voice dropped. Tactfully, Mitzi went to sit on the side of the canal and dip her boots in the liquid. "What do you know about the League of Musician-Assassins?"

Lemmy began to chuckle. "That hasn't come up in a long time."

"But you were supposed . . ."

"It was ages ago. A different era. A different universe, probably."

"Then there's some truth in it."

Lemmy became cautious. "I couldn't take a job like that. I've got enough to do as it is."

"There's money . . ."

"It was never a question of money." Lemmy drew a battered packet of Bensons from his top pocket and lit one. "We soldier on, you know."

"But what about the other one? The one who's supposed to be sleeping somewhere in Ladbroke Grove?"

"Your old mucker? What about him?"

"You're in touch with him."

"I see him occasionally, yeah."

"Couldn't you ask him?"

"He gave it all up. He said there wasn't any point in it any more. You know as well as I do."

"Does he really think that?"

"Well . . . He *has* been having second thoughts. He was round at his mum's the other day . . ."

"So he's not asleep."

"It depends what you mean." Lemmy was losing interest. He rubbed at his moustache and sighed.

"Could you put me in touch with him?"

"He's not working. I told you. None of us are. Bullshit-saturation does it to you in the end. Haven't you found that out yet?"

"Would his brother know . . . ?"

"His brother doesn't know a fucking thing about anything. His brother spends his whole bloody life trying to work out what's going on. Whenever he thinks he's found it, he tries to exploit it. He's been doing it for years. But him and his mates seem to have won." Lemmy looked up at the black buildings. "They sort of linked hands and formed a vacuum."

"It's important to me," said Mo. "I mean, I wouldn't be asking if I wasn't desperate . . ."

"You've only lost a battle, my son. We lost a war."

Stepping Stone

"You said he could never be revived." Frank was frightened. Even his grip on Mitzi's hair was weak.

Miss Brunner was at a loss. "It's what we all understood. Why should he want to come back?"

"He's been resurrected." Bishop Beesley spoke through mouthfuls of Maltesers. "Before."

"But never like this." Frank helped himself to a few of the bishop's chocolate-covered Valiums. "We'd blanked out every bit of possible music. He has to have it, to recover at all. To sustain himself for any length of time. It's the one thing we were sure of."

Miss Brunner pushed her red hair back from her forehead. "Something got through to him. There's no point now in wondering how. Couldn't have done it. He didn't know anything, did he, Mitzi?"

"Ow," said Mitzi, "I'm getting tired of playing both ends against the middle. It hurts."

"Did he?" Miss Brunner drew out her special razor.

"Not as far as I know."

"He's a demon," said Bishop Beesley. "And he can never be completely exorcised, I'm certain of that now. Just when we thought we had everything under control."

"Who got the music to him?" Frank let go of Mitzi "You?"

Mitzi shook her head and tried to get her father's attention.

"Lemmy?"

"Might have been."

"Nothing came through on the detectors," said Miss Brunner. "There's always someone on duty. You know that."

"We were squabbling amongst ourselves too much. It's that money problem."

216

"A very real one," said Bishop Beesley.

"I'll have the equipment checked." Miss Brunner shrugged. "Not that there's much point now. I could have sworn he was stuck in 1957 for the duration. Still, it's no use crying over spilt milk, is it."

"The problem we have now," said Bishop Beesley, "is where he's got to. We found most of his bases and destroyed them. Any clues?"

"You'd better ask your mum," suggested Mitzi.

Silence is Golden

The blimp was drifting towards the coast of Brazil. The flying boat had been abandoned in Florida. The blimp was losing gas.

"I thought you still had your old touch."

Mo was unshaven. "We've been in this bloody thing for days!"

The last of the Music-Assassins blew his nose. "I haven't been well. Anyway, all my equipment's old."

"It was never anything else, as far as I can see."

"I prefer stuff that doesn't work properly. I always did. How many bloody times do you think I've been resurrected? I'm coming apart all over the bloody place."

Mo was used to the self-pity by now, but the smell remained dreadful.

"Stand by," Jerry croaked.

The blimp bumped onto the beach. Blondes scattered, screaming. "Here we are. I'll stay while you get the tapes I told you I needed."

"I'm going to be embarrassed." Mo took off his coat and hat, revealing a T-shirt and shorts.

"Don't worry. They all talk English here." The last of the Musician-Assassins frowned. "Or is it German?"

"I don't mind about the Hendrix . . ."

"Well, just make it Hendrix, then. But hurry. You want help, squire, you'd better help me first. I never expected to pick up a bloody snob."

Steve opened the door and put his big toe onto the warm sand. "It's nice here, isn't it?"

Behind him, Jerry uttered a feeble sound. "Get—the—fucking —music . . ."

Purple Haze

Miss Brunner studied the computer breakdowns. "You were right about Hendrix," she said. "He always resorts to it in the final analysis. But there are other factors to consider. He seems to be finding boosters elsewhere, these days. Do you think that's what they're offering him?"

"Fresh energy?" Frank pushed the long sheets aside and looked blankly at the instruments.

She began to punch in a new programme. "I've got a feeling it is. What's bothering me, however, is where they're getting through. I could have sworn we'd blocked every channel. And, moreover, that we'd got them to believe that that was what they wanted."

Frank flicked an uninterested whip at the little body of Mitzi as she swung gently in her chains above the CRYPTIK VII computer. "You can never afford to relax for a second. We'd become lazy, Miss Brunner."

"What else did your mum say?"

"Nothing. He came to see her at her job, watched a bit of the film, had about fifteen bags of popcorn and ate all the hot dogs, then left in his Duesenberg."

"Which was found in?"

"Cromer."

"We didn't know about Cromer." She bit a nail.

"We're spread too thin," he said. "Those of us who are prepared to guard the borders. It's like the collapse of the Roman Empire. That's what I think, anyway. My own brother! When will he ever grow up?"

"He's got to be in Rio," she said. "Or, failing that, Maracaibo."

"What's in Venezuela?"

"Airships."

"And Brazil?"

"Failures. Exiles. The usual stuff he goes for. You'd better get someone to check all the record shops in Rio. After that, see what recording studios they have out there. It can't be much."

"Has Mo broken through to him yet, do you think?"

"Nothing available on that."

"And if so, who is it? Or how many of us?"

"I've got a feeling we're all going to be targets this time."

From overhead, Mitzi's muffled titters phased in with the click of the CRYPTIK.

Cruel Fate

"Mrs T. no more created the situation than Hitler started World War II. But once it had happened he had to pretend it was deliberate." Martin Bormann was closing up for the evening. "Of course I didn't know him very well."

"Hitler?"

"Nobody knew him very well. He tended to go with the tide. Do you know what I mean?"

"Not really," said Mo, pocketing the tapes.

"Well, we were all heavily into mysticism in those days. How's my old mate Colin Wilson, by the way?"

"I think he lives in the country."

Bormann nodded sympathetically. "It's what happens to all of us. I envy you young lads, with your cities and your ruins. We never liked cities much. In the Party, I mean. I sometimes think the whole thing was an attempt to restore the virtues of village life. It's still going on, I suppose, but on a modified level. I blame the atom bomb. It's had the absolutely opposite effect it was meant to have. No wonder all those hippies are fed up with it. I had hopes . . ." His smile was sad. "But there you go. I'm not complaining, really. Anything else you need?"

"I'm not sure."

"That's the spirit." Bormann patted Mo's shoulder. "And not a word to anyone about this, eh?"

"All right." Mo was puzzled.

"I wouldn't want people to think I was merely justifying my mistakes."

As Mo walked up the street, looking for a tram to the beach, Bormann began to pull down the shutters.

It was a fine evening in the Lost City of the Amazon.

CLAIM FIVE:

JUBILEE JAMBOREE: JAMBUK
LEGISLATION: JOKE JIVE

In October they signed with EMI. They released the hit single "Anarchy In the UK" and they were all set for an extensive, triumphant tour of the country. Then they were invited onto the Today show. Bill Grundy got what he asked for—and the Nationals had a bean feast. The band who had been playing week after week all over the country for more than a year were suddenly front page news, branded "filth" and made Public Enemies No. 1.

All but five dates of the tour were hysterically banned and the band returned to London on Christmas Eve with the dramatic news that EMI was about to rescind their contract. In January EMI asked them to leave the label. Glen Matlock decided to form his own band called the Rich Kids. Sid Vicious replaced him. Everyone cheered when in March, it looked like the Pistols had found shelter at A&M.
—*Virgin Records Publicity, 1977*

J erry was looking a shade or two less wasted. He removed the headphones and signalled to Mo to turn up the volume. Very bored, Mo did as he was told. He was beginning to regret the whole idea. In front of the Assassin was a collection of peculiar weaponry, most of it archaic: needle-guns, vibra-guns, light-pistols, a Rickenbacker 12-string.

The gondola of the little airship swayed and the hardware slid this way and that on the table. The Assassin seemed oblivious. He took another pull from his Pernod bottle.

"Have a look out of the window," he shouted. "See if we're near Los Angeles yet."

All Mo could see was silver mist.

Strange, garbled sounds began to issue from Jerry's lips.

Steve winced.

He had a feeling the Assassin was singing the blues.

His colour was better, at any rate. His skin was changing from a sort of LED-green to near-white.

Old And Tired But Still Playing His Banjo

"If ants ever had an Ant of the Year competition," said Miss Brunner disapprovingly, "Branson would be the winner. It's the secret of his success."

They were all uncomprehending. Only Maggy said "What?" and nobody listened to her.

Frank was biting his bullets to see if they were made of real silver. He began to load them into the clip. His hands were shaking terribly.

"Why don't we all go to Rio?" asked Bishop Beesley.

"Because you'd never squeeze into Concorde." Miss Brunner checked the action of her Remington. "Have you oiled your bazooka?"

"It doesn't need it." He unwrapped a Twix and sulked in his own corner of the bunker. "Did you try all the A&R men?"

"We can't get through to Virgin."

"They've probably been used in the ritual sacrifice, ho, ho, ho." Frank slid the clip into the Browning automatic he favoured.

"I said we weren't going to mention all that. It's poor publicity."

Mitzi grinned to herself. She now had a Banning cannon all her own. "When do we start to fight?"

"As soon as we run out of other choices," Miss Brunner told her.

"You divided," Mitzi was smug, "but they kept re-forming. It's just like real life now."

"We'll be changing all that." Bishop Beesley was no longer confident, however. He scraped ancient Cadbury's off his surplice and carefully carried the bits to his lips. "I wish I'd stayed in the drug business now. You don't get this sort of trouble from junkies."

"Do you mind?" Frank was offended.

. . . Down The Drain And What She Found There

"That's not bloody Los Angeles," said the Assassin petulantly. "That's Paris! Isn't it? Don't I know you?"

"It's got to be." Mo rubbed at his ear, which was hurting. "Unless there's another Eiffel Tower."

"Right. No harm done. I'll drop you off in Montmartre, if that's okay with you."

"What are you going to do?"

"Well, you've told me all I need to know. I'll be in touch." The Assassin combed his lank hair with his fingers. "Mo Coalman, isn't it?"

"You going to kill someone?"

"I'm going to kill everyone if I can get enough energy." The thought seemed to revive the Assassin. He cheered up.

He began to turn his steering wheel, cursing as the ship responded badly.

A little later he pushed open the door and started letting down a steel ladder.

"There you go. You should be able to get a taxi from here."

Mo didn't like the look of the weather. He put on his trenchcoat and hat.

"What did you say to Mr Bugs?"

"Biggs," corrected the Assassin. "Oh, I just needed a couple of addresses in South London and the name of his tailor."

Mo lowered himself onto the swaying ladder. "I hope you know what you're doing."

"I never know what I'm doing. There's no point in working any other way in my business."

It was raining over Montmartre now. It was cloudy. Mo became cautious. "Are you sure this is the right district?"

"The district's fine. You should be worrying whether I've got the time right. For all we know it could be 1990 down there."

"Stop trying to frighten me," said Mo.

The Assassin shrugged. "They're all pretty much the same to me, these days. You should have tried the fifties, mate." He began to shiver. "Hurry up. I want to shut the door."

Spirit of the Age

More data was coming through to the bunker Miss Brunner pursed her lips as she studied the printouts.

"He's getting stronger. Five Virgin shops and the EMI shops in Oxford Street and Notting Hill have been raided and a significant list of records stolen. Three of the places were completely destroyed. And there's been a break-in at Glitterbest. That probably isn't him. But three recording studios have had master-tapes taken. Seven managements have lost important demo-tapes."

"It might not mean anything," said Frank. He was fixing himself a cocktail, drawing it into the syringe.

They ignored him.

Frank laid the syringe on the table and put his head in his hands. "Oh, bloody hell. Who could have predicted this? I was *certain* it was all under control again. Bugger the Sex Pistols."

"I told you so," said Mitzi. Her eyes heated.

Miss Brunner pushed a pink phone towards her. "Get in touch with Malcolm. Tell him we've got to stick together. He'll see sense. I'll try Branson again."

Mitzi picked up the receiver. "If you think it's worth it."

They were all beginning to get on one another's nerves.

I Wanna Be Your Dog

Mo walked into the Princess Alexandra in Portobello Road. It had taken him ages to get from Paris and he had a feeling he was no further forward. All that he seemed to have done was start a lot a trouble he couldn't begin to understand.

The pub was full of black leather backs. He reached the bar and ordered a pint of bitter. The barman, for no good reason, was reluctant to serve him.

Various overtired musicians clocked him, but nobody really recognised him or he them. Lemmy was nowhere to be seen.

There was an atmosphere in the place, as if everybody was hanging about waiting for World War Three.

The talk was casual, yet Mo sensed that a great deal was not being said. Was the whole of London keeping something back from him? Was the Revolution imminent? If so, what Revolution was it? Whose Revolution? Did he really feel up to a Revolution?

He finished his pint. He was down to his last fifteen pence.

As he was leaving he thought he heard someone whispering behind him.

"Who killed Sid, then?"

"What?" He turned.

All the backs were towards him again.

Sleazo Of The Month

"They think they're heavily into manipulation, but really we just let them play at it.'' Mr Bug's representative sat comfortably in the darkness of the limousine. "Nobody who really believes they're manipulating things is safe. Sooner or later people lose patience. And people are very patient indeed. Most of you don't actually want to make anyone else do anything."

"Live and let live," said Mitzi. "It's time I got back to the bunker."

"I'm interested in human beings," said Mr Bug's representative, squeaking a little as he moved in his rubber. "I've studied them for years."

"Do you understand them?"

"Not really, but I've learned a lot about what triggers to pull. And I know enough, too, not to think that I can keep too many balls in the air."

"Have you seen Jerry? That's who I was looking for, really."

"We've all seen too much of Jerry, haven't we?"

"Has he left your club?"

"You could try it. But hardly any of us go there any more."

"Aliens?"

"Call us what you like. I prefer to think of myself as a student person. But I'm not sure I'm going to make the finals."

Mr Bug's represenatative uttered a cheerful wheeze and opened the door so that Mitzi could step out.

"It's quite a nice morning, isn't it?" he said. "It was Clapham Common you wanted?"

"It'll do," said Mitzi.

"The malady lingers on." Mr Bug's representative flicked his robot driver with his whip. "We'll try Hampstead Heath again now."

The driver's voice was feminine. "What are we looking for, sir?"

Mr Bug's representative shrugged. "Whatever they're looking for."

"Do you think we'll find it, sir?"

"I'm not sure it matters. But it's something to pass the time. And we might meet some interesting people."

"Are there any real people left in London, sir?"

"I take your point. The city seems to be filling up with nothing but the ghosts of old anarchists. Not to mention Chartists and the like. Have you seen any of the Chartists?"

"Not recently, sir."

"There's bound to be a few on Hampstead Heath. What London really lacks at present is a genuine Mob."

It Was A Gas

"Any news?"

Frank Cornelius looked anxiously at the CRYPTIK. It didn't seem a patch on some of Miss Brunner's other machines, but she put a great deal of faith in it.

"A few more record companies have been broken into. Tapes and records stolen. Some accounts. Majestic Studios have been blown up. Rockfield have had a fire. Island's sunk."

"And the casualties?" Bishop Beesley mopped his brow with an old Flake wrapper.

"They don't look significant. Everybody seems to be evacuating."

"Mr Bug?"

"Not sure. No data."

"Why are we sticking it out, then?" Frank gave a swift, resentful blink. "Why should we be the only ones?"

"Because we know best, don't we?" Miss Brunner reached absently towards where Maggy had been sitting. Now there was just a little pile of clothes. Maggy had been absorbed some hours ago. "Someone's going to have to go out for some food. I think it's you, Frank."

"You're setting me up. If my brother finds me, you know what he'll do. He's got a nasty, vengeful nature. He's never forgiven me for Tony Blackburn, let alone anything else."

"He's too busy at present." She waved the printouts. "Anyway, he hardly ever bothers you unless you've bothered him."

"How do I know if I've bothered him or not?"

Miss Brunner became impatient. "Go and get us a meal."

"And some chocolate fudge, if possible," said Bishop Beesley.

Frank put his Browning in the pocket of his mack. He sidled reluctantly towards the door.

"Hurry," hissed Miss Brunner.

"Any special orders?"

"Anything tasty will suit me." She returned her attention to the CRYPTIK. "At this rate we'll be eating each other."

This made her feel sick.

Through The Mirror

There was a bouncer on the door of the New Oldies Club as Mo
tried to go through.

"No way, my son," said the bouncer.

Mo blinked. "You know me."

"Never seen you before."

"What's going on? Who's playing tonight."

"Deep Fix."

"Is the Captain there?"

"Not for me to say. Not for you to ask."

"But I'm with the band."

"What band?"

"What band do you want me to be with?"

"Off!" said the bouncer. "Go on."

"Ask the Captain."

"You, mate, are persona non bloody grata. Get it?"

"Is the Captain in there?"

"You're a persistent little sod, ain't ya." The bouncer hit him.

"What did you do that for?"

"Security."

Mo nursed his lip. "Oh. You shouldn't be afraid of me."

"It's not you, chum. It's the people you're hanging around
with."

As Mo reached the street again, and began to walk in the general
direction of Soho, he looked up. Over the rooftops was the outline
of a small, sagging airship. It seemed to be drifting aimlessly on the
wind.

To the North, quite close to the Post Office Tower, a fire was
blazing.

United Artists, thought Mo absently.

What We Found There

Mr Bug's representative said: "Things look as if they're hotting
up."

They were crossing over Abbey Road. Police were making a
traffic detour around the ruins.

"All the old targets." Mr Bug's representative lit a fresh cigarette and put it to his tube. "Still, what new ones are there?"

The driver pressed the horn.

EMI Unlimited Edition

Mo leaned on the gates of Buckingham Palace and dragged the book from his inside pocket.

The book was called *The Nature of the Catastrophe*. He opened it up. All the pages were blank. He was getting used to this sort of thing.

"Oh, there you are!" Mitzi came running over from St James's Park. "We thought we'd lost you."

"I don't trust you, Mitzi. You're with them again."

"Why not join us?"

"What for?"

"There's safety in numbers."

"So you say."

"Anyway," said Mitzi, "you shouldn't be hanging about here, should you? Everyone's getting very security conscious. They might arrest you. Or shoot you. SAS and that."

"Everything else has been arrested, by the look of it."

"I'm worried about you, Mo."

"Don't be."

"We can help you."

"That didn't work the last time."

Army trucks were coming down the Mall. Garbled voices called through loudspeakers mounted on the tops of the trucks.

Mo decided to follow Mitzi round the corner into Buckingham Palace Road. She took his hand. "Coming along then?"

"No," he said. "I think I'll catch a train from Victoria."

CLAIM SIX:

LET'S GO WITH LABOUR

STEVE JONES: Twenty. Born in London. Lives in a one-room cold-water-only studio in Soho where the band rehearse. Ex-approved school. He was the lead singer with the Sex Pistols before he took up the guitar.

He has the reputation of being a man of a few words. But his sound intuition and low boredom threshold makes him great fun to be with. He's always looking for action. Of the four he probably had the most difficult childhood. His real father was a boxer whom he never knew. He never got on with his step-father and since the family lived in one room only, this led to a very fraught home environment. The first record he remembers being impressed by was Jimi Hendrix's "Purple Haze". He always wanted to play electric guitar.

—*Virgin Publicity, 1977*

"Delusions of grandeur will get you a very long way in this world." Martin Bormann leafed through his cut-price deletions. "You just missed him, I'm afraid."

Una Persson handed him the album she'd selected. "I'll have this, then. Do you know the times of the planes to New York?"

Bormann looked at his watch. "There's one in an hour. You'd better hurry. It could be the last."

God Save The Short And Stupid

"Ain't she fuckin' radiant, though?" Mrs C. studied the blue and white picture on her jubilee mug before putting it to her lips. "Thassa nice cuppa tea, Frank. Wotcher want?"

"Jerry." Frank was furtive. "Mum, I haven't got much more margin. Have you seen him?"

"Yeah."

"When?"

"Yesterday."

"Where?"

"At work. 'E watched ther picture four times."

"Why?"

"I fink 'e wanted a rest. 'E was asleep through most of 'em."

"When he left, did he say where he was going?"

"'E said 'e 'ad a few jobs ter do. Somefink abart pushin' a boat aht?"

Frank remained puzzled. "That's all?"

"I fink so." She puckered her brows. "You know what 'e's like. Yer carn't fuckin' understand 'alf o' wot 'e says."

"Was he with anybody?"

"I dunno. Maybe wiv that bloke in a kilt. Like in ther film."

Frank dropped his cup into the saucer. "God almighty."

"I didn't catch 'is name," said Mrs Cornelius.

Sod The Sex Pistols

From where he stood on the Embankment, near the cannon, Mo could see the half-inflated airship tied to one of the spikes of Tower Bridge. Either the Assassin was stranded, or he was becoming more catholic in his targets.

As he climbed up the steps to the bridge, he thought he saw a flash of tartan darting down the other side. He hesitated, not sure which lead to follow. It had to be "Flash" Gordon.

"Oh, bugger!"

The last of the Musician Assassins, clambered unsteadily down his steel ladder, a Smith and Wesson Magnum held by its trigger guard in his teeth.

"You look a lot better," said Mo.

"Feeling it, squire." Jerry dusted off his black car coat and smoothed his hair. "I've been eating better and getting more exercise. What's the time? My watch has stopped."

Mo didn't know.

"It doesn't matter, really. We'll be all right. Come on." The Assassin took Mo's arm.

"Where are we going?"

"I had a nasty moment last night," said the Assassin obliviously. "Somebody must have tried to slip some disco tapes into my feeder. Nearly blew my circuits. I think they're trying to get rid of me." He strode rapidly in the direction of Butler's Wharf on the South side of the bridge.

"Where are we going?"

"1977."

"What?"

"Nineteen bloody seventy seven, Mo. We've got a bloody gig to do. And this time you're going to do it properly."

Abolishing The Future

Miss Brunner was white with rage. "What on earth possessed you, Frank?"

A dozen dogs growled and grumbled as Frank tried to untangle their leads. "I had nowhere else to bring them. And I need them."

Bishop Beesley crouched in his corner munching handfuls of Poppets. "This is a very small bunker, Mr Cornelius."

"I've worked out what my brother's up to. He's made a tunnel into 1977."

"Oh, no." Miss Brunner began to punch spastically at her terminal. "That was why he was doing all that stuff with record companies. To get the energy he needed."

Frank nodded. The dogs began to pant. "We're going to have to follow him. He's got that little wanker Collier with him and maybe the rest of them, I'm not sure."

Bishop Beesley clambered to his feet. "What are his plans?"

"To create an alternative, obviously. If he succeeds it means curtains for everything we've worked for."

Miss Brunner was grim. "We managed to abort it last time. We can do it again."

Frank stroked the head of the nearest Dobermann. "This could be the end of authority as we know it."

"Aren't you being a trifle apocalyptic, Mr Cornelius?" Bishop Beesley reached a plump hand for the Walnut Whips on the steel table. "I mean, what can he do with a couple of guitars and a drum kit?"

"You don't know him." Frank unbuttoned his collar. "He's reverting to type, just when it seemed he was getting more respectable at last."

"He's fooled us before," said Miss Brunner. "And we should have known better." Her hands were urgent now, as she fed in her programme. "1977 could have been a turning point."

The CRYPTIK began to give her a printout. She grew whiter than ever. "Oh, Jesus. It's worse than we thought."

"What?" Frank's arm was yanked by a sudden movement of his dogs.

"I think he's trying to abolish the Future altogether. He's going for some kind of permanent Present."

"He can't do it." Bishop Beesley licked his fingers. "Can he?"

"With help," said Miss Brunner, "he could."

"How can a few illiterate and talentless rock and rollers be of any use?"

"It's what they represent," she said. "There's no getting away from it, gentlemen. He's playing for the highest stakes."

"Can we stop him?" asked the Bishop.

"We're under strength. Half our usual allies are in stasis."

"What will wake them up?"

"The Last Trump," said Frank. He was panting now, in unison with his dogs.

Living In The Past

"Are you sure you know what you're doing?" said Mo, not for the first time.

Jerry was hurrying through the corridors of the vast warehouse. It had become very cold.

"I told you. I never know what I'm doing. I have to play it by ear. But I've got a shifter tunnel and I've got a fix and I'm bloody sure we can make it. After that it's up to all of us."

"To do what?"

"The Jubilee gig, of course."

"But we've done it."

"You've *tried* it, you mean. Just think of that as a rehearsal."

"I wish I'd never got in touch with you."

"Well, you did." The Assassin was humming to himself. It seemed to be some sort of Walt Disney song.

Mo tried to pull back. "I'm fed up with it all. I just want . . ."

"Satisfaction squire." Cornelius glowed. "And I'm going to give you your chance."

"All I wanted was the booze and the birds," said Mo weakly. "I was enjoying myself. We all were."

"And so you shall again, my son." The Musician-Assassin turned a crazed eye on his old comrade. "Better than ever."

The walls of the warehouse began to quiver. A silver mist

engulfed them. From somewhere in the distance came the muffled sound of bells.

"We're through!" The Assassin cackled.

He burst open a rotting door and they stood on the slime of a disused wharf. Beside the wharf was a large white schooner with a black flag waving on its topmast. The schooner seemed to be deserted. On the poop deck a drum kit had been set up and Mo noticed PA all over the boat.

The Assassin paused, checking his wrist. "My watch's working again. That's good. We made it. The others should be along in a minute."

"That equipment looks expensive."

"It's the best there is," said the Assassin confidently. "Megawatt upon megawatt, my son. Enough sound to shake the foundations of society to bits! Ho, ho, ho!"

"Will Malcolm be here with the money?" asked Mo.

"You won't need money if this works," said the Assassin.

"I haven't had any wages in months." Mo set a wary foot on the gangplank.

"There are bigger things at stake," said the last of the Musician-Assassins. "More important things."

"That's what they always seem to wind up saying."

The white schooner rocked in the water. The Assassin began to hurry about the decks, checking the sound system, following cables, adjusting mikes.

"Power," he said. "Power."

"Wages," said Mo. "Wages."

But he was already becoming infected. He could feel it in his veins.

Glory Daze

"Hurry up, Bishop." Miss Brunner was being dragged along by four of Frank's dogs. She had her Remington under her arm.

Frank was in the lead with six more dogs. The bishop, with two, rolled in the rear. It was dawn and Goldhawk Road was deserted apart from some red, white and blue bunting.

"If you ask me," said Mitzi catching up with her dad, "he's using all this for his own mad ends. All we wanted was a bit of publicity. Are you sure this is 1977?"

"Miss Brunner is never wrong about things like that. She's an expert on the Past. That's why I trust her." Bishop Beesley set his mitre straight on his head with an expert prod of his crook. "She stands for all the decent values."

He wheezed a little. "You haven't got a Tootsie Roll on you, or anything I suppose?"

They had reached Shepherds Bush. On the green people were beginning to set up marquees and stalls. Pictures of QEII were everywhere.

Miss Brunner paused, hauling at the leads. "This could have achieved what the Festival of Britain was meant to achieve. A restoration of confidence."

"In what?" asked Mitzi innocently.

"Don't be cynical, dear."

They took the road to Hammersmith.

"It's just your interpretation I'm beginning to worry about," said Mitzi.

The Management Fantasy

Everyone was on board. Nobody seemed absolutely certain why they were here. The assassin was checking his rocket launchers and grenade-throwers, which lined the rails of the main deck.

"Hello, Sid," said Lemmy. "You're not looking well."

Sid plucked at his bass. John cast a suspicious eye about the schooner. "Ever get the feeling you're being trapped?"

"Used," said Maggy with relish, "in a game of which we have no understanding."

Automatically Mo was tuning up. "Has anybody seen Harrison?" He thought he'd spotted a flutter of moleskin on the yardarm.

The schooner was full of musicians now, most of them dead.

"Raise the anchor!" cried the Assassin.

The band faltered for a moment, astonished at its own magnificent volume. The sound swelled and swelled, drowning the noise of the rocket launchers as Jerry took out first the bridge and then the White Tower. Stones crumbled. The whole embankment was coming down. Hundreds of sightseers were falling into the water, clutching at their ears.

Overhead, police helicopters developed metal fatigue and dropped like wounded bees.

On board the schooner everyone was cheering up no end.

Mrs Cornelius lifted her frock and began a knees up. "This is a bit o' fun, innit?"

Soon everyone was pogoing.

The Assassin ran from launcher to launcher, from thrower to thrower, whispering and giggling to himself. On both sides of the river buildings were exploding and burning.

"No future! No future!" sang Jimi.

London had never seemed brighter.

The schooner gathered speed. Down went Blackfriars Bridge. Down went Fleet Street. Down went the Law Courts. Down went the Savoy Hotel.

It wasn't World War Three, but it was better than nothing.

Number One In The Capital Hit Parade

Miss Brunner, Bishop Beesley and Frank Cornelius had managed to get through the crowds and reach Charing Cross. With the dogs gnashing and leaping, they stood in the middle of Hungerford Bridge, watching the devastation.

The schooner had dropped anchor in the middle of the river and the sound-waves were successfully driving back the variable-geometry Tornados as they attacked in close formation, trying to loose Skyflashes and Sidewinders into the sonic barrier.

"You have to fight fire with fire," said Miss Brunner. "Come on. We still have a chance of making it to the Festival Hall."

They hurried on.

Mitzi let them go. She clambered over the railing of the bridge and dropped with a soft splash into the river. Then she struck out for the ship.

Behind her, the dogs had begun to howl.

The water had caught fire by the time she reached the side and was hauled aboard by the Assassin himself. He was glowing with health now. "What's Miss B up to?"

"Festival Hall," Mitzi wiped a greasy cheek. "They're going to try to broadcast a counter-offensive. Abba. Mike Oldfield. Rick Wakeman. Leonard Cohen. You name it."

The Assassin became alarmed for a moment. "I'll have to boost the power."

"No future! No future! No future!"

From over on the South Bank the first sounds were getting through.

"They're fighting dirty." Jerry was shocked. "That's the Eurovision Song Contest as I live and breathe. Look to your powder, Mitzi."

He gave the National Theatre a broadside.

Concrete blew apart. But the counter-offensive went on.

"We're never going to make it to the Houses of Parliament at this rate," said the Assassin. "Keep playing."

It had grown dark. The fires burned everywhere. The volume rose and rose.

The schooner began to rock. Planes and helicopters wheeled overhead, hoping for a loophole in the defences.

"God Save The Queen!" sang The Sex Pistols.

"God Save The Queen!" sang the choir of what was left of St Paul's Cathedral.

Mrs Cornelius leaned to shout into Mitzi's ear. "This is great, innit? Just like ther fuckin' blitz."

Another broadside took out the National Film Theatre. Celluloid crackled smartly.

The schooner creaked and swayed.

The Assassin had begun to look worried. They were being hit from all sides by Radio 2.

"Suzanne takes you to the kerbside
  and she helps you cross the street,
Sits beside you in the restaurant,
  tells you what there is to eat
And she combs your hair and cleans your trousers
  leads you down to smell the flowers
And fills out all your forms for you
And reads to you for hours . . .
Yes, she makes a perfect buddy for the blind . . ." sang Jerry.

Slowly, through the flames and the smoke, the schooner was making it under the bridge and heading for Vauxhall. There was still a chance.

CLAIM SEVEN:

MAGGIE PROMISES VICTORIAN FUTURE

Malcolm first thought about the film when the group were banned. The idea was if they couldn't be seen playing, that they could be seen in a film. That was probably just after they got thrown off A&M in Spring 77.

Obviously with "God Save The Queen" and the kind of global attraction that the whole episode had, he began to think more seriously about it and he approached Russ Meyer in early Summer 77 and he went out to Hollywood and talked to him . . .

I think (Meyer) intended it to be a Russ Meyer film using The Sex Pistols, whereas Malcolm obviously intended it to be a Sex Pistols film using Russ Meyer. So there was a basic conflict from the start. He thought it would be the film that would crown his career . . . Meyer thought Malcolm was a mad Communist anti-American lunatic and he was demanding more money because the thing looked risky. Meyer was very, very angry when it fell through. Kept referring to Malcolm as Hitler. "Sue Hitler's ass" and all this stuff.

—*Julien Temple, interview with John May, NME, October 1979*

"We've lost a battle, but we haven't lost the War." Petulantly, Miss Brunner switched off the equipment. Her face was smeared with soot. The dogs lay dead around her, bleeding from the ears.

Through a pair of battered binoculars Frank surveyed the ruins. "They got the palace before they sank."

"Did they all make it into the airship?"

"I think so."

Bishop Beesley finished the last of his toasted marshmallows. "They're a lot further forward," he said. "Aren't they."

Miss Brunner glared at him.

Smoke from the gutted Houses of Parliament drifted towards them.

"It's a state of emergency all right," said Frank.

"Somebody's got to teach the Sex Pistols a lesson." Miss

Brunner's lips were prim as, with a fastidious toe, she pushed aside a wolfhound.

"They have a lot of power now," said Bishop Beesley.

She dismissed this. "The secret there, bishop, is that childishly they don't want it. They'll give it up. They don't want it—but we do. Half the time all we have to do is wait."

"I suppose so. They're not fond of responsibility, these young hooligans." Bishop Beesley took off his dirty surplice. "It makes you sick."

Miss Brunner looked with horror at his paisley boxer shorts.

Hello, Julie

"You weren't breaking any icons," said Nestor Makhno. "You were just drawing bits of graffiti over them. And helping the establishment make profits. You went about as far as Gilbert and Sullivan."

It was a somewhat sour evening at The Café Hendrix.

"You have to go solo," said Marc Bolan. "It's the only way."

"Don't give me any of your Stirnerist rationalisations." The old anarchist poured himself another large shot of absinthe. "*The Ego and his Own*, eh?"

"*My* anarchists were always romantic leaders," said Jules Verne, who had dropped over from The Mechaniste in the hope of finding his friend Meinhoff.

"Which is why they were never proper anarchists." Makhno had had this argument before. He turned his back on the Frenchman. "It's all substitutes for religion, when you come down to it. I give up."

"If you want my opinion, they should never have put a woman in charge." Saint Paul, as usual, was lost in his own little world.

Big Money

Having failed to find what he needed at The Jolly Englishman public house, Mo put his disguise back on and went to Kings Cross, heading for The Hotel Dramamine.

He was sure, now that a few things had been settled along the embankment, Jerry would want to explain.

The lady at the door recognised him. "Go up to Room 12, dear," she said. "There'll be someone there in a minute."

He didn't tell her what he was really after.

He got to the first landing and went directly to the cage room. This was where Mr Bug had kept his special clients. It was empty apart from a miserable Record Company executive, who whined at him for a moment or two before he left. No information.

Other doors were locked. The ones which yielded showed him nothing he didn't already know. It was obvious, however, that Mr Bug wasn't here.

Room 12 had been prepared for him. He suspected a trap. On the other hand the lady on the waterbed looked as if she could take his mind off his problems. He decided to risk it.

"You don't know where Mr Bug is, I suppose," he said, as he stripped.

She opened her oriental lips.

"Love me," she said, "you're so wonderful."

He flung himself onto the heaving rubber.

The door opened. One of Mr Bug's representatives stood there. He had a wounded Alsatian with him. From beyond the window a car began to hoot.

Mo scrambled out of the bed. As he made for the window he was certain he heard the dog speak.

It was better than nothing. He plunged from the window and into Jerry's car. "Let's rock."

I Need Your Tender Touch

"Monarchy's only a symbol," said Mr Bug's representative to Mitzi as the car moved slowly through what remained of St James's Park, "but then so are the Sex Pistols."

Near the pond, groups of homeless civil servants were jollying each other along as they erected temporary shelters, prefabs and tents.

"I don't think anyone meant it to go this far." Mitzi frowned. "Could you hurry it up a bit? I've got a train to catch."

"Jerry did. A bit of chaos allows him more freedom of movement."

"Malcolm has the same idea. Keep 'em fazed."

Mr Bug's representative placed a rubber hand on her little knee. "Instant gratification," he said. "Where are we going?"

"To rock."

Mr Bug's representative tapped the chauffeur with his whip. "Did you hear that?"

"Yes, sir."

The car bumped up the path through the park towards Piccadilly. All the roads around the Palace were ruined.

"It's peaceful now, isn't it?" Mitzi wound down the window. "I love the smell of smoke, don't you?"

"I can't smell a thing in this exoskeleton. My usual senses are cut off, you see."

"I suppose that's the point of it."

"It does allow one a certain kind of objectivity."

"Like being a child?"

"Well, no. Like being an ant, really."

Anarchy Dropped Out Of The Top Twenty

Mo and Jerry panted on the platform, watching the train as it pulled away.

"I saw him." Jerry scratched. "Jimi."

"Or someone like him." Mo rubbed his nose. "Should we find out where the train's going?"

"He could get off anywhere."

"True."

"You spent too long in that bloody hotel," said Jerry.

"You could have arrived a couple of minutes earlier." Mo was bitter.

"This is pointless. Let's give it up."

"I want my wages."

"He hasn't got them, though has he? Or if he has, we're not going to get them now. What are you really after, Mo?"

"I need some answers, I told you."

"Don't we all? But you never got them, did you?"

Slow Train Through The Occident

Miss Brunner settled herself in the first class compartment. "We're going to have to deal with them."

"I tried to get into the next carriage," said Frank, "but it seems to have been locked. I think there's some trouble going on."

"It's locked at the other end as well." Bishop Beesley wiped the sweet sweat from his cheeks. "I think it could be part of the emergency regulations."

He relished the phrase. It was like coming home.

The regular rhythm of the train was soothing them all.

"What are you going to offer him?" Frank asked her. "I mean, what have we actually got?"

"Experience," she said. "Ambition. A sense of right and wrong. Everything you need to put things into proper order. Sooner or later the balloon will burst."

"It seems to have burst already."

"A pinprick. It'll be patched in no time."

"I admire your resilience, Miss Brunner." Bishop Beesley was feeling in his pockets for the remains of his chocolate digestives. "I suppose you didn't notice if there was a buffet?"

"Not in this carriage," Frank told him.

"They always come back to us." Miss Brunner looked out at the windows. "Cows," she said.

Change Your Masques

The last of the Musician-Assassins put his vibra-gun into its holster. "They'll be wanting a martyr," he told Mo. "A proper martyr to the Seventies."

"Well it isn't going to be poor old me. All I'm after is my wages and maybe a chance to do the odd gig. I should never have got mixed up with you, Mr C."

"You summoned me, remember?"

Mo shrugged. He sat hunched over his Bacon Burger in the Peckham Wimpy, watching the dirty rain on the windows. "I've got a feeling I'm being used. Has it after all come down to Peckham?"

"You keep saying that. I'm only doing what you said you wanted me to do."

"There's always a snag about making deals. Particularly with old hippy demons."

"Do you mind? I was around long before that."

"Maybe that's your trouble. Are you trying to recapture your lost youth?"

Jerry dipped into his Tastee-Freeze. His whole attitude was self-pitying. "Maybe. But probably I'm trying to recapture those few moments when I felt grown-up. Know what I mean? In charge of myself."

"How did you lose it?"

"Equating action with inspiration, maybe. Or 'energy', whatever that is."

"You've done quite a lot. You're just feeling tired, probably." Mo wondered how he came to be comforting his old boss.

The Assassin gave a deep sigh. "Bands begin breaking up when they're faced with the implications of what they've started. When it threatens to turn into art, or something like it. Look at the problems the Dadaists had. Successful revolutions bring their own problems."

Mo's attention was wavering. "You really can be a boring old fart sometimes, can't you? Hippy or not."

Jerry seemed chastened. "It comes with analysing too much. But what else can I do these days? Imposition hasn't worked very well, has it? Analysis is all you're left with. Am I right or am I wrong?"

"Suit yourself." Mo swivelled his red plastic seat round. "You should do what you feel like doing."

The Assassin toyed with his Tastee-Freeze.

"Look where that's got me." He cast a miserable eye around him. "The bloody Peckham Wimpy."

Every Room Was A Dead End

"Isn't the train ever going to stop?" Miss Brunner couldn't recognise the countryside. "Whose idea was this, anyway?"

"Yours," said Frank. "Or mine. I forget." He was beginning to fugue a bit. "Tra la la. Hi diddle de de. Ta ra a boom de ay."

Bishop Beesley was of no use at all. He desperately needed a fix. His fat was turning a funny colour and the flesh was loosening even as she watched.

"We're out of control," she said, "and I don't like it."

"I thought you said we knew what we were doing?" Frank wiped drool from his lips. "Hic."

"We do. But I didn't expect the corridors to be blocked. That little bastard has outmanoeuvred us."

"But only for the moment, eh?" said Frank. He was being dutiful. "What do you want me to say?"

"You're bloody useless!"

He winced.

"I have to do everything myself."

Bishop Beesley mewled. "A Milky Way would be all right."

It became dark. The train had entered a tunnel. It stopped.

Miss Brunner thought she saw a white face press itself against the window for a second, but she was losing faith in her own judgment.

This realisation made her very angry.

She kicked Frank in the shin.

Frank began to giggle.

Holidays In The Sun

Mrs Cornelius had her sleeves rolled up. She was doling out soup from the specially erected canteen in Trafalgar Square.

"Hello, mum." Jerry held his tin cup to be filled.

"Oxtail," she said, "or Mulligatawny?"

"Oxtail, please."

"You've done it this time," she said. "There's a lot of people pissed off wiv you. I told 'em it was just your way of celebratin'. But look wot you've caused. Pore ole Nelson's got 'alf 'is bleedin' body missin'. It's gonna take ages ter clear up ther mess."

"Sorry, mum."

"No use bein' sorry now. You'd better keep yer 'ead down for a while. I thought you'd bloody learned yer lesson."

"Lesson?"

"You 'eard me."

"Can I have the key to the flat?"

"Oh, so ya fuckin' wanna come 'ome ter mum now, do yer? Littel sod." She softened. "'Ere y'are. Now move on. There's a lot more people waitin'."

She watched him shuffle off, sipping at his soup. "They just fuckin' use yer when they need yer. An' then they're fuckin' off again."

But the crowd had recognised him. They were beginning to converge.

With a yelp of terror, Jerry scuttled towards the National Gallery.

Mrs Cornelius watched impassively. "E'll be okay," she said to herself. "Unless they actually tear 'im ter pieces."

She ladled Mulligatawny into the next outstretched cup.

When she looked again, the crowd was rushing through the doors of the Gallery.

Ten minutes later they were all coming out again, like spectators whose team had lost.

She grinned to herself. "Shifty littel bastard," she said. "At least 'e knows when ter scarper."

I Shot The Sheriff

The train had begun to move again, but by now Bishop Beesley was catatonic and Frank Cornelius was completely ga-ga, dribbling and whistling to himself. Miss Brunner went into the corridor and tugged at the door. It wouldn't open. All the windows were jammed.

She ran along the corridor, looking for help. All the other compartments were filled with old rubber suits, as if Mr Bug's representatives had dematerialised.

"What's going on?" she cried. "What's going on?"

The train groaned and clattered in unison with her voice.

She clawed at the connecting door. It wouldn't budge.

"Somebody's going to pay for it." She was livid. "I'm not used to treatment of this kind. Who's in charge? Who's in charge?"

The train grunted.

"Who's in charge?" Now her voice became pathetic. A tear appeared in her right eye. She adjusted her blouse. She whimpered.

The train was moving faster. It swayed wildly from side to side.

Miss Brunner began to scream.

CLAIM EIGHT:

A PROPERLY OWNED DEMOCRACY

JULIAN TEMPLE (DIRECTOR): Went to Cambridge University "For the same reasons as one applies for an American Express Card". Attended National Film School "so that I didn't have to wait 20 years to be able to do something". The Great Rock 'N' Roll Swindle was his graduation film. Since then he has made Punk Can Take It, featuring the UK Subs and narrated by John Snagge, who once declared the end of World War II on BBC Radio and ghosted for Churchill's speeches while it was still on.
—*Virgin Publicity, 1980*

The last of the Musician-Assassins was crawling along rooftops overlooking Portobello Road.

He was looking for his airship. He was certain he'd left it in the vicinity of Vernon's Yard.

"Bugger," he muttered. "Oh, bugger."

He was not feeling at one with himself.

Every so often a demonic grin, a memory, crossed his poor, ravaged face.

"Why am I always getting mixed up with bloody bands? What's happened to my complicated vocabulary of ideas? Why do I prefer rock and roll?"

It was familiar stuff to him.

Flies clustered around a faded chimney stack, rising as he groped.

"Monica?" His mind cast about for any anchor. "Mum? Colonel? David M?"

His cuban heels scraped slate. Something fell away from him and smashed in the street. The sun was rising.

He drew a scratched single from the pocket of his black car coat and put it close to his eyes, studying it as if it were a map.

He was crying.

The flies hissed rhythmically. A stuck needle. He held on to the chimney, pulling himself up, his feet slipping.

There had to be something better than this.

The Uncertain Ego

"Passion feeds passion and then we are left with a small death." Mr Bug's representative was trying to comfort Miss Brunner.

She stared at the strangled corpse.

A young man in a trenchcoat and a trilby stepped backwards.

"Is anyone really dying?" she asked. "Or are we all just very tired?"

"Some of you are really dying, I'm afraid." Mr Bug's representative plucked at his mouth-tube. "Time is Time, no matter how much you struggle against it."

"Then we're done for."

"I haven't come to any conclusions about that." He was apologetic. "I'm honestly only an observer."

"You've interfered."

"I've taken an interest. It's the best I can offer."

Miss Brunner shrugged him away.

A whistle blew.

"I'm getting off this train," she said.

Mr Bug's representative made a peculiar gesture with his right glove.

"There'll be another one along in a minute."

Difficult Love

Very sluggishly, the airship was lifting.

The last of the Musician-Assassins lay spreadeagled on the floor of the gondola. A faint tape was playing *Silly Thing*.

"It's what the public wanted," murmured Jerry. "Or at least some of them. I did my best. It was good while it lasted."

The ship gently bumped against a church steeple. He pulled himself to a window. He recognised Powys Square. There was a bonfire.

Something bit at his groin.

He scratched.

Framed against the flames, a tartan-clad figure and a dwarf were dancing.

"I think I'm missing all the fun again." The Assassin switched on his engine.

It faltered. It was apologetic.

He tried again.

Something clicked.

The Laughing Policeman

"We're going to have to split up," said Miss Brunner firmly. Her colleagues had revived enough to get off the train and sit, shaking, on the platform seat.

"I think I have already," said Frank.

"You mean diversify, don't you?" Bishop Beesley wrenched a wrapper off a Mars.

"Disintegrate?" Frank was thinking of himself as usual.

Miss Brunner had recovered a bit of her composure.

"Captain Maxwell is the only one who will know how to deal with all this. So much of it is his fault."

"Oh, come on," said Frank. "We were partners. Maxwell's as decent as the rest of us underneath. He pretends to be a revolutionary but he's really just an ordinary businessman."

Miss Brunner shook her head. "In different ways, Mr Cornelius, you're as gullible as your brother. We're facing a genuine attempt to take power."

"The Pistols."

"Of course not, you idiot. You very rarely get that sort of trouble from the musicians. They want different things, most of them. Subtler things."

"The Pistols want subtler things." Bishop Beesley appeared to be trying to recondition his mind.

"That's hard to believe," said Frank.

Miss Brunner yawned and glanced away. "At least they're all good looking."

"I haven't been well," said Frank. "What's this about breaking up?"

"Diversifying," said Bishop Beesley.

There was a peculiar lack of noise around the station. The train had long-since pulled away.

"Splitting up," she said. "To find them."

"Who?" said Frank. He watched a butterfly settle on the track.

"Anyone," she said.

"Divide and Rule," said Bishop Beesley. "Where in hell are we, anyway?"

He began to snore.

Miss Brunner peered into the countryside. "Is that real, do you think? It's such a long time since I've been anywhere."

Familiar Air

"There must have been something in the marketing," said Mo. He stood in the deserted office complex holding a phone without a lead. "Badges and that. T-shirts."

"There's a lot to be made from marketing," agreed Mitzi. "Posters. Programmes. People get a good profit off all that. Special books."

"Masks. Sweets."

"Tie up marketing and it's far less hassle than actually managing a band," said Mitzi. She had seen it all. "Often a better turnover. And there are no people to get in the way and spoil things."

"Maybe the marketing company could pay my wages."

"Ah, well, Mo, it's a separate organisation, you see. They would if they could. But they have their accounts."

"Maybe I should look at their accounts."

"Only accountants understand accounts. You need an accountant to check it for you."

"A lawyer?"

"A lawyer and an accountant's what you need."

"To keep an eye on the manager?"

"It isn't as simple as that, Mo."

Dead Loyal

Mrs Cornelius stuck her neck through her strap. "Ter tell yer the truth, Sarge, I'm glad ter be back at me regular job. 'Ow's business?"

"Who?" said Sergeant Alvarez.

"Not 'oo—wot." She flashed her torch on and off. "Somebody's got ter earn a livin'."

She paused at the door of the auditorium. "O' course, it's in troubled times like these, people see a good picture, don't they?"

"Killed," said Alvarez.

"Oh, yeah. That, too."

Before she could go through, Mr Bug's representative entered.

"Everything all right here?"

"Loverly," she said. She had never liked the look of him.

"Plenty of stock?"

"Ask the Sarge."

"Any more handcuffs? Whips? Lengths of chain?"

"We're orl right for most o' that, far as I know," she said. "But it's Sarge does the stock, doncher, love?"

"We've got to look after the housewives," said Mr Bug's representative. "Can't have them getting bored, can we?"

Mrs Cornelius frowned at him. He seemed to be attempting a joke.

"Are you the usual fellah?" she asked.

"I'm filling in for him."

"You 'aven't—I mean, it's not a takeover or nuffink?"

"Just a change of territory. It'll all settle back to normal soon. Are you sure you don't need any more gags?"

Mrs Cornelius tittered. "Not if they're anyfink like ther last one."

Mr Bug's representative didn't get it.

"What do you need?" he said. "You must need some replacements."

"New feet," said Mrs Cornelius, "would be nice."

He looked at her shoes.

"Something elegant in rubber?"

She turned back towards the doors.

"I've got them in the car."

"It's no good," she told him. "I 'ave ter rely on the National 'Ealth."

"Business is bad all round at the moment, even in entertainment. I remember when you couldn't go wrong in entertainment, so long as there was plenty of crisis and stuff. Cash from Chaos, eh?"

"Chaos?"

"It's not the same as entropy. Not superficially, at any rate. Still, it's all the same in the end."

"Wot the bloody 'ell you talkin' abaht?"

"Stuff." Mr Bug's representative felt about his person. "I'm having a spot of trouble with my tubes. It's hard to remain attached. Do you find that?"

"Ask bleedin' Alice in bleedin' Wonderbloodyland," said Mrs Cornelius. She sniffed. "Blimey! You don't arf pong."

"Ping," said Alvarez pulling at his beard.

Mr Bug's representative slouched away. "Everything's rotting."

"You could've fooled me. You're enough to give ther fuckin' 'otdogs a bad name. An' that's sayin' somefink."

She backed through the doors with her tray.

On the screen they were shooting extras.

Voices In The Night

The airship was drifting over the debris near the river. People had already set up stalls and were selling various souvenirs: bits of ship, parts of planes, twisted singles.

The Assassin could hear their voices.

"Get yer genuine Prince Philip bandages."

"Johnny Rotten's safety pins. All authentic."

"Fresh Corgi!"

Not a lot had changed.

He watched the shadow of his own ship as it passed over the ruins, over the dirty water, over the collapsed bridges.

He was feeling more depressed than ever.

"I need . . ." he murmured. "I need . . ."

But his memory was failing again. He had seen too many alternatives. All the directions were screwed up. All the pasts and all the futures. They rarely seemed to make a decent present, which was only what he'd been aiming for. A bit of relief. But Time resisted manipulation, finally.

"Time's a killer," he said. He tried to turn up his volume, but the music remained a whisper.

With an effort he moved the wheel and set a course for what had once been Derry and Tom's Famous Roof Garden. Now it was some sort of posh nightclub. He had relinquished his interest in 19–.

He had all but relinquished his interest in the 20th century.

He checked his instruments.

"There's never a World War Three around when you need one."

**Please Leave The State In The Toilet In Which
You Would Wish To Find It**

Sid had lost another game of pool at the Café Hendrix. He went over to a window seat and looked out into the grey mist of eternity.

"I don't think it's going to clear up," said George, Lord Byron, arm in arm with Gene Vincent. They had been having a medical boot race. "Don't mope, lad. You didn't do so badly. And think of all those Sid Is Innocent badges they won't be able to sell now."

"What about all the Sid Still Lives badges they *will* be able to sell?"

"There's a lot more money in death, these days, than there was when I coughed it," said Shelley. "Although it didn't do any harm to the poetry sales. Just think what they could have done for me? I did get a funeral pyre, though, and all that. Shelley posters would have gone over a treat, don't you think. Shelley pens."

Jesus came over, chewing on a toothpick. "I've never had any problems," he said. "My marketing's been going strong for a couple of thousand years. Gets better all the time. But then none of you were crucified, were you."

"Don't listen to him, the snob." Oscar Wilde put his hand in Sid's lap. "You still on for that game of skittles?"

"You have to aim for universal appeal," said Jesus. "And that means your middle classes, I'm afraid. Without them, you'll never do it."

"Sid didn't understand that, did you Sid?" said Nestor Makhno. "And neither did I. And neither would I want to."

"I did it my way," said Sid. "I think."

Grumbling Bums

Miss Brunner sighed with pleasure. "What a terrible trip. I'm glad to be home."

"We achieved nothing," Frank complained.

"Not true, darling. We found out certain things by a process of elimination."

"It was a wild goose chase."

"It was a field trip. Trust me, darling." She stroked her CRYPTIK. "We'll just feed in what we know and then run another complete programme. Be a good boy, Frank, and put the kettle on."

Bishop Beesley said: "You still think we might be able to get the concessions."

"We've the experience and the knowhow. Show me a product, bishop, and I'll show you a profit in a very short while. How have I managed to stay in business so long? We'll need a few ideas to show the captain."

"But we can't find him. No-one can find him."

"Wait until he hears what we have to show him. For the Mirror."

"You're an incurable optimist, Miss Brunner," said Bishop Beesley. He began to force a chocolate orange into his mouth.

Remixing

The Assassin opened the door and manhandled the bomb out.

He watched it sail down towards the new estate opposite Rough Trade in Kensington Park Road.

It landed with a clang in the street. People began to come out of their doors and look at it.

Faces stared up at the last of the Musician-Assassins. He spread his hands.

"Sorry."

"Is it a dud?" shouted the grocer.

"I was told it would go off." Jerry shrugged. "Win a few and lose a few, eh?"

When, a couple of seconds later, the bomb did explode and bits of the crowd were scattered in directions, the Assassin was struck in the face by the grocer's left foot.

He wiped the blood from his cheek.

"What a lovely bit of fragmentation."

CLAIM NINE:

YOU KNOW IT MAKES SENSE

He violently dislikes Rotten because Rotten insulted him all the time. Rotten used to talk to him in words that he didn't understand, like English swear words. It was quite amusing to see Meyer trying to make sense of it.

Meyer took Rotten out to dinner and Rotten was incredibly rude and disgusting over his food. He was trying to alienate him because it was Malcolm's project. By that stage Rotten really didn't get on with Malcolm, so the film was one of the major causes of a rift in the group that led to the break up.

. . . Apparently they spent three days tracing down this deer until they found the right one, and Meyer shot it himself.

The focus puller was thrown off for being squeamish about the thing. Meyer wouldn't have anyone anti-American on his set.
—*Julian Temple, Interview with John May, NME, October 1979.*

"The fabric's wearing a bit thin, isn't it?" Mr Bug's representative sat in his static limo. People moved like ghosts through ghostly trees. "Is there any way of compensating?"

"It's a write-off," said Jerry sheepishly.

"You're losing your touch."

"I haven't got the help I used to get."

"True. You'd had hopes for the Pistols, then?"

"It isn't their fault." Jerry shifted as far away from Mr Bug's representative as possible. He cleared his throat. "Would you mind if we opened a window, squire?"

"Not at all. But the fumes . . . ?"

"The fumes are fine. It's quite pleasant. The scent of dissipating dreams."

"I'm afraid . . ."

"What?"

"I can't follow you."

"Just as well, squire. I'm on my own. I have to be. People try to turn you into leaders. Do you find that?"

"Not exactly. I just tend to the sick. When I do anything at all."

The car started up again and moved at less than ten miles an hour through the strangely faded park. Mr Bug's representative pointed at a distant outline. "The Palace is springing back again. Isn't it?"

"Oh, I wouldn't be surprised, squire."

A large mob, all greys and light browns, ran through the car, carrying torches. They wore 18th century clothes. "The Gordon Riots," said Mr Bug's representative. "But they seem to be burning the Pistols in effigy. Look over there."

The Assassin nodded. "Everything's out of focus, at present. This happens when you mess about the way I was. Still, it might have gelled. You never know."

"You manipulate Time?" Mr Bug's representative was impressed.

"I pretend to."

"I pretend to manipulate people. On Mr Bug's behalf, of course."

"Who is Mr Bug?" asked Jerry.

"Have a guess," said Mr Bug's representative.

Boo-boo-boogaloo

The Cessna came in to land on the deserted airfield. Its wheels bumped on the broken tarmac and it narrowly avoided the collapsed remains of a small airship.

Mr Bug's representative and the last of the Musician-Assassins crouched behind a ruined wall and watched.

Jerry held his vibra-gun in a trembling hand.

"It's the Americans," said Mr Bug's representative.

A figure in a red and blue diving suit emerged from the plane.

"Their technology's so sophisticated." Mr Bug's representative was admiring. "You'd hardly know there was anyone inside would you?"

"I'm not even sure about you." The Assassin wet his lips.

Mr Bug's representative nodded in agreement. "Yes." His breathing became erratic. "Yesssss."

Jerry had the feeling that, given half a chance, Mr Bug's

representative would begin some kind of mating ritual with the American suit.

Moleskin glowed in an abandoned control tower.

Jerry leaped from cover. "Flash!"

"Not yet!" hissed Mr Bug's representative. But it was too late.

Aiming the vibra-gun, Jerry hit the American just as he was reaching the tower. The suit fell to the ground and began to thresh as the sonics shook him to death. Part of the tower broke away and crashed onto the corpse.

Tartan dodged from window to window as the vibra-gun swept the building. Concrete cracked. Glass shivered.

Mr Bug's representative grabbed Jerry's arm. "Too ssssoon. Oh, dear!"

A helicopter swished into the sky.

"Bugger," said the Assassin.

"I'm not sure you have any understanding of anyone's best interests," said Mr Bug's representative, walking with slow, sad steps towards the American corpse. "It could be the culture gap, but I'm beginning to think you're past it. I must have a word with Mr Collier."

"He wants his wages. I thought . . ."

A strange, high-pitched hiss came from Mr Bug's representative. It took the Assassin a while to realise that he was whistling *Dixie*.

Gather At The River

"The Captain's in America, I'm afraid," said Clivey on the phone. "I'm sure he'll want to get in touch the minute he comes back."

Mo replaced the receiver.

Mitzi said: "I told you so. You ought to go there."

"Why?"

"For the same reason he's gone. For the same reason everyone goes. Because you've run out of possibilities here. Desperate times require desperate journeys."

"I never thought it would come to this."

"Distance makes the bank grow fonder."

"Do what?"

"Everyone else is going. You can bet your life on it."

"This job involves a lot of travelling, doesn't it? And very little money."

"Don't start whining." He was in an unusually brisk mood. It probably meant that she was keen to go to America for her own reasons.

"I can't afford it."

"I can get us a lift."

"I could do with a lift," Mo said feelingly.

"We'll have to hurry."

"Where to?"

"Brighton," she said.

Mo offered her an enquiring scowl.

Mitzi shrugged. "It's where the plane leaves from."

Tragic Magic

"Americans always think British bands are setting out to shock, when half the time the band is just behaving with its habitual rudeness." Frank had his new denim suit on.

Miss Brunner pursed her lips. "We have so many complaints from abroad."

"They were right about Captain M," said Bishop Beesley. "If not the band itself. But then the Captain must be easily shocked himself."

"He had his finger on the pulse of the public for a moment or two, I'll give him that."

"He had his hands in their pockets, too," said Frank. "That's what I'm complaining about."

"Times are hard," she said. "Everyone's got their hands in everyone else's pockets. Groping about for the pennies they're sure someone must have."

"Disgusting," said Bishop Beesley.

"Hurry up, Bishop. Are you packed?"

He was trying to close the lid on a large suitcase of Toffee Crunch.

"I have every admiration for American Management." Frank became pious. "They handle things so well over there."

"They have nicer musicians, that's why."

"Even the cowboys?"

"Hearts of gold, underneath."

255

"Rough diamonds," said Bishop Beesley sentimentally.

"Any kind would do me, right now." Frank looked at his ticket. "This had better work."

"They love me," she said. "It's my accent."

Touching Base

"Half the time you think you're flying." Jerry fiddled with his controls, "and when you get out you discover you've been in a Link trainer the whole time."

"Try and keep quiet and concentrate," said Mitzi. They were all fed up with him. "Are you sure you know this type of plane?"

"I love it," he said. "Therefore I know it."

"A classic romantic delusion." Mr Bug's representative wriggled in the navigator's chair.

"Get on with it, you stinking old hasbeen." Mo sat with the rest of the group in the passenger seats. He lifted a bottle of Wild Turkey to his lips.

"Will we get to meet Bugs Bunny?" asked Flash. He was well out of things.

"I'm having a hard time," said the Assassin with characteristic self-pity.

"Getting them good times." Only Mitzi was really looking forward to the trip.

The old Boeing Clipper lumbered through the water, its Wright Double Cyclone engines screaming and burping as they gave all they had left.

"You ought to be running a bloody transport museum," said Mo without disapproval. "You're living in the past."

"I think he simply wants the whole 20th century at once," said Mr Bug's representative. "It's greed, really. And romance, of course."

Jerry pulled down his goggles. "I'm just heavily into technology," he said.

"Well, I suppose I can't complain about that." Mr Bug's representative crossed his legs, if they were legs. "It's been my problem for years."

The ancient Boeing heaved itself into the wild, blue yonder.

Mitzi clapped her little hands. "Look out, Land of Opportunity, here we come!"

"If we're lucky," said Mo enthusiastically

The Assassin had a strange grin on his lips. "Manifest Destiny. We'll be fine."

"I think I'd feel safer in a bleedin' covered wagon," said Jimi, waking up for a moment and not enjoying the experience.

Buddy, Can You Spare A Dime?

"Yanks," said Mrs Cornelius reminiscently. "I saw a lot of 'em durin' ther War."

"War?" said Alvarez rolling a hot dog between his hands.

"Ther last one. Ther last bit one, that is. Thaes wot I liked. Mrs Minniver, innit? Well, you wouldn't know abart any o' that. Yore too fuckin' young."

"Who?"

"You."

"Killed?"

"You, if ya don't fuckin' shut up, I'll tell yer one fing. I'm gettin' bleedin' bored wiv this picture, ain't you? I could do wiv a nice bit o' John Wayne."

Ladies Love Outlaws

"Self-conscious, self-involved, chauvinistic and just downright bloody terrified." Miss Brunner dragged Frank off the plane at LAX. "Where's your sense of the International Brotherhood of Man, Mr Cornelius?"

"I've been here before." Bishop Beesley wiped his brown lips.

"I never did like it." Frank was miserable. "It's hardly ever the way it is in the pictures."

"A fact of life which your family has always failed to accept." They moved towards the Immigration desks. "And take that silly Stetson off."

"Will they give us the money?" asked Bishop Beesley, in the rear as usual. "In Los Angeles? Sunset Boulevard?"

"Sunset something," she said. "This could be the end of the line."

Frank cheered up a little. "You getting cold feet?"

"My feet are never hot, Mr Cornelius."

She was sensitive about her inability to sweat.

Dead Puppies

They pushed Sid out first. He went down over the Bay, rolling and twisting in the air before his parachute opened.

"Go," shouted the Assassin, circling the Golden Gate Bridge. "Go!"

One by one they jumped.

"At least it's sunny," said Mitzi, passing Mo on the way down. "It's amazing what a difference a bit of sunshine makes."

"Have a nice day." The Wild Turkey and Crème de Menthe hadn't mixed well. He began to vomit in the general direction of Haight-Ashbury.

They drifted over the city.

Mr Bug's representative hung limp in his harness. Stuff was oozing from his suit. "Can this be a propaganda drop?"

"I've never tried them," Jimi tugged at one of his ropes. "This is all right, though, isn't it?"

One by one they hit the ocean.

The Boeing Clipper circled over the spreading blobs of silk.

Jerry was beginning to revive a trifle. He swung the plane out to sea and flipped a toggle. His vibra-cannon were now At Go.

He turned and headed back towards the city as fast as he could go. The tapes rolled, straight into the cannons' ammo-storage.

"Time for a little earthquake."

He gave them *Anarchy In The UK*. It seemed appropriate.

He whistled to himself as the buildings began to bounce.

Honky Tonk Masquerade

Mitzi Beesley stood dripping on the wharf while the cutters continued their search.

"Americans take everything so *seriously*. They're worse than the French."

Mr Bug's representative was incapable of standing. Someone had tried to remove his suit but had stopped when they had seen what was inside. "They're too polite. And when politeness fails, they're too violent."

"There were at least four more went in." The policewoman was staring wonderingly at the blasted city. "What did they have to do that for?"

"Jealousy," said Mitzi. "Also revenge."

"What for?"

"Oh, they're all looking for the Captain. We thought he was here."

"And Tenille?"

"If you like."

The Boeing Clipper had disappeared out to sea, pursued by helicopters and coastguard planes.

"Who's the pilot?" asked the policewoman. It was obvious that she still didn't believe what had happened. She looked suspiciously at Jimi and Sid.

"Just an old fart."

Three familiar figures were picking their way over the tattered wood and concrete. "Are we too late?" Miss Brunner wanted to know.

"Too late?" asked Frank and Bishop Beesley in unison.

"Too late," agreed Mitzi.

"Poor lads." Miss Brunner grinned like an ape.

"Will the Captain be at the funeral?"

"There's got to be an inquest first," said Mitzi.

"Questions are going to be asked, eh?" Frank prodded at the shoulder of Mr Bug's representative. It hissed back at him, a dying snake. "Phew! He must have been gone for months."

"It's what we're all beginning to realise." Mitzi wandered off in the direction of Fisherman's Wharf. She was hoping she could still buy a postcard.

CLAIM TEN:

I KNOW WHO KILLED THE EMPIRE

Said Lydon in his statement: "McLaren hoped that our record sales would be enhanced if the public were under the impression that we were banned from playing. That was certainly untrue. Some halls wouldn't have us, but others applied to Glitterbest for gigs during 1977 and were either refused or else received no replies." In the end, he claimed, the Pistols resorted to doing three gigs under assumed names.

. . . Sid Vicious rang Lydon one morning at 5.00 a.m. to inform him that McLaren had just visited him. McLaren had complained to Vicious about Lydon, and Vicious himself told Lydon that he had had enough of the Sex Pistols. "Vicious sounded incoherent," said Lydon's statement. "I've since heard that he took an overdose of heroin shortly after McLaren's visit." Subsequently, Wilmers claimed, Lydon and McLaren had a face-to-face showdown at which Lydon said he didn't like getting publicity out of a man who had left a train driver like a vegetable.

The judge asked whether Rotten had changed in view of his refusal to become involved with Biggs. "The image projected is one in which violence is not opposed," he commented.

Mr Wilmers said that Rotten did not approve of killing people.
—*New Musical Express*, 24th February 1979

Manager As Voyeur

"It was just another wank," said Sid, picking at himself in the Café Hendrix.

"But a seminal wank, you must admit," said Nancy. She had been allowed in on a visit. She had always been fond of bad jokes.

Nestor Makhno looked up from the next table, a spoonful of ruby-coloured bortsch near his lips, his woolly hat slipping down over one eye. "It's the politically illiterate who start revolutions. And it's the politically literate who lose them. You mustn't blame yourself."

"I blame the Chelsea Hotel," said Dylan Thomas. "Have you ever stayed there? In the winter? Brrr. It brings you down, boyo."

Since arriving at the Café Hendrix he had adopted an appalling Welsh jocularity.

"What would you do?" asked Nancy. "If they gave you the chance of a comeback?"

"Tell them to stuff it."

"I know what I'd do," said Nestor Makhno. "I'd go all the way. Nihilism. I would have in the first place, I think, but the wife didn't like it."

"Blow 'em all up," said Bakunin cheerfully.

"Now there speaks a true wanker," said Jesus. He went up to the counter to get another espresso. "Who did you ever assassinate?"

"That's scarcely the point, is it?" Bakunin was hurt. But he knew he was talking to an ace.

Everyone was aware of it.

Sid winked at the pouting Russian. "You can't compete with him. He's sent millions and millions off."

"It's a question of style." Bakunin waved a gloved hand. "Not of numbers killed."

"You've probably got a point there." Keats and Chatterton went by arm in arm. "And Sid had a lot of style. A lot of potential."

"Well, I might yet realise it," said Sid. He was having a think.

Great Moments With The Immortals

"Maybe it's the Gulf Stream." Flash and Mo were dragging themselves ashore at last. They had arrived on the beach at Rio.

"It's fate, lads!" Martin Bormann, wearing only red and black swimming trunks, a discreet swastika on his saluting arm, came marching up. "I was only thinking about you this morning."

"Have you seen the Captain?" Mo asked.

"You've just missed him, I'm afraid. But Ronnie's about. He wants to join the group. I hear you're a couple of members short. I don't wish to push myself forward, but I used to be very fond of music . . ."

"We'll think about it," said Flash.

"Pistols, pistols über alles," sang Martin, striding along beside them. "You look defeated. I know a great deal about defeat. You mustn't let it get you down."

"You wouldn't happen to have seen an old Boeing Clipper, would you?" Mo cast an eye on the sky.

"Oh, you know about that, do you?"

"Has one been here?"

"It's the plane the Captain left on."

"Betrayed!" said Mo.

"It's probably a coincidence," said Flash.

"The entire German people betrayed me," said Martin sympathetically. "They weren't worthy of us, you see. But what do we actually mean by this word 'betrayal'? Don't we in some ways betray only ourselves . . . ?"

They hadn't time for his third rate Nazi metaphysic. They began to run up the beach.

"We've got to earn some money," said Flash.

Mo stopped.

"We'll have to do a few gigs." He turned. "Have you got any bookings, Martin?"

"Amazon, three nights starting from tomorrow. Then there's the Mardi Gras . . ."

"We'll take 'em," said Mo.

Human Conditioner

Miss Brunner set the crudely printed invitation on top of her CRYPTIK and frowned at it.

"Maybe they're willing to deal at last?" said Frank. He had his areas of optimism.

"It could be a joke," said Bishop Beesley.

She hovered over her keyboard, but nothing came to mind.

"A farewell gig, though," said Frank. "I thought they'd already done that." He sniggered.

"Captain Maxwell will be there." Bishop Beesley waved an important Crunchy. "And we need to raise some cash."

"We'll make a few contacts." Frank reached towards the invitation but had his wrist slapped away by Miss Brunner.

"It's another trap," she said.

"What can they do to us? We've survived everything."

"Your brother's involved. He's been resurrecting people again. You know what he's like."

"Everyone who is everyone—or was anyone—will be there. Let's give it a go." Frank stroked his hand. "Please. My mum'll be there. She works at the venue. He wouldn't hurt our mum."

Miss Brunner was letting him convince her.

"And I've never seen him live," said Bishop Beesley. "If live is the right word."

"It'll be a relaxing night out." Frank gave a stupid grin. "Well, it'll make a change."

"It'll make a change," Miss Brunner agreed. "Do we get to see the film as well?"

"It doesn't say."

The CRYPTIK made a peculiar peeping noise.

"I think it's laughing," she said.

The Mysteries

"I hope to god this is my last bloody comeback." Jerry Cornelius bit his mouldering lip and stared at his disintegrated fingers. "There just isn't the energy around now."

"It's because you've used it all up," said Captain Maxwell. "Jilly where's the cheque book?"

"They took that as well."

The Captain began to look in the backs of his desk drawers, as if he hoped to find a little cash. "This is silly."

"What happened to the money?" asked the Assassin.

"It was won in a dream and lost in a nightmare," said Jilly. She seemed to be quoting somebody.

"Where did it go?"

"Ask the bloody Official Receiver."

"Isn't that what he's asking you?"

"Everybody's asking the wrong questions." Jilly glared at the Assassin. "Leave him alone. Can't you see he hasn't had any sleep in months?"

"That always happens when you try to make a dream come true, doesn't it?"

"I don't need you sitting there, rotting in my last good chair," said Maxwell. "Have all the invitations gone out, Jilly?"

"I'm not moralising," said the Assassin defensively, "exactly, I'm speaking from several lifetimes of experience."

"All gone out," said Jilly.

"Isn't the dream better than what we've got?"

"Are you Mr Bug?"

"Let's just say I do his tailoring."

"Where is he?"

"Where he always was. Zurich. Watching telly."

"I never thought of Switzerland." Jerry tried to recover a fingernail which had dropped onto the bare boards.

"Few people ever do."

"It could just be the suit that's in Switzerland."

"The suit is Mr Bug." The Captain paused in his search. "I should know, shouldn't I?"

The Assassin drew himself onto unsteady feet. He dusted a little light mould from his black car coat.

"Well, that clears everything up. Thanks. I'll see you at the gig."

"See you there," said the Captain. He crossed the room and began to feel in the pockets of a pair of discarded bondage trousers.

The Assassin paused by the door. "Oh, by the way, who really did kill—?"

"Get off," said Captain Maxwell.

As the Assassin went down the stairs, Jilly came trotting after him. She whispered:

"It was Richard. But the Captain set it up."

The Assassin had already forgotten the question.

When You Wish Upon A Star

The Concorde landed on schedule at Margaret Thatcher Airport.

"England looks very clean, these days," said Martin Bormann with some satisfaction. "I always knew there was a chance for her."

An old robber, disguised as an ex-boxer, said through his balaclava: "A return to proper standards. And about time."

Mo settled his trilby on his head. "As soon as I see Captain M I'm going to . . ."

"Give it up," said Flash. "Just for a bit, eh?"

Martin Bormann was disappointed. "I thought there'd be a crowd waiting for us. Like the Beatles."

"Crowds need organising," said Mo, "and the Captain's too busy for that. Besides, he's not managing us any more."

"Are you sure?"

"Well, you can never be absolutely certain."

Reaching The Market

"I'm glad I'm not dead. I'm glad I'm not dead," mumbled the last of the Musician-Assassins to himself. He had put on his old pierrot suit and had plastered his face with white make-up to hide the worst of the decay. "You've got to think positive."

He shuffled through the streets of North London. He was lost. He seemed to remember that he had been on his way to some kind of party. Possibly he had missed it during one of his rests. The rain had started. His silk suit began to stick to his skeleton as he turned into Finchley Road.

Everything was getting very hazy.

Requiem Mc2

"Two Rotten Bars, please." Jilly looked at her own little dolls on display in the foyer. She still thought she should get the bars free, but she paid for them anyway. Alvarez began to sing at her.

"You stop that, Sarge," Mrs Cornelius came round the corner. "Don't let 'im bovver you, love. 'E wants ter be discovered. Will Captain M be along later?"

"Discovered?"

"Like America." She laughed heartily so that her goods in her tray bounced beneath her bouncing breasts. "An' all them ovver bleedin' colonies."

Jilly went inside. She wanted to be sure of a good seat.

They were all beginning to arrive now. Nearly everybody was in some form of fancy dress. Mickey Most, in lugubrious and inappropriate corduroy, Jake Riviera, Tony Howard, Peter Jenner, Andrew Lloyd Webber, Martin Davis. A lot of denim and fur. A lot of vain leather.

Shuffling in and standing in the shadows, the half-collapsed pierrot looked at them going by. It was like a gathering of Mafia dons, old and new. Richard Branson, Michael Dempsey, Miles Copeland: some of them in modifications of demi-monde styles, some in grotesque parodies of dandyism. The Nouveaux Noires arrived, singly or in couples, with their girlfriends.

The pierrot noticed how comfortable they all were. It was probably because not a single punter had been on the invitation list. Some of them complained that they had to pay, but in the main they were not discontented.

Elton John, Rod Stewart, Olivia Newton-John, Cliff Richard and Barbra Streisand. Bishop Beesley, Miss Brunner, Anne Nightingale. Frank Cornelius didn't notice his brother. He was walking on air. He felt euphoric in the presence of cash. The slightly self-conscious members of the musical press were trying to look like musicians, and as usual were not absolutely certain of their social status: their expressions changing constantly as they tried for an appropriate mode.

They were piling in, drawn by curiosity, greed, a wish not to be left out.

Music publishers, record company executives, the owners of studios; agents and managers.

"What a lot of controllers," mumbled Jerry vaguely. "What a lot of mortgages."

Elegant cowboys, smoothed-up Hell's Angels, Beverly Hills punks. Nobody required any hope, only confirmation. They confirmed one another.

The pierrot was reminded of a bunch of burghers going into church.

Mo and Flash wandered in. Mo's trenchcoat was covered in a variety of old food, vomit and semen. He had lost his hat. A bouncer appeared from nowhere. "Sorry, you've got to have invitations."

Ronnie Biggs and Martin Bormann said in chorus: "It's all right. They're with us."

"Johnny won't come," said Mo to no-one in particular. He hadn't noticed the pierrot in the shadows either.

Wasting It

"I've seen this before," whispered Miss Brunner to Frank as the film came on.

"We've all seen it before," said someone behind her. "That doesn't mean we can't enjoy it."

Mo was crawling between the seats, still looking for Captain Maxwell.

He found a tartan knee. "Flash? Wake up."

"Give him a break," said Jilly. "Can't you leave him alone for a minute?"

It was standing room only for the old pierrot. He held on tightly to the rail at the back, trying to focus fading eyes.

His mother popped in. "Jerry. Yore lookin' terrible. There's a chap in the foyer. Sez 'e's Mr Bug's bailiff. Is it ther Receivers?"

"They're not playing tonight."

"I'll tell 'im." She disappeared.

"Mum . . ." He stretched out his wounded hand. "My wiring's gone . . ." But she didn't hear him.

He could only dimly detect the soundtrack now. There was a lot of plummy laughter coming from the seats. The film was reassuring its audience while pretending to shock them; a perfect formula for success.

"It's sure to be a winner," said Mitzi B, slipping out for a pee.

The pierrot gasped. Everything was going round and round.

Sometime later, as he desperately tried to revive his attention, he saw Sid at last. The operation had been a success. He wasn't absolutely sure by now if Sid was actually on stage or on film. He was singing *My Way* with all his old style.

Mo crawled up and began to tug at the pierrot's suit. Bits of it tore away in his hand. "This is where I came in."

He crawled on, towards the exit.

The volume rose higher and higher. There were a few murmurs of complaint.

The pierrot felt a shade better. He managed an appreciative groan.

The song ended.

Gunfire began to sound in the auditorium.

The pierrot sank to the dirty floor with a happy grunt. "It worked, after all. We did it, Sid."

The hall became filled with the sounds of terror. Blood and bits of flesh flew everywhere. The audience was tearing itself to pieces as it tried to escape.

Eventually there was silence. A dark screen. A vacuum. An avenged ghost.

Mrs Cornelius opened the doors. She had an expression of resigned disgust on her face.

"'Oo the bloody 'ell do they expect ter clear up this fuckin' mess, then?"

"Jimi?" said Alvarez behind her.

He began to sing again.

Ladbroke Grove, 1980
Marrakesh, 1988

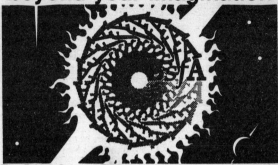

CRITICAL WAVE

THE EUROPEAN SCIENCE FICTION & FANTASY REVIEW

"CRITICAL WAVE is the most consistently interesting
and intelligent review on the sf scene."
- Michael Moorcock.

"One of the best of the business journals...
I never miss a copy..." - Bruce Sterling.

"Intelligent and informative, one of my key sources of
news, reviews and comments." - Stephen Baxter.

"I don't feel informed until I've read it."
- Ramsey Campbell.

"Don't waver - get WAVE!" - Brian W Aldiss.

CRITICAL WAVE is published six times per year and has
established a reputation for hard-hitting news coverage, perceptive
essays on the state of the genre and incisive reviews of the latest
books, comics and movies. Regular features include publishing
news, portfolios by Europe's leading sf and fantasy artists, extensive
club, comic mart and convention listings, interviews with prominent
authors and editors, fiction market reports, fanzine and magazine
reviews and convention reports.

Previous contributors have included: MICHAEL MOORCOCK, IAIN
BANKS, CLIVE BARKER, LISA TUTTLE, BOB SHAW, COLIN
GREENLAND, DAVID LANGFORD, ROBERT HOLDSTOCK, GARRY
KILWORTH, SHAUN HUTSON, DAVID WINGROVE, TERRY
PRATCHETT, RAMSEY CAMPBELL, LARRY NIVEN, BRIAN W
ALDISS, ANNE GAY, STEPHEN BAXTER, RAYMOND FEIST, CHRIS
CLAREMONT and STORM CONSTANTINE.

A six issue subscription costs only eight pounds and fifty pence or a
sample copy one pound and ninety-five pence; these rates only apply
to the UK, overseas readers should contact the address below for
further details. Cheques or postal orders should be made payable to
"Critical Wave Publications" and sent to: M Tudor, 845 Alum Rock
Road, Birmingham, B8 2AG. Please allow 30 days for delivery.

Bedlam

HARRY ADAM KNIGHT

An hallucinatory novel of urban terror by the author of the classic pulp novel *The Fungus*.

'Another superior chunk of splatter' – *The Times*

'A nasty compulsive tale . . . if you like your horror in ten-foot high blood-red neon capital letters then this is definitely the book for you' – *Time Out*

0 575 05347 X £3.99 net

Little Boy Lost

T.M. WRIGHT

'More than a master of quiet horror – a one-man definition of the term' – Ramsey Campbell

The eighth in Gollancz's series of horror novels from the author of *A Manhattan Ghost Story*.

0 575 05026 8 £3.99 net

Bill, The Galactic Hero on The Planet of The Hippies From Hell

HARRY HARRISON & DAVID BISCHOFF

Harry Harrison, bestselling author of *West of Eden* and *The Stainless Steel Rat*, and David Bischoff, author of *War Games* team up to send Bill, the Galactic Hero on another lunatic quest through time, space and sobriety.

0 575 05526 X £3.99 net

How The World Was One:
Beyond the Global Village

ARTHUR C. CLARKE

Clarke brings all his storytelling flair and scientific expertise to this fascinating account of one of the century's greatest achievements; the story of how communications technology, through cable and satellite, changed the world.

'A passionate narrative . . . every bit as enthralling as any of his fictions' – *Locus*

'A fascinating story, full of amazing events and no less amazing people, told with flair. He blends history, his own ideas, and speculation, and makes it all so readable' – *Croydon Advertiser*

0 575 05546 4   £6.99 net

Aztec Century

CHRISTOPHER EVANS

In the late twentieth century Britain falls under Aztec rule, a pyramid dominates the Thames at Westminster, and Princess Catherine and her sister are in hiding in Wales; soon to be betrayed and drawn into war and political intrigue.

Aztec Century is an epic novel of war, politics and romance, set in a brilliantly imagined alternate Britain, from the acclaimed author of *Chimeras* and *Cappella's Golden Eyes*.

Paperback   0 575 05540 5   £8.99 net
Hardback   0 575 05538 3   £14.99 net